Scared Witchless

AMY BOYLES

This book is dedicated to my mother, Cheryl, and my mother-in-law, Sharon. Without their help with my little ones, I never would have been able to get this book written.

ACKNOWLEDGMENTS

I want to acknowledge the awesome girls of SASS. They are always there to listen to me whine and mope. Your support and cheer have meant a ton.

Thanks to Lea Ann, for never being afraid to pull punches when it comes to suggestions.

Thanks to Ruth Vincent, for reading an earlier version of this and many other books I've written. You've always taken the time to pour over my work and offer your help.

Scared Witchless

ONE

"If that ain't the other side of stupid, I don't know what is."

Reagan Eckhart, all platinum-blonde ninety-eight pounds of her, shoved a newspaper in my face. I winced, barely avoiding a massive paper cut to the nose.

"Those idiots put you in Arts and Leisure. You should have been on the front page of the *Birmingham News*." She tapped the newspaper with a single red fingernail. "With as much business as you do, Dylan Apel, you should have been the main story of the day."

"Don't you think technically they should have put me in the business section?" I said.

Reagan fluffed the foot of hair teased up at her crown. At least it looked like a foot. Okay, it wasn't a foot—only six inches. But those were a tall six inches. Big enough to practically be their own person. "Whatever," she mumbled.

The debutante was in rare form today. Reagan was dressed to the nines in a black halter top and pants that resembled Spandex. Personally, I was waiting for her to break out into the chorus of "You're the One That I Want," à la Olivia Newton-John. Harry Shaw, her fiancé—a smallish, bald financial advisor—definitely wouldn't join her if she did. His idea of playing John Travolta probably resembled hot-and-heavy talk about how gross grease and lightning were and why would you want to put the two together?

I grabbed the paper and scrutinized the picture of me and my sisters, Seraphina and Reid. Bright, beaming smiles on our faces, we stood in front of our side-by-side stores—Perfect Fit and Sinless Confections. Seraphina, tall and slender, her hair shimmering like glass in the sunlight, looked absolutely perfect. Even Reid, my eighteen-year-old baby sis, looked cherubic and innocent, her doe eyes and cheeky smile radiating youthful exuberance.

Then there was me. I sighed. It had taken two hours to smooth my hair, and it had still frizzed on the edges. I wasn't as tall or slender as Seraphina. But what I lacked in athletic build, I made up for in curves. Good for me. I might not look statuesque and perfect, but I could put on a slutty dress and have enough T and A to get noticed.

Was that a zit on my cheek?

"When I realized you had this store, Dylan," Reagan said, "and I saw how beautiful the dresses were, I told Harry—I said, 'Harry, that's who's going to design my wedding dress.' Didn't I, hon?"

Harry, nose-deep in the business section, remained silent. Reagan kicked him.

"Ow!" Harry rubbed his ankle. "What'd you do that for?"

"Didn't I, Harry? Didn't I say that?"

Harry shrank a little, his bald pate looking even balder under the fluorescents. "Yes, of course you did, dear."

Poor guy. He probably wouldn't last a year in the marriage. He'd be whipped, beaten down and likely castrated after two months.

Did I say that out loud?

"Anyway," Reagan continued, flitting about the room. "I told Harry, Dylan Apel and I were best friends in high school—"

"Mortal enemies," I corrected.

"—and of course she's going to be the one to design my dress." Girlfriend didn't miss one beat. I don't think Reagan listened to what people said. Did she even hear them when they talked?

From the corner my assistant, Carrie Dogwood, snickered. I shot her a look of warning. She turned a deep shade of red and pretended to straighten a rack of sequined gowns.

"Reagan, do you want to see your dress again?" I asked.

"Of course," she squealed. "I can't get enough of it."

Carrie crossed to me. She leaned over, kept her voice low. "Wonder what she'll complain about this time."

I turned away from Reagan. "Hopefully nothing," I whispered. "Can you grab the dress?"

"Sure thing."

An unfinished blue gown caught my attention. The color of a robin's egg, the dress would be the envy of the Silver Springs solstice banquet, what with its deep vee neckline and overlay of chiffon. I needed to finish it before the dance, which was barely two weeks away.

I sighed. I'd been working a lot lately, thanks to Reagan's never-ending changes to her gown. There was less than a week until the wedding, and after that I'd have plenty of time to work on my own dress. That is, if I survived Reagan for a few more days.

I stared vacantly at the gown until a bodiless hand thrust the newspaper into my face once more. Reagan popped up in front of me and wiggled the now crumpled article. "But this reporter nails it. She absolutely gets it right. I could have gone anywhere for my dress, but there's just something about your gowns and your sister's food. It's like I'm transported to another place. I don't know how to describe it."

I had heard the same mantra over and over from clients. *There's something about your clothes that I can't put my finger on. It's almost like they're magical.*

Yeah. Right. Not that I didn't appreciate the compliment. Believe me, I did. So did Sera. If it weren't for the folks in our lakeside community of Silver Springs, Alabama, we'd be beggars. Hoboes maybe. Vagabonds most likely. And not the good kind. Not the sexy kind you see on the covers of romance novels.

Wait. There weren't hoboes on those. Well, anyway, we'd be dirty, covered in rags that smelled of oil and sweat, with grit under our fingernails that not even the best manicure technician could lift.

"Here's the dress," Carrie said.

Reagan's smile vanished. "Oh."

My dreams, my hopes, my wishes for a beautiful future crashed and exploded like a car careening off a cliff in a 1970s B movie. What could possibly be wrong this time—the hundredth time? I swear, every occasion this girl saw her dress, she found something to criticize. It was a wonder I hadn't strangled her before now.

I smoothed the lines of frustration that were forming on my forehead. "What's the problem?"

Reagan wrinkled her nose. "It's just...well...that's a lot of sequins."

I took a deep, cleansing breath and thought happy thoughts. "Last week you wanted more sequins. You said it didn't have enough *bling*."

Carrie bit back a giggle.

I flashed her a seething look. I mean, seriously. I knew it was funny, but it was only good service not to laugh at the customer while she's standing right in front of you. At least wait until the door hits her backside as she's leaving.

"Well," Reagan said, "last week there weren't any sequins. What were there? Like five on the whole thing?"

I steepled my fingers beneath my chin. "There were two hundred."

"Oh. How many are there now?"

"Five hundred."

"It's too many. Listen, Dylan, just because we were best friends in high school—"

"Mortal enemies," I said.

"—doesn't mean you can take advantage of me. If this dress isn't to perfection by Saturday, then I'm getting it for free. Right?"

Whoa, Nelly. "I'm sorry?"

Reagan batted her fake eyelashes. "That's just plain old good business. The customer is always right. I mean, we go way back. Too far back to let a little disagreement over some sequins ruin what we had."

I poked the air with my index finger. "Once again, we were *mortal enemies.* Reagan, you have brain damage when it comes to what high school was like."

A tittering laugh escaped her throat. It sounded like a thousand butterflies taking flight. That was right before I lifted my imaginary rocket launcher, aimed high and fired, sending the beauties crashing to the ground in a blazing explosion.

"You're so melodramatic, Dylan. We had a little disagreement about prom; that was all."

I crossed my arms. "Reagan, let me remind you of exactly what happened in high school."

"Why don't you do that, since you're so convinced we had nothing to do with each other." Reagan pulled one of her eyelashes. Ouch. Didn't that hurt?

I shook my head and said, "You had Colten Blacklock ask me to prom for the sole purpose of standing me up the night of." I pointed to her and then to me. "You and I—we were never friends, and I'm not giving you this dress for free. We've done a dozen fittings, and you've found something wrong with each and every one. You can either take it or leave it."

Reagan's mouth fell. She swung to Harry. "Are you going to let her talk to me like that?"

Harry squashed the grin on his face and cleared his throat. "Ahem. Well. You *have* tried the dress on a lot, and Miss Apel has been more than accommodating."

Reagan stomped her foot. "You," she said, wagging a finger at him. "You wait until we get home."

Oh no. I didn't want Harry to be in the dog house because of me. I reached out and rubbed Reagan's arm, trying to soothe the savage bridezilla. "Reagan, I'll lose some of the sequins. Stop by tomorrow and see what you think."

She flashed a tight, bitter smile. "What you have better be good, or I'm taking my business elsewhere. And that means your sister won't be doing the catering, either." She squared her shoulders, swiveled on her heel and stormed out of the shop. Harry gave me an apologetic smile and followed. The little bell above the door tinkled as they left.

"Do you think she'll back out?" Carrie asked.

I shook my head. "Of course not. Not unless she wants a dress off the rack and a cake from Walmart."

Carrie laughed. "She's something else, isn't she?"

"She's certainly something." I rubbed my neck. Tension latched to the cords of muscle. I'd have a headache pretty soon if I didn't take an ibuprofen. Extending my palm, I gestured for Carrie to hand me the wedding gown. "I guess I'll alter her dress."

Carrie stuffed the layers of silk in my hands and nodded to the blue cross-necked dress. "But when are you going to finish that one?"

I peeked out from behind the mass. "I don't know. We have, what? Two weeks until the summer solstice? I'll work on it soon."

The bell above the door tinkled. Seraphina crashed in, a whirlwind of flour following her. Her blue eyes sparkled with delight. How I envied those eyes. Mine were poo brown. Some said chocolate, but I knew better. Those folks were just being Southern polite.

"Oh my God! Did y'all see the article?" She waved the paper like a flag of surrender.

"I did!"

"It's incredible. The reporter went so far as to say our work is, and I quote..." She scanned the article. "Where is it? Where did that passage go? Oh, here it is." She jabbed it. "She said our work is 'inspired by the gods themselves.' Ha! You couldn't pay for better advertising."

"You probably could," I said.

Carrie flipped the ends of her chestnut hair. "Listen, y'all, I just got this new gel manicure machine in the mail. Do you mind if I go freshen up these bad boys?" She wiggled her perfect coral nails. To my eyes, they needed no refreshing. But hey, every girl has some sort of vice. Carrie's happened to be that she was ADD about her nails. In the three years she'd worked for me, I'd never seen one chip. Ever. Mine, on the other hand, looked like Godzilla had tried to paint them—there were broken wedges of color that Carrie would have deemed unforgivable.

"Go ahead. We'll be here," I said. She picked up a shipping box and exited to the back.

I hung Reagan's wedding dress on a rack and brushed my hands of any rogue sequins that hadn't been sewn on properly, which was actually impossible since I'd done the work myself. But my grandmother had always taught me to be humble, so that was my attempt.

Sera chewed her bottom lip. "The reporter says, 'Dylan Apel's dresses will transport you to another time and place. A claim I can attest to personally, for I experienced this peculiar phenomenon first-hand when I tried on one of her gowns. When I saw my reflection in the mirror, for a split second I was taken back to the cotillion ball where I met my husband thirty years ago. If that wasn't enough to put a spring in my step, one bite of Seraphina's baked treats and I was back in my grandmother's kitchen as she created confections on the stove. Truly a magical experience.'" Sera paused, looked up at me. "Seriously. That's some good stuff."

"Yeah, it's good," I said. But the reporter's description about trying on my clothes bothered me. I shrugged off the uncomfortable feeling and smiled. "Though I have been accused on occasion of drugging my clothes."

Sera frowned. "That's the stupidest thing I've ever heard."

The bell tinkled. I stepped forward, my most welcoming smile on my face.

My sister glanced at me. "You look like a piranha. Tone it down."

I settled into a half smile. "Good morning! Welcome to Perfect Fit."

A towering redhead sauntered into the store. Bangles covered both her arms, clinking pleasantly as she walked. Emerald-green eyes fixed on me and Sera. I squirmed. Couldn't help it. At five-five I wasn't short. Not by any means. But this was a tall woman. Five-ten easy. And all that hair. A cloud of silky crimson and honey curls cascaded down her back. I don't even think she had any product in it. It was a totally natural head of hair.

I hated her.

Kidding. But envy did surface.

She smiled brightly. My envy turned into instant like. "Mornin'. I wanted to try on some clothes," she said in a throaty voice, the kind that drove men mad. I'd never seen her before, and Silver Springs was a minuscule town. From the look of interest on Sera's face, I guess she hadn't seen this woman before, either.

I stepped forward. "Absolutely. What are you looking for?"

"Just some regular day-wear stuff."

My time had arrived. I had a knack, a sixth sense really, about clothes and people. In one try I could create an entire body-fitting wardrobe and not even know the size of the person. What can I say? It came naturally to me.

"Are you looking for sportswear or business?"

"Both."

Cha-ching! "Let me pull a few items and see what you think."

"I'm gonna head back," Sera said. "I'm sure there's something I need to make."

I waved. "Bye."

She waved back and left, leaving me to focus on my client. Five minutes later I had two armfuls of pants, jackets, and blouses. "Let me get you in a dressing room. After you're done, come out and see what you think in the three-way mirror."

None of my dressing rooms had mirrors. People thought it weird, but I wanted to be around when my clients saw themselves in my clothing for the first time.

The woman disappeared behind the door, a roomful of clothes at the ready. Two minutes later she reappeared in a pair of jeans and a loose blouse.

"Take a look."

She stepped forward. The air contracted as if the very atmosphere had been sucked away. The mirror shimmered, and the woman's image bowed and straightened. It happened fast, so fast no one ever noticed. No one except for me.

So, this is where I tell you what that's all about. I would if I could. The easiest explanation is that my clothes make people feel great. From what Sera's told me, putting on one of my garments reminds you of an amazing time in your life. For instance—you're a fifty-year-old woman buying a dress for your daughter's wedding. You try something on and *poof,* you're transported back to the wondrous feeling you experienced at senior prom. Of course, that would be you, not me. My prom stank thanks to Reagan Eckhart.

At least, that's what I'd always thought. It's also why the reporter's story bothered me. She saw her younger self in that mirror. That had never happened before—at least not that I knew of. My clothes blanketed clients in a wondrous feeling. They didn't make anyone see visions.

Sera's baked goods do something similar. Every time I eat something she's made, I feel amazing, like I could take on the world. One bite of a buttery croissant and I'm totally superwoman. Minus the red cape. And the tights. Now that I think about it, I wouldn't be caught dead in that outfit.

But why are we like that? We're *gifted;* that's what our grandmother always called it. We have a *gift.*

"What do you think?" I asked.

She stared at her image. After a long moment her lips curlicued into a smile. She licked the bottom one, her eyes shining.

9

"Your clothes are breathtaking."

Thirty minutes and three hundred dollars later, I placed the last package in the redhead's hands.

"How'd you hear about us?" I asked.

"I saw the article in the paper."

I clicked my tongue. "Wow. News travels fast." Sweet. Today might be a crazy, busy day.

She smiled, her eyes glittering. "You don't even know the half of it."

"Oh?"

She pinched her brows together, giving her a dark, ominous expression. "In one week I guarantee you won't recognize your life."

An awkward laugh escaped my lips. "Oh. Ha-ha. I hope it's all good."

She shook her head. "That little article that came out about you? The one that was supposed to help your business? Well, you just did the opposite. You stirred up a bed of fire ants." She leaned forward and gave me a stern look. "And in case you need remindin', the sting from a fire ant lasts a long time. Take this as your warnin'."

I was so confused. "What do you mean, a warning?"

"Watch your back."

With that she left, her cloud of hair billowing behind her. I stood stone still. Numb shock tingled over my body, filtering down into my fingers and toes.

What the heck just happened?

TWO

That was just plain weird. Who walks into a shop and tells the owner they just stirred up a fire-ant bed? I mean, what does that even mean? I had to tell Sera.

"I'm going next door," I shouted.

"All right," Carrie said. "I'll watch the front."

"Be right back!"

I stepped outside. The bright June sun warmed my arms. I smiled, letting the rays kiss my face. Shielding my eyes, I looked around Main Street. Shops lined both sides of the road, from the upscale children's boutique Butterfly Days, to Gus's, the local fried burger joint. Yes, fried hamburgers. Patties floured and dropped into hot peanut oil. Yum. Seriously. Don't knock it till you've tried it. The line at Gus's threaded out the door, spilling onto the sidewalk. My stomach growled. The beast would be fed later. But now I had some sister business to attend to.

I stepped inside Sinless Confections, expecting the scents of roasted coffee beans and vanilla to seduce me, but instead, noxious fumes filled the air. Gray smoke puffed from the kitchen. Not being one to stand on ceremony, I charged into the back and found Sera and Reid, a mop bucket of smoking liquid sitting on the floor between them.

"What did you do?" Sera said, edging back from the fumes.

"What are you talking about?" Reid said. "I'm cleaning, like you asked."

"With what?" Sera said. "What's in that bucket?"

Reid coughed. "Bleach and ammonia."

"What? Are you trying to kill us?"

"What are you talking about?" Reid said.

Through racking coughs, Sera picked up the bucket, signaled for Reid to open the back door and then flung the stuff into the alley. She tossed the bucket in the sink.

"Reid, get the fans going."

"Why?"

"Because ammonia and bleach make a poison when mixed together. I don't want the next person who walks into my store to die a violent death because my little sister isn't smart enough to know not to mix those two chemicals!"

Reid grumbled as she plugged in a small circulating fan. "If this is how I'm going to be thanked for doing what I'm asked, I'm going to work for Dylan."

"Oh no you're not," I said. "I've got Carrie, and she's all I need right now. Besides, the way things go with you, you'll have my shop burned down within a week."

"I was only trying to clean," Reid whined.

"Yes, and just narrowly managed to avoid suffocating yourself," I said.

"And me," Sera added.

Reid shot us both a scathing look. "I have no talent!"

"That's not true," I said. It was, though. Totally true. But I couldn't let my sister feel bad, now could I?

"It is true! You make amazing clothes, and Sera bakes pure heaven into her food. What can I do? Kill people by combining poisonous chemicals."

Sera wrapped an arm around Reid's shoulders. "One day, Reid, you'll find your gift."

"And when she does, it'll probably kill us."

"And the entire town," Sera added.

Reid pouted out her lips and huffed. "Ingrates. Both of you." She untied her apron and pulled it over her head. Her burgundy curls, restrained by the marmiest of school-lunch-lady hairnets, tumbled out onto her shoulders. The net itself clung to her head by a stubborn hairpin. Yanking out the pin, she threw it to the floor and stomped on it.

Sera giggled. "Ah. Teenage angst. Isn't it cute?"

Reid threw her head back in defeat. "I can't do anything right!"

Restraining my own laughter, I took my sister by the shoulders and guided her to one of the slick red bar stools in the dining room. "Want some hot chocolate?"

Reid sniffled. "Maybe."

"Chocolate always makes things better," Sera said, moving to heat a pot. After she'd melted shards of dark chocolate and added milk, she served it to a sniffling Reid with a dollop of whipped cream on top. Sera and I rolled our eyes as Reid took a couple of pathetic sips.

"Better?" I asked.

Reid wiped a dramatic teenage tear from under her eye. "Better."

I stole a sip from her cup. As soon as the chocolate hit my tongue, I felt my bones melt. Warmth and happiness washed over me, and I knew I had a dreamy-eyed look on my face.

"Oh, to be eighteen and stupid again," I said.

"I'm not stupid," Reid said.

"I know that. But you can get away with things at your age that I can't at mine."

"Yeah, old woman." Sera rolled her eyes. "Twenty-eight is so old."

Reid fisted her hands on her hips and glared at me and Sera as if she wanted to burn us alive. "Look, y'all, I'm an adult." I threw her a steely glance. Biting her lower lip, Reid backpedaled. "Legally, that is."

"Right," I quipped. "And when you stop trying to accidentally kill people, I will treat you as such. Until then..."

"Until then?" she asked.

I patted her on the head. "Until then, you will be my little teenage sister." I gave her a warm smile and ruffled her hair.

She swatted my hand away. "Stop."

"Never," I said in my most Vincent Price–like voice. "But anyhoo." I slid onto the swivel bar stool beside her. "Something crazy weird happened to me a few minutes ago."

Sera brushed flour off one bronzed arm. Oh, I was so jealous of those toned limbs of perfection. "You mean other than our sister trying to kill us?"

"Well, yes indeed."

Sera leaned her elbows on the counter. Her eyes lit with amusement. "Do tell."

So I filled them in. "And then she basically said that because of that interview in the Birmingham News, we'd stirred up a bed of fire ants."

Sera quirked an eyebrow. "That makes no sense."

"Yeah. That's stupid," Reid added. She sipped her cocoa. "Doing that should increase business, not make a mess of things."

I tapped the Formica counter. "I know. It's weird. Totally weird."

Sera wove her fingers through her chin-length bob. She glanced up. A vacant, whimsical expression sequestered her face. "You don't say."

I turned. A man with a shock of sandy hair strolled down Main. He wore indoor soccer shoes and green pants that weren't fit for anyone except an old man playing golf.

I pinched my nose. "Ugh. Don't look and maybe he won't notice us."

Too late. Tim Harper looked up at us.

"Sera," I said, my voice sharp. "Don't even think about—"

She lifted her hand and waved.

"—waving at him." My sister beamed at the man who, six months ago, had broken her heart.

Tim waved back. He smiled at me. I shot imaginary darts from my eyes, silently warning him not to ravage her heart again. He walked right on by. Either he took my hint, or he had someone else to meet. From the recent rumor mill, my bets were placed on Tim having a girl to see.

"Sera, you've really got to focus on other guys," I said. "Tim's not the only man out there."

She scrubbed her fingers through her hair. "I know. I'm just not over him. He's really great, you know?"

I rolled my eyes. "Yeah, really great. He broke off your engagement and now flirts with you from the sidewalk. Classy guy."

She stuck her tongue out at me.

Reid dropped her cocoa spoon to the counter with a clank. "Speaking of other guys out there—who is that?"

I turned my head. Standing across the street and blatantly staring into the store, stood a man wearing black from head to foot as if that were a totally normal thing to do in June in Alabama. His jaw looked like it had been carved with a straight razor, and his blond hair was tied back. Dark shades masked his eyes, and his cool expression looked almost too cool. Like, I'm too cool for school, dude.

Loser.

"Why's he wearing that coat?" Reid said. "It's like a thousand degrees outside."

"It's not a coat. It's a duster," I corrected.

"Whatever. Who wears that sort of thing?" Reid said.

"Assassins," Sera said.

Reid and I scowled at her.

Sera shrugged. "What? That is what assassins wear. I've seen enough movies to know. Besides, who other than an assassin would wear that this time of year?"

She wasn't kidding. Temperatures easily topped ninety degrees in early June in Alabama. Most everyone wore shorts during the summer.

"A homeless person would wear a duster," I said.

Sera flipped the ends of her hair. "We don't have homeless people in Silver Springs. Besides, he's too hot to be homeless."

"Yeah," Reid said, leaning over to see him better. "He's way too hot to be homeless."

I pulled her hair. "Don't even think about it, Reid. That guy is trouble. T-R-O-U-B-L-E."

She jerked her head away. "Ow."

"Good. I'm glad it hurt. He's too old for you and clearly mentally off to be wearing such a ridiculous outfit." I clicked my tongue. "Well then, never mind about my news. That guy takes the meaning of weird to a whole new level."

He crossed the street, heading straight for the bakery. Was he coming in? Why would he do that? Assassins didn't eat muffins or croissants or brownies. They ate people—everyone knew that.

My insides jumped and jittered. There was no reason to be nervous, but I was. As the clutches of fear gripped me, I moved to my best defense—I chewed my fingernails.

"Oh my God. Do you think he wants to eat us?" Reid said. "Should I offer myself first?"

I smacked the back of her head. "Reid! Shut it."

He extended his hand, grabbed the door and swung it open. The three of us held a collective breath as the stranger filled the door frame. Up close it was obvious that this was no ruffian. Well, not that obvious. His black shirt hugged his chest, revealing the outline of pectorals cut from marble. He could have lifted the entire building on those broad shoulders of his, and that jawline—the one I thought was carved with a straight razor? Well, good God almighty, I could have slit my wrists on it. Not that I wanted to. I didn't want to. Really.

Sera leaned over. "Stop drooling."

I closed my mouth.

A woman's voice broke the spell. Imagine rocks being pressed through a cheese grater while your first-grade teacher runs her nails over a chalkboard, and you'll almost—and I mean almost—come close to understanding the exact timbre of Jenny Butts's voice.

"Um, thank you," Jenny said to the assassin as he held the door open for her. Okay, so her voice didn't really sound that bad, but just wait. Her personality totally made up for what her voice lacked.

The man nodded, released the door and disappeared down the street. I shivered.

"Bye," Reid said faintly.

Sera turned to the newcomer. "What can I do for you today, Jenny?" she asked brightly.

I slid off the stool and crept toward the front door. I was not, I repeat, not in the mood to deal with Jenny Butts.

Jenny pumped her hands to emphasize each word. "Y'all. Y'all. Y'all." She stopped as if expecting us to bow down. Not going to happen. When we didn't, she continued. "I cannot believe I'm standing in one of the most famous stores in Silver Springs. Y'all. Seriously. I mean, I can't deny that I wasn't disappointed that they didn't interview me for my home decor shop, but they did y'all right by that article."

"Thanks," Sera said.

Jenny smiled, walked over to the counter and snatched a brownie out from under a glass dome. She took a bite. "Oh, Sera, these are phenom. I mean it. Best ever."

"Thanks again," Sera said.

"Y'all's stuff is amazing, but my shop probably does twice the business you do. I don't understand why I wasn't featured as well."

See what I mean? Totes annoying.

"Bless your heart, Jenny. I don't know why you weren't interviewed. Do you know why, Dylan?" Sera said.

Crap. Jenny whirled to look at me. She traced a finger over

the brownie. "It's not that my feelings are hurt. But I've been here longer than the two of you, and I just don't understand it. People love my store. I mean love it. They like y'all's stuff, too, but I sell things hand over fist. I mean, folks come from Birmingham just for my homemade decorations, so I really don't understand it."

Dear Lord, once Jenny got on a roll, she never shut up.

She laughed. "One of the girls suggested that perhaps Dylan slept with the interviewer, but I said that was ridiculous. Dylan would never do that. First of all, the article was written by a woman. Secondly, the whole town knows she hasn't slept with anyone since high school, since Colten Blacklock stood her up at prom. Besides, Olivia Helm was in my shop the other day—you know she just got engaged—"

"That's great, Jenny. Thanks for stopping by. Next time the News asks us for an interview, we'll be sure to mention you." I grabbed her by the shoulders and scooted her toward the door. "You can pay for the brownie later."

"Oh," Jenny whispered. "Sera doesn't know, does she?" She lifted a hand to her face, her eyes wide with concern.

"No, she doesn't, and I want to keep it that way," I whispered back. With your big mouth, I'm surprised she doesn't, I wanted to add, but I stayed quiet. I would not have put it past Jenny to spread doom and gloom on Sera just to make herself feel better since her store was overlooked for that interview. Well, not on my watch.

Jenny twisted back to look at Sera. "Don't forget you're doing the confections for the solstice dance. And," she said, locking her legs, "the dance committee wants to make both of you guests of honor for the solstice party. Will you do it?"

I yanked her by the arm. "Sure. Of course. We'll do anything the committee wants. Now, time to go." And with that, I shoved her out the front door.

When I turned back, Sera smirked. "What was that all about?"

I wiped my hands on my jeans. "Oh, nothing. I just thought it was time for Jenny to spout her big mouth off somewhere else."

"Good riddance," Sera said. "Though it will be fun to be the guests of honor at the dance, even though I'm not looking forward to all the baking."

"You volunteered weeks ago," I said.

She shrugged. "I know."

"Guests of honor," Reid said. "That should be cool. Hey, is it true what she said?"

"About what?" I asked.

"About that Colten guy?"

Dang that Jenny and her Mouth of the South. "Of course not. I don't know what she's talking about."

Reid picked up her empty mug and rose. "Seemed pretty true. So is that why you hate men?"

I gave her a good, long look. "I don't hate men."

"You never date any."

"That doesn't mean I hate them."

Reid shrugged. "Okay. Whatever. But it seemed true. You got your panties in a wad pretty quickly after she said that."

I did get my panties in a wad, but not because of that part of the monologue of vomit. I stopped Jenny because she was about to spill the beans that Sera's ex-boyfriend, the worthless Tim Harper, whom she'd waved at only moments before, was now engaged to Olivia Helm. I didn't need that drama. Not right now.

I sliced the air with my hand. "What she said is absolutely not true about me."

Sera patted me on the shoulder. "Of course it isn't. We believe you."

I needed a glass of wine. To heck with it, I needed the whole box.

"And with that, I'll see you both later." I pushed out the door, flipping them off as I left.

***

As soon as six o'clock hit, I put the CLOSED sign up on the shop. "Good night, Carrie. See you tomorrow."

Carrie shouldered her purse. "You going to work on your dress tonight?"

The blue gown beckoned me. Mostly finished, I really only needed to add a few sequins here and there and finish the hem. I'd taken it home several nights in a row but didn't feel up to it tonight.

"Nah. I'll work on it tomorrow."

"See you then," she said.

I locked up and met Sera and Reid out front. "Think Grandma and Nan will want pizza?" I asked.

Reid shrugged. "If they don't, I do."

"Okay," Sera said, pushing Reid into the backseat. "We'll just give you their slices, not even feed them."

"I was only saying," Reid grumbled.

"Great! Pizza it is," I said, trying to force a truce between the two. Though after the near fatal ammonia-and-bleach episode, I had the feeling it would be a long time before Sera fully trusted Reid in the back of the store. Or the front. Or anywhere, for that matter.

We jetted off through town. Let me be honest here, my ten-year-old Nissan is not going to "jet" anywhere. If you consider "jetting" burping and sputtering, then it does that. But if you're thinking it goes from zero to sixty in eight seconds, I laugh at you.

We passed Gus's, home of the fried burger, the train depot, and Jenny Butts as she locked up Rustic Touch and Travel. You heard correctly. There was also a travel agency in her store. No comment.

We wound our way up the hill toward First Baptist. The squat building sat stoic with its Roman columns and red brick. It quietly guarded our sleepy town. A lone summer breeze wafted over its face, lazily blowing the dwarf gardenias set in front of it. A couple of minutes later we entered our neighborhood of one-hundred-year-old craftsman homes.

"Nan! You want pizza?" Reid called out as we entered.

Sera wrung her finger in her ear. "Way to make me deaf, Reid."

She glanced back and grinned. "You're welcome."

Nan came out of the kitchen. "Sure thing."

"How is she today?" I asked, bending over and kissing the papery cheek of Hazel Horton, my grandmother, who was, unfortunately, frozen in a state of mutism. That meant she didn't talk and she barely moved.

Nan tilted her head back and forth. "The same. She ate a full lunch, though."

Reaching down, I wrapped my hand around my grandma's and squeezed. I didn't do it too hard, though. I'd hate to hurt her. Not that squeezing her hand would do any sort of permanent damage—I'm not dense, you know. It's just that when you see the same person day in and out respond to very little stimuli, it's hard to know what causes them pain.

"Hi, Grandma."

She didn't react. She hardly ever did. With Nan's prodding, she would walk and eat, but not much more. I felt like Grandma could hear us, but a barrier stood in her way of responding. Right now, if I grabbed her hands and helped her stand, she would do it, but that's all she would do—stand board still and wait for me to move her around.

The doctors didn't know how long it would last or even what caused it. There were no drugs to help her. Sometimes mutism occurred in stroke victims, but Grandma hadn't experienced a stroke. So we were at a loss as to why this afflicted her. Without the help of Nan, her live-in nurse, I think we as sisters would be lost, too. Literally. Grandma raised us after our parents died in a car accident. I was ten, Sera was eight and Reid just a baby. So she'd been both mother and father to us for all our lives. I can say with confidence that we loved her deeply.

Though I have to admit, she had been a little nutty before the frozen state occurred. Like she'd say strange things sometimes—talk about unicorns and such. I know, right? A little off, that's all.

"Do you think Grandma will eat pizza?" I asked.

Nan ran a hand through her short pepper-colored hair. "Why not? Who doesn't like pizza? And girls, I read today's paper. Loved the article. Those folks at the News did the town justice."

"You think so?" Sera asked, plopping onto a floral-patterned wingback chair.

Nan smiled, her wise eyes sparkling. "I know so."

***

"Want to go to Java Joe's tonight?" Sera asked after we had eaten the pizza.

I sat up on the couch, the weight of food making it hard to move. "Ugh. I think I ate too much. So tired."

She threw a napkin at me. "Which is why you need coffee. Want to go?"

I shook my head. "No. I need to fix Reagan Eckhart's dress. She's going to stop by tomorrow and try it on."

"What's wrong with it now? Is it the wrong dress?" she joked.

Sera knew all too well my problems with Reagan and The Dress, as it had come to be known. At first it was the wrong design, then the wrong color (how many different shades of white could there be?) and now, of course, the bling issue.

"Too many sequins," I said.

Sera patted her full belly. "She told you last week she wanted more."

I sighed. "I know, and now she wants less."

"Lord help that man who's about to marry her. Does he know what he's getting into?"

I pulled my hair over one shoulder and started to braid it. "Pretty sure. He doesn't seem too gaga over her if you ask me."

Reid chimed in. "Would you be gaga over her? I mean, she's pretty and all, but she's a total witch."

"Agreed." I yawned. "Anyway, I'd better go down to the shop and fix that dress so that I don't have to deal with her wrath."

"Why didn't you bring it home and work on it here?" Reid asked.

"Because it's huge. Too much train to cram into a car."

Sera caught my yawn. "Good luck on both fronts. Since you don't want to get coffee, I guess we'll be here watching B horror movies."

Crap. I hated missing B horror movie night. "What are you going to watch?"

Reid scrolled through the Netflix options. "Tonight it's Killer Klowns from Outer Space."

"Oh man, I didn't want to miss that one. Let me know how it is, and be sure to turn the volume down so Grandma and Nan don't get scared."

"We will."

With that, I was off to fix Reagan's dress. I hit the Unlock button on my key ring. The car beeped softly. When I reached it, I stood and looked up and down the street. It was completely empty, the quiet hum of the streetlights the only sound. A slow tingle spread over the back of my neck.

If it was so empty, why did I get the feeling I was being watched?

THREE

Perfect Fit jumped and jangled the next day. Okay, so I was the one doing the jumping, and it was really more like jiggling than jangling given the girly parts God blessed me with. But we were slammed. And I mean slammed. The article in the paper had certainly done its job and all too well.

The ever awesome Carrie kept each and every client watered and replenished with snacks until I could give them my undivided attention. Part of the Perfect Fit experience was that I pulled the garments I thought best for whatever occasion a client needed to be outfitted for. My knack for finding the correct size and style was legendary. At least in my own mind. Not that I'm super tooting my own horn here, but I have sewn every article of clothing in my store. I know it inside and out, so I'm best qualified to find what someone's looking for.

"I need an assistant," Carrie said as I whizzed past.

"You're my assistant," I said.

"Yes, but it's impossible to make coffee, keep the cucumber sandwiches replenished and refill the nut bowl."

I glanced at the snack area. She was right. We were out of everything. "Run to Sera's and ask for some scones or croissants or something. Be quick."

She returned with an armload of confections. I loved my

sister. I owed her one. Or a thousand. A few hours and a dozen or so treats later, the rush finally settled down. I collapsed on the lounging couch.

"Thank goodness that's over," I said.

"I know. I'm exhausted," Carrie said. She inspected her nails. "Drat. I chipped a nail."

"It's a gel manicure. They don't chip."

"Well, this one did." She showed me her finger.

"Oh, so it did."

"Can I go fix it?"

I threw her an incredulous look. "Right now? What if we get another rush?"

"But my nail. It needs it," she pleaded.

Seriously. Girlfriend had a problem. "Okay. But be quick."

I closed my eyes and relaxed. The bell tinkled as the door opened. I groaned. Time to get back at it. "Welcome to Perfect Fit."

"Hey, Dylan!"

Reagan Eckhart. Noooooooo! I opened my eyes and rose. "Reagan, so glad to see you."

She beamed. "I'm guessing you've got my dress ready?"

"And how," I said. "Let me go get it."

I passed Carrie, who wasn't bothering to fix just the one nail. She was redoing both hands. Sheesh. How I ever managed to get any work out of her was beyond me.

I presented the dress to Reagan.

"It's gorgeous. Just the way I always envisioned it."

Sure. Right. At least today. Ask her tomorrow and she'll probably change her mind again. "I'm so glad you like it. That's what I aim for here, a satisfied customer at every corner."

"Well, I am."

"Great. I'll store it until the wedding."

I placed the gown in back. When I returned, Reagan stood beside my blue dress, the one I had been making for the solstice dance. Carrie stood beside her.

"I don't know," Carrie said. "That's Dylan's gown."

"What's going on?" I asked, raising my eyebrows as intimidatingly high as I could.

Reagan rushed over and grabbed both my hands like we were best freaking friends. I thought we'd already covered this. Mortal enemies. At least in high school. Tenuous friends in the present at best.

"Oh Dylan, that dress is simply gorgeous. I absolutely love it."

"Thanks. I'm wearing it to the solstice banquet."

Her face fell in true dramatic princess fashion. "But it would be absolutely perfect for the rehearsal dinner on Friday. I mean, it's a one-of-a-kind Dylan Apel. When everyone finds out I'm wearing a dress made especially for me, your sales will skyrocket."

"Um. I make every dress by hand. They're all one of a kind."

She scoffed. "You know what I mean, Dyl."

Dyl? Were we chums now?

I plastered on my best sincere smile as I unhinged her claws from my arm. "Reagan, I love that you want to wear it, but it's really been made just for me." I scanned her waif-thin form. "You and I aren't the same size."

"I'll give you three thousand dollars for it."

My ears must not be working. "What?"

"Make it four thousand."

Suddenly all bad thoughts about Reagan were thrown on the floor and squashed beneath my foot. "Carrie, get the dress ready for Ms. Eckhart."

I was not selling out. Really, I wasn't. Of course one of my wedding dresses cost a fortune, but a regular dress—I would never charge four grand for it. More like five hundred. So yes, I see dollar signs the same as anyone else. Besides, paying Nan to take care of Grandma wasn't exactly cheap. Insurance didn't cover most of it. So all my extra money went to her salary. The same can be said for Sera. Reid, so far, hadn't discovered anything she was good at—besides teenage whining, that is—so she couldn't contribute to the family fund.

Carrie wiggled her nails at me. "Can't. They're wet."

For goodness' sake. Why was she my assistant again? "Come on, Reagan. Let me put it in a room for you."

I unzipped the back and pulled the dress off the mannequin. The fabric felt warm, but it was hot in the store, what with the rush of bodies we'd had earlier, so I didn't give it another thought. After hanging the gown in the dressing room, I left Reagan to try it on.

After a few minutes of straightening clothes on hangers, I noticed Reagan still hadn't emerged. Odd. I made my way down the hall and knocked on the door.

"Reagan?"

No answer.

I knocked harder. "Reagan, are you okay?"

Still no answer.

Okay, do I barge in? What if she's naked? I didn't want her to kill me. I gave it one more round of hard knocks.

"Reagan?"

When she failed to answer for the third time, I turned the knob. She hadn't locked it. That was awfully brave of her. Not that anyone would charge in and try to see her unclothed. But I never entered a dressing room without locking the door. Did that make me paranoid?

I edged the door open a tad. The acrid sent of sulfur assaulted my nose. Reagan must have ripped the biggest fart ever for the room to smell that bad. I pinched my nostrils shut.

"Reagan?" I pushed the door all the way open. She stood in the middle of the room, the blue dress hanging limply from her body. Her peachy flesh was no more. In its place, blackened skin sizzled as if it had been fried to a crisp. A sulfurous smell wafted off her body, filling the room.

Dear Lord.

My dress had killed her, which meant—

I'd killed Reagan!

FOUR

Ten minutes later, half the town was swarming outside the building, trying to see what all the fuss was about. I swear, I hadn't seen a line so deep in Silver Springs since Gus's reopened after they updated the interior. That's how this town was—the slightest hint of new or different and everyone plus their mother showed up.

Sera handed me a Styrofoam cup of sweet tea. I smiled weakly. "Thanks."

She hugged me. "Sure thing."

Trying to drown my sorrows with refreshing liquid sometimes worked, but I doubted it would wash this guilt away. Somehow a dress I'd made had killed Reagan. How could that be? I was making it for myself, not her. Not that I could kill someone even if I tried. My clothing always made people happy. It didn't physically hurt them. Never. Ever.

I shook the cup to break up the ice clumps, and took a sip. The sugar very nearly crystallized on my tongue. If it hadn't, the tea wouldn't have been sweet enough for my taste. This one was perfect. Of course it was. Sera had made it.

"So she was burned up?" Sera snapped her fingers. "Just like that?"

"Yeah," I murmured, my heart heavy. I rubbed a patch of goose bumps from my arm.

"Like a chicken on the spit too long?" Reid asked.

"Shush," I warned her. "It's awful as it is."

"Is Carrie okay?" Sera asked.

I nodded toward the hall of dressing rooms. "She's talking to the police now."

A tall, dark-skinned detective in a navy-blue suit jotted down notes on a pad while Carrie told him what she knew. He'd introduced himself as Detective Blount. His suit jacket hung a little loose on him. Hmmm. I should start making men's clothing. I could really improve on what was currently out there. Was that wrong of me? Thinking about business when a woman had died in my store?

"Have you talked to him?" Sera asked.

I nodded. "Told him what I knew, which wasn't much." Only that I was a total murderer, if by accident.

Detective Blount made his way over to us. He gave me a weary smile. "We should have the scene cleaned up pretty quick. I'd like to ask you to keep the victim's name to yourself until we've had time to contact the family."

"Of course," I said.

He placed a hand on his hip. "Your assistant mentioned that you were making that dress for the town banquet."

"Yes," I said. "I was working on it here, and Reagan happened to see it and wanted to try it on."

He wrote in his notepad. "And you let her?"

"Yes. After she offered me four grand for it."

He raised an eyebrow. "Four thousand dollars for a dress?"

"Detective Blount, in case you didn't know, the Eckharts are wealthy."

"Fabulously," Reid confirmed.

"This is my sister, Reid," I said, answering his question before he asked. "Reagan could easily afford a four-thousand-dollar dress."

"Had you let anyone else try it on?"

"No. It was obviously an unfinished piece. It had a ragged hem and strings at the shoulders."

"But you let her try it on."

The room felt very hot. Stifling, in fact, as I realized the detective's questions pointed more and more toward me doing bodily harm to Reagan. Which apparently was true. I wanted to tell him the truth, admit my guilt, but what was I going to say? Officer, my clothing has a strange effect on people. Normally this doesn't harm them, but this time I managed to kill someone.

I wanted to puke.

"Do you know anyone who's an expert in chemicals?" he asked, changing gears.

"You mean like a chemist?" I asked.

He nodded.

"No. Why?"

He shrugged. "Just trying to figure out what happened. I have a dead woman, her skin cooked like she'd been baked in an oven, and a dress that's perfectly intact."

"That is super odd," Reid said. "Good luck with that."

I gave her a scornful look.

"Who are you again?" he asked.

I shoved Reid back. "My little sister who likes to butt her nose into places it doesn't belong. Detective, I'll tell you anything I can."

"Great. How about a list of where you get your fabric from?"

"I'll get it for you right now."

A couple of hours later the police and bystanders were gone. I had sent Carrie home to recuperate. I hoped she wouldn't be forever scarred by this. I sank onto a lounging couch, trying to figure out the best way to turn myself in.

Sera called from the back hall. "At least she didn't leave a mark."

"Sounds like you're talking about a dog," Reid said.

"Reid, have some compassion," I snarled.

She shrugged. "It's not like I'm spouting off that Reagan was a mega-meanie from hell. I only said the way Sera made it sound, it

31

seemed like she was referring to a dog who'd pooped on the carpet, and not a dead woman."

"That's awfully ladylike of you," I said.

"Thank you."

"That wasn't a compliment."

Reid scoffed. "Sorry for saying it like it is."

"You're forgiven."

Sera appeared from the hallway. She brushed her hands together. "It's not so bad in there. I was afraid there'd be some sort of grim stain, but there's nothing."

"Nothing except the fact that somehow a dress I made killed her. I mean, I know we're gifted and all, but I've never, not once in my life, killed someone!"

Sera and Reid exchanged glances.

"You can say it," I said. "It's the absolute truth. I killed Reagan Eckhart."

"You didn't kill her."

We did a collective head turn toward the front door. I'd been so lost in my self-deprecating announcement that I hadn't heard the bell above the front door tinkle. But it had, and in the doorway stood the redhead from the day before. She wore bangles on her wrists again, and they clinked as she crossed her arms over her chest.

"Like I said, you didn't kill her."

I didn't know what to say. I didn't talk about my gift with strangers. None of us did. I wasn't sure if the best course of action was to laugh off what I'd said or listen to her. I glanced at Sera for backup, but she looked just as dumbfounded as me.

I had to say something. "Okay? Thank you for your input, but the store's closed. We've had a tragedy occur."

She dropped her purse to the floor, apparently settling in for the long haul. "I know. I told y'all you'd stirred up a fire-ant bed with that article."

"Yeah," I said. "Want to explain what that meant?"

She smiled. "Sure thang. You know when that reporter wrote

that she looked younger when trying on one of your dresses? Only one way that can happen. That little article let the whole wide world know exactly what you are."

I swiveled my hips and planted my feet on the floor. "And what exactly is that?"

Her upper lip curled into a half smile, half snarl. "Darlin', you're a witch. And now someone wants to kill you."

FIVE

I yanked my ear. I must have missed some wax when I cleaned it this morning. "What?"

"Did she just call us the B word?" Reid asked.

"That's what it sounded like," Sera said. "That's pretty rude."

"That ain't what I said. I called you witch—"

"That's what I thought she said, too!" I added.

The redhead adjusted her clanking bangles. "That ain't what I said."

Reid crossed her arms defiantly. "Then what did you say?"

"I called you witches."

My sisters and I exchanged glances. Then we busted our guts in laughter.

"Oh, y'all," Sera said. "That is so funny."

I wiped a tear from the corner of my eye. "I needed a good laugh. Ha! Witches. So if we're witches, who are you, the boogeyman?"

We laughed again. The woman's cheeks shifted to bloodred. Seriously. Who walks into a store and calls people witches? Obviously she was crazy. Had she recently escaped from the loony bin? Were people looking for her? I reached for the phone in my pocket. Time to dial 911.

The woman rubbed her forehead. "Good grief. Couldn't

Hazel have told you anythin'?"

I jerked my head at the mention of my grandmother. Attention! New level of creep factor achieved. "How do you know about her?"

She pouted her lips while sucking in her cheeks. Even creepier. "I've known your grandmother since she was a little girl."

Okay, crazy lady. "Don't you mean, since you were a little girl?"

A trill bubbled from the back of her throat. "Girls, it's about time someone told you exactly who you are." She grasped the back of a chair and dug her nails in. "Y'all are witches. I'm Esmerelda Pommelton, Queen Witch of the South. And I am ninety-eight and a half years old."

I snickered.

"Don't people stop counting halves when they're like ten?" Reid asked.

"Apparently until you reach your nineties. Then it's back in again," Sera said.

I stood up. I'd had it with this crap. "I appreciate you stopping by, but I have no idea who you are, and this is a sensitive time. Someone just died. Thanks but no thanks." I crossed to the door and opened it.

Esmerelda snapped her fingers.

A small ball of fire hovered over her hand. Orange and red flames licked the air, crackling as they fed on oxygen. The orb started spinning.

Holy crap.

Crimson and orange twirled like a barbershop pole. The ball tightened and elongated, taking on the form of a curvaceous woman rocking her hips back and forth. The doorknob slipped from my fingers. Well, okay then. I guess this kind of changed things.

"Wow. That's a neat trick. Can you teach me how to do that?" Reid asked.

"I don't think that's a trick," Sera whispered.

35

I exchanged dumbstruck looks with my sisters.

The woman smiled. "Now that I have your attention, your lives are in danger."

***

"We've been watchin' your family for a while," Em (she preferred that to Esmeralda) explained. "When your grandmother left Savannah nearly twenty years ago, she never told any of us where she was headin'. We eventually found her and have spent the last few years watchin' from a distance."

"Until now," I said.

"Until now." She folded her hands and delicately cupped them over one knee. Her long, tapered fingers reminded me of a woman in a classical painting. Ivory skin, long, well-constructed bones—the type an aristocrat owned. Too bad her redneck accent ruined it.

"So you're still holding tight on being ninety-eight," I said. It's not that I didn't believe her. I mean, the woman lit fire from her hand, and she wasn't even wearing sleeves. But come on, she didn't look a second over thirty.

Em threw me a disdainful glance—the kind old ladies perfect. Maybe I was wrong. Perhaps under that creamy skin lay a shriveled-up octogenarian. I know, technically an octogenarian would be in their eighties. I am aware, thank you.

"Like I said, I'm ninety-eight and a half years old. One of my talents is longevity. I age, but very slowly. Y'all will probably age like ordinary Joe Shmoes, but I've placed a lot of my magic in stayin' young."

"Why's that?" I asked.

Her eyes widened like it was the stupidest question on earth. "Because I'm Queen Witch of the South." Like, duh. "It took me a long time to get here, and I ain't lettin' my throne go to waste because of somethin' as silly as death."

That made sense.

Not at all.

Sera held a hand over her mouth, hiding a smile.

"What do you find so funny?" Em said.

"I can't help it. Whenever you say Queen Witch, all I can think of is Queen Bit—"

She threw her arms into the air. "That's enough! If y'all want to survive until the summer solstice, by all means, make jokes. Laugh at the fact that a witch is trying to kill you. Go ahead. If you don't want my help rootin' out who spelled your dress, continue to act like idiots. But if you want to live—and by that I mean survive to see your next birthday—shut up and start acting like adults."

Someone was certainly testy. We sat in silence. Reid braided a strand of hair, Sera rubbed her arms and I simply watched.

"Now then. I take it I have the floor." She looked at each of us before continuing. "There're witches who choose to increase their power, not by learnin' and refinin', but by stealin' magic. They seek out other witches and take their power. So when ignorant kittens like yourselves go around announcin' to the world, in a newspaper article of all things"—she shook her head in disgust—"that you're witches, you draw bad elements to you like a ship to a lighthouse."

"What if the lighthouse is turned off?" Reid said. "Won't the ship crash and burn?"

"It's too late for any turnin' off. Half the state knows what you are, and since plenty of witches aren't officially registered, that makes it impossible for me to know who's trying to kill you."

"Witches are registered?" Sera asked. "Like in a book?"

Em ran a finger under her chin like she was feeling for coarse hairs. "Yes. That's how we keep track of each other. But like I said, plenty don't register, choosin' to stay unknown."

"But I don't understand what happened with my gift," I said. "I've never known anyone before to see an image of themselves from their youth. My clothing may offer the feeling, but never a mirage, or a vision."

Em shrugged. "There aren't always answers to every question. Magic is a strange beast. Most likely it changed, morphing as you've aged—like our bodies going from childhood to puberty to adulthood."

Okay. "So let me get this straight," I said. "We're witches, apparently, and there's another witch out there trying to kill us because they want our power."

She plucked something from her face. Probably one of those hairs her fingers had been searching for. "Bingo. Y'all are descended from a long line of witches. It's a shame your grandmother never told you, but there ain't nothin' I can do about it now."

I squinted as if that would help me understand this craziness any better. "So you don't know who killed Reagan because they're not registered in your book?"

"Right."

"That's not very helpful," I said. "I mean, if you're going to show up and turn our worlds upside down, then maybe you should've had an idea about where to start looking for clues."

Em pulled out a compact and powdered the tip of her nose. "I'm a witch, not a mind reader. And watch your tone, little girl." She snapped the compact shut with a click.

Who was she calling little girl? "Sorry," I said drily. "I've never met a Queen Witch before. I don't know how people talk to you, but I'm not about to bow down just because you can do some silly parlor trick."

"Silly parlor trick?" Em's eyes narrowed to slits. A sudden breeze blew through the store, lifting my hair. My clothes fluttered, fighting against the wind. Something told me it wasn't the air conditioner kicking on.

"Uh-oh," Sera whispered. "I don't think you should've said that."

I turned to her. "I don't appreciate being told someone wants to kill me, and then not have the faintest clue where to start looking."

Sera's eyes grew bigger. "I think you should apologize."

Clothes swayed on the racks. The hangers ground against the metal bars as they swung to and fro, higher and higher. A stack of papers on my desk lifted and flapped like a deck of cards being shuffled by an invisible hand. In the corner a miniature tornado tumbled about. It edged to the center, where it caught the papers and swallowed them in its whirling cyclone. The funnel danced through the room, heading straight for a line of my best gowns.

Fear gripped my throat. I did not, I repeat, did not want to have to remake any of those dresses. It had taken practically forever to get them out, and the last thing I needed was some witch lady with a bad temper ruining them.

I jumped to my feet. "Okay! I'm sorry. You're a witch. These aren't parlor tricks, and I appreciate you warning us about the killer."

The wind vanished, sending a storm of papers fluttering to the floor.

Em tucked a strand of hair behind one ear. "If you're finished complainin', I'm here to help you."

"That's good," I said in my most cheery voice. Sera scowled at me. "I'm for real. I'm not being fake," I said as I slowly sank back into my chair.

Em rose. "Dylan, let's get one thing straight—it wasn't your magic that caused that girl's death. Someone placed a spell on that dress. That spell was meant for you. Not your sisters. You."

I rubbed my thighs. It wasn't cold in the store, but I couldn't help but feel chilled, as if the entire situation had zapped the warmth from me. "Whoever did this killed Reagan. We may not have been best friends, but she didn't deserve to die—especially when she wasn't even the intended victim." A thought occurred to me. "Em, you said bad witches want to steal power from others. How can they do that if the spell kills the person? Like, if I'd put on the dress, would it have killed me and the person then somehow got my power?"

Em paced the room. "You can't take magic if the victim is dead. That there spell backfired."

"So you're saying the person isn't a very good witch," Reid said.

Em paused. "Honey, she ain't good at all."

I shuddered. "And the person who did that to the dress—they had obviously been in here."

Em nodded.

I dropped my head in my hands. "Someone who was a customer got close to my dress and spelled it, as you say."

"Do you have a record of everyone you helped in the last few day?" Sera asked.

I shook my head. "No. We've been so busy since the article, I haven't kept track. Besides, I didn't even recognize half of them." Great. Super great. There was no way to narrow down who the killer was.

Sera raised her hand.

"Yes?" Em asked.

"One question. If you can't take the power when someone's dead, how do you take it?"

Em regarded us for a moment. "You skin 'em just like a rabbit. Only the witch is alive."

Ew. Super ew. I did not plan on dying by being skinned alive. Gross. And seriously painful. Who would do that? Only some sort of deranged person.

"So someone wants to skin me alive?" I asked.

"Yes." She stopped, stared at us. "And y'all need to be ready for 'em. In your current state, y'all are completely vulnerable. I need to awaken your power. That way, you'll be able to learn the magic you need to protect yourselves."

"Awaken our power," Reid said. "How?"

"Join hands," Em said.

Sera whispered in my ear, "Are you sure we should do this?"

"Right now I'm not sure of anything. But it's not like it can make things worse. Besides, you might be able to learn that little fireball trick."

"Good point," she said.

We formed a circle.

Em chanted a few words under her breath. A flash of light filled the room while a surge of electricity streamed down my spine. My entire body tingled, and my breath balled up in the back of my throat.

"You can release each other."

I let go of my sisters' hands. My head swam as if my brain had been dunked in nitrous oxide. I stumbled forward. Em caught me.

"Steady. The power takes a little gettin' used to, but by dinnertime you won't notice a thing."

I sat down and massaged my temples. My sisters joined me on the couch.

Em arranged the bangles on her arm. "Chicklets, your power has been released. You're officially witches."

"What were we before?" Sera asked.

"Before, you were a little more than ants and a lot less than a witch." Em gave me a weary smile. "Now you can perform magic and hopefully"—her gaze swept from our feet to our crowns—"not be as bad as you look."

I tried not to be insulted by that.

"However," she said, "since y'all are freshly born witches, that also means that from now until the summer solstice, your magic will peak. It will grow stronger by the minute, until the longest day of the year. After that your magic will settle down. This is normal. Every witch goes through it, but most have the skill required to protect themselves because this is also a dangerous time, you know, since you have more power to steal."

I raised my palm, indicating for her to stop. "Let's rewind. Someone wants to kill me for my power—power that I didn't even know I had. And now, for the next two weeks that power will peak, which means if they kill me before the solstice, they get even more of that power."

"Y'all are some fast learners."

"Which also means they'll probably try harder to kill me."

Em cocked her head back and forth. "Yep. But the good news is, I'm here to protect you."

"Why will you protect us?" Sera asked.

Em pulled a tube of lipstick from her purse and applied a layer of red. She smacked her lips. "It ain't good to have rogue witches stealing people's magic. That much power could make someone…let's just say, unstoppable. They could do real damage to the council, never mind upper management."

"Council?" I asked.

"Of witches," she said. "Eliminate us, cause a witch war. There hasn't been one for sixty years, and I'm not about to see one happen on my watch."

"You said Dylan and Sera," Reid said. "Am I a witch, too?"

Em crossed to her, grasped her chin in her hand and turned Reid's head right and left. She inspected her face with care until finally releasing it.

"No."

"Oh," Reid said, dropping her gaze. Poor girl. All she wanted in the whole wide world was for her gift to come in. She'd need some chocolate-sundae therapy after this. I'd be happy to oblige.

"It might still come, but as of now, you ain't got a stitch of power." Em lifted her finger. "Which, if you think about it, is good for you. No one wants to kill you."

"I guess," Reid grumbled.

Em shouldered her purse. "Tomorrow we'll begin basic lessons on protection," Em said. "Y'all need to close your shops for the week. We'll work here."

"But the solstice is two weeks away," I said. "What could we possibly learn that will protect us from some crazy witch murderer?"

Em smiled. "If you work hard, I think you'll be satisfied with the results. Get a good night's sleep. You're going to need plenty of rest. Oh. And bring lots of water. Hydration is key to good spelling."

Okay, Mom. Should I also bring my yoga mat so I can nap after lunch?

Em left, and the three of us looked at each other.

"Looks like we're in some serious shi—"

"At least you didn't kill Reagan," Sera said.

That was true. Upside—I didn't kill Reagan Eckhart. Downside—someone wanted me dead. One point for downside. Darn it. I should've stayed in bed today.

SIX

When I got out of my car, a tingle washed over the back of my neck. There it was again. I felt that someone was hiding in the darkness, watching me. Who would be watching me?

It hit me—the killer. Of course! I had been the target of the spell that killed Reagan. That meant—

I ushered my sisters inside and bolted the door behind us.

And wedged a chair beneath the knob.

And looked for a plank of wood so I could nail the door shut.

Sera grabbed my arm. "What's going on?"

"I think someone's spying on us."

She turned off all the lights. I heard the low hum of a television coming from the back. Nan's usual nightly routine involved unwinding with the boob tube. She'd probably already put Grandma to bed. Good. I didn't want to have to explain what was going on.

We crouched over to the large window in the living room and nestled on the couch. I lifted the blinds to see out.

"You realize the porch light is on," Reid said. "If someone's watching the house, they can see us peeking out."

"Turn it off, then, Miss Smarty-pants," I said.

"I think I will."

She did. We glanced up and down the street. Rain earlier in the day had washed the road clean. Streetlights reflected in shallow pools that on a dry day were normally potholes. Drops of water lay scattered over cars that had been parked during the shower. Since I'd arrived later, there weren't any drops on mine.

"See if there are any cars that look dry," I said.

We scanned up and down. "There," Sera said. "That black SUV. It looks dry."

I squinted, unable to make out if someone sat in the car or not.

"Where are your binoculars?" I asked her.

"The ones from when we played 'spy' like, fifteen years ago?"

Was that supposed to embarrass me? It didn't. "Yeah, those."

"Reid has them."

I pushed a strand of hair from my face. "Why do you have them?"

"I use them for bird-watching."

"Right. And cardinals poop on my head. You better not be watching Rick undress."

"I'm not," she said with a load of guilt.

Rick Beck lived next door. Tall, dark-headed, and twenty-two. When he moved in six months ago, Reid had deemed him the perfect guy. It also helped that Rick was in the habit of mowing his yard shirtless like, every day.

I cocked my head toward my youngest sister. "I don't need the police to stop by with an arrest warrant for a peeping Tom."

"I'm not spying on him."

"How hot is he? I mean, I've seen him in the yard, but I haven't really paid much attention," Sera said.

"You can't even begin to believe," Reid said.

"Just go get the binoculars," I growled.

Reid pushed off the couch. "Okay, missy miss. Someone is certainly a crab apple today. Personally you don't know when to thank your lucky stars. You two are witches, and I'm a big nothing."

Crap. I'd forgotten all about the ice cream sundae. I'd get on that right after this. "Someone is trying to kill me, Reid. Can you

AMY BOYLES

please keep things in perspective?"

She huffed and went to fetch the binoculars.

"You could be a little nicer," Sera said.

I ignored her. "So Grandma's a witch, right? I mean, Em said that."

Sera pursed her lips. "Seems so. But why did she keep it from us?"

"I don't know. It's hard to swallow." I chewed a hangnail and spit it out. "I guess all this is real."

Sera rolled her eyes. "I'm pretty sure we're dealing with the otherworldly. Queen Witch, or whatever she is, made flames with her fingers, for goodness' sake."

"I know. I know."

Sera curled her legs underneath her. "You're such a skeptic."

Reid returned. She handed me the binoculars, and I aimed them at the vehicle. It was dark, but I swore I saw someone in the SUV.

"There's someone there."

"There is?" Sera said. "Let me see." She took a good look and exhaled. "You're right. Do you think it's the witch?"

A shiver rolled down my spine. "I don't know, but I'm not going to lay here and let whoever it is barge in and start skinning me. We'll take watches."

"Watches?" Reid asked.

"Yep. I'll go first. You two get some rest. Sera, I'll wake you up in a few hours."

***

No one came to kill me that night. Thank goodness. All I had for defense was a termite-eaten baseball bat. With my luck it would break on the first swing. I really needed a better weapon. Or perhaps I needed to learn some magic.

I still didn't know how I felt about that. I watched Grandma

46

the next morning, looking for any sign of magic in her. Of course when someone's frozen in a state of unresponsiveness, it's hard to garner any info from them.

I called Carrie, told her I'd be closing for the week but would still pay her normal wages. She seemed glad for the time off, and I couldn't blame her. I wouldn't want to walk into a place where I'd seen a dead body the day before.

Em sat waiting for us inside Perfect Fit. She wore a velour sweat suit. Dude. Someone needed to inform the ninety-eight-and-a-half-year-old that velour went out in the seventies. Though I had to admit, the purple outfit did look great with her red hair. So maybe I was a tad jealous. Or still bitter that this woman I didn't know had upturned my life.

I made a decision as I walked in the door. Unless I could make magic after a few hours, this lady was full of BS.

"Don't let a little lock stop you," I said.

Em laughed. "I didn't. Never do. Locks are easy to get around."

"How's that?" I asked.

She wiggled her fingers. "Y'all will find out soon enough." Her gaze floated from me to Sera to Reid. "Oh. You brought the talentless one. That's okay. We can use you as a third person. Magic always works best when done in threes, so even though you ain't got a lick of the gift, you're still strong in body."

Reid scrunched up her face. "What does that mean?"

"Never mind. Stand in a circle."

"It means you're a body, plain and simple," Sera said.

Reid pouted.

I ruffled her burgundy curls. "Cheer up. At least you're not on someone's hit list."

We circled round.

Em floated her arms to her side. "The first thing I'm goin' to teach you is a basic protection spell. This is the simplest and yet most powerful magic you can learn. If you'd known this the other day, you could have avoided someone enterin' your store and spellin' your dress." Em cleared her throat. "Ahem. Now. Link hands and think about protection. Think about staying safe."

"Me staying safe, or the three of us staying safe?" Sera asked.

"Good question," I said. "I was wondering the same thing."

"I don't think it matters," Reid added.

We looked at Em. She pressed the tips of her fingers to her chin. "The talentless one is correct." Reid shot us a triumphant smile. "It don't matter. Think about overall protection. That's the point."

"Should we close our eyes?" Sera asked.

"It helps," Em said.

I closed my eyes and concentrated on feeling safe.

"Focus on your core of power. Feel it in the center of your stomach. Think real hard on it."

I quirked an eyebrow. Yes, I was ready to think real hard on my core of power. Ha! I did eventually, focusing on my stomach. It growled at me. One slice of toast for breakfast hadn't done a very good job of filling me up.

"Focus. Concentrate," Em said.

So I did. I thought about keeping my family safe—all of us staying absolutely safe. I also thought about my growling stomach. It snarled in reply. I located a bubble of energy in my gut. As I focused, the air changed. It felt charged, as if a buzzing electric current had centered itself in our midst. Starting in my middle, a tingle washed over my body, energizing me. The hairs on my arms stood straight up, and I could feel it—power. Like nothing I'd ever experienced before.

"Open your eyes," Em said.

I did. A blue iridescent ball of…I don't know…energy, bobbed up and down in the midst of our circle.

"That is so cool," Reid said. "Did I do that?"

"No. They did," Em said.

Reid's face fell. "Oh. Well, didn't I at least help?"

"Not really."

Poor Reid. Dying to have her power.

"That is what I call a sphere of protection," Em said, circling the globe. "When placed right, it'll prevent anyone who wants to harm you from enterin' a buildin'. But in order to use it, you have to walk it over to the doorway and let it pop in the frame. That'll seal it. You ready?" She smiled at us expectantly.

We shrugged.

"Walk it over."

We stepped; it shimmered.

"Careful, y'all. Pretend this is one of those egg baby things you had to take care of when you were a kid. Don't break it."

"Egg baby?" Reid said.

"Before your time." I gritted my teeth, trying not to destroy the ball.

"Egg baby?" she repeated.

Sera sighed. "Every year at summer camp, we always had to blow the yolk out of an egg and pretend it was a baby. Get it? It was fragile. Now stop asking questions and focus."

"I don't know how she knew that," Reid said.

Em smiled. "There's a lot of stuff I know."

"Come on, let's go," I said.

I stepped forward, Sera stepped to one side and Reid stepped to the other. The sphere of protection, as Em called it, wobbled and shimmered.

"Y'all created it together; move it together."

"Let's go straight back," I said.

"There's a couch right behind me," Sera said.

I sighed. "Okay, Let's take a step to the right."

"Which right? My right or your right?" Reid asked.

"Your right."

The ball shook. The blue swirls on it vibrated. I bit my lower lip. We'd break the stupid thing before we made it to the door.

"Let's go," I said.

We moved right and then back. As we reached the door, I

said, "Okay. Now Reid, swing around so we can position it right."

"Why do I have to swing around? Why can't Sera?"

"There's a table in my way," Sera grumbled.

"Just someone swing around," I said.

Reid swung around, all right. She moved so fast the ball shook.

"Hold it, everybody. Stop."

The ball wobbled, flexing in and out like a muscle. And it popped. All over me. Blue magic-bubble gunk dissolved on my body. It didn't feel bad, sort of like a wave of warm air.

"Good job, y'all. Way to go," I said.

"Well, at least now you're protected," Reid said.

That was an upside. "How long does it last?" I asked Em.

"A few days, tops. Every spell is different, and since every witch is different, it's hard to say."

"Way to be specific," Sera whispered.

"You can keep practicin' on your own. I recommend tryin' it at home to see if you can create it individually. For training purposes it's best to work with each other, but in the real world you'll need to master these techniques."

Not such a bad idea. At least alone I wouldn't be contending with two bickering sisters.

"How about we take a little break?" Em said.

"Sure."

"Drink some water. It may not seem like it, but magic takes a lot out of you."

Reid saluted her. "Aye, aye, captain."

Em frowned. "In the witch world, there are specific rules. The first is being respectful to your elders. Witches who aren't learn that lesson the hard way."

"I'm not a witch," Reid shot back.

"That's true. You ain't got power, but you never know. Your magic could come in." She stared at Reid's head. "You have such pretty, pretty hair. I'd hate for you to lose it."

Reid's eyes widened. "My hair?"

Em patted Reid's cheek. "Mind your tongue, sweetie. It would be a shame for those curls to disappear."

Em exited to the back, leaving Reid to wring out the ends of her tresses. "You don't think she'd cut my hair, do you?"

"Of course not," I said.

Reid exhaled in relief.

"She doesn't have to. She'd spell it off or something."

Reid gasped.

Sera pointed out the window. "Hey, isn't that the SUV from last night?"

I glanced out. Sure enough, sitting across the street was the same black vehicle. "That's it."

"How can you tell?" Reid asked.

"Out-of-state plates," I said. "The back license on the vehicle last night was blue. See the one on the front fender of that one? Same color blue."

The driver's side window rolled down, revealing a man with dirty-blond hair.

"Oh my God," Sera said. "It's the assassin."

I grabbed the doorknob. Sera placed a restraining hand on my arm. "What are you doing?"

"I'm going to ask him why he's following us."

"You think he's following us?" Reid.

"Obviously. Why else would he keep popping up?"

Sera's grasp on my arm tightened. I looked at her. Tears welled in her eyes. "What if he tries something?"

I unhinged her hand from me. "Oh please. It's broad daylight. That guy's not going to try anything. If he does, there's witnesses." I yanked open the door and stormed out. The assassin, seeing me coming, looked up in what may or may not have been surprise. Dark shades shielded his eyes, so I really couldn't tell.

I stopped in front of his door, crossed my arms over my chest and tapped my toe. An intimidating stance, I know. "Just what do you think you're doing, following us?"

"Excuse me?" he asked.

Deep voice, kinda husky. Very sexy. My knees turned to jelly. Whoa. I needed those to stand. Couldn't have them collapsing out from under me now. I locked my legs and pursed my lips.

"You heard me. Following us. Who are you? What are you doing?"

He rested his arm on the lip of the window. Veins popped out from the taut skin. Strong, masculine fingers drummed the door. His smooth flesh looked so inviting. I wanted to run my fingers down it. I wiped a tinge of drool from the corner of my mouth. Why was I here again? To invite him in for cookies and coffee? Oh my gosh, what if he was spelling me and I didn't know it?

"Listen, you'd better explain why you're following me, or else I'll call the cops."

"No one's told you?" he asked in that deep, übermasculine voice of his.

I took a step back. "Told me what?"

He opened the door. "Come on. Let's go get you some answers." He stalked off toward my store. Not once did he bother to look back to make sure I was following him.

Well, that was rude.

***

"You haven't told them?" The assassin pointed the question at Em.

A slight blush smeared her cheeks. "I forgot."

The assassin leaned against a wall. He crossed massive arms over his chest.

"Hubba, hubba," Reid whispered.

"Hush," I said.

Reid shrugged. "What? I can't help it."

I shook my head. What was I going to do with her?

"Told us what?" Sera asked.

Em smiled. "I'm providin' you with a bodyguard."

"And I take it this is said bodyguard," I demanded.

The assassin nodded.

"So he's not an assassin?" Sera asked.

Em scowled at her. The assassin chuckled. "Not today," he said.

Oh. So did that mean he could be an assassin? Perhaps a question for another time. "So that's why you've been following us?"

"I'm keeping you safe," he said.

I snorted. So unsexy. "You're keeping us freaked out, is what you're doing. Stalking us, following us."

He frowned. "It's not my fault no one told you about me."

"Don't you think you should've introduced yourself?" I huffed.

"I was going to the other day, but then that girl walked in the bakery, in case you've forgotten." He meant Jenny Butts, when she came in to gab about something. I don't remember what.

"You've had plenty of opportunity since. Usually—and I can't be certain about the etiquette here because I only just discovered that I'm a witch and all—but it seems to me that if you've been hired to protect someone, the least you can do is introduce yourself."

He rocked back on his heels, smiled at us. "My name's Roman," he said. "I've been hired to protect you. How's that?"

I flipped the end of my ponytail over my shoulder. "It's a start, but don't expect me to welcome you with open arms. Folks with manners introduce themselves. Tell you they're guarding you."

He smirked. "I'm telling you now."

"Thanks, but no thanks. We don't need a bodyguard."

The assassin, all six foot whatever of him, took a towering step toward me. I tried not to cower, because really, he was a rock of man. "Listen here. I don't care what you want. I've been hired to guard you, and that's what I'm going to do. Whether you like it or not."

I swallowed the egg in the back of my throat. "Well, don't expect me to like it."

"I don't care if you like it. That's not my concern." He glanced at Em. "Now if we're done here, I'd like to get back to work."

Em swatted her hand. "We're done."

"Don't fall asleep, Mr. Bodyguard," I said.

He stopped, turned around and glared at me. "Don't worry. I never sleep on my watch." Then he opened the door and slammed it shut behind him.

"If I were you, I wouldn't get on his bad side," Em said.

I wiped a line of sweat off my forehead. "Why's that?"

"Because he's killed before. I wouldn't put it past him to kill again."

I bit my lip. Maybe I should have been nicer.

SEVEN

I rubbed the back of my neck, trying to work out a tension knot. "How could you forget to tell us about him?"

Em shrugged, appearing unimpressed with my concern. "Like I said, it slipped my mind. In case you haven't noticed, a lot has happened in the past few days."

I shook my head. The nerve of this woman. "Of course I've noticed. You've upturned our lives more than anyone."

"No, dearie," she said in a fairy-godmother sort of tone. That was if the fairy godmother liked playing You Might Be a Redneck If... "Y'all are the ones who went and did that. You are the dirt, and I'm the cleaner. I'm fixin' what should have been done long ago. And mind this: you need to practice as much as you can, because if the Queen Witch of the North has any say, she'll skin you herself."

"That's not very nice," Reid said.

I whacked the back of her head.

"Ow."

"Don't say stupid things. Of course it isn't nice. It's terrible."

"What are you talking about?" Sera said to Em.

Em stretched her spine. She contorted her body in some sort of yoga pose that made my muscles ache to look at. "The North Queen wanted to have y'all skinned. That way we wouldn't have to worry about this situation one way or the other."

"Skinned," Sera said. "What do we do? Where do we go?"

Em straightened herself. "Calm down, chicklin'. Since I know Hazel, I convinced the queen not to make a move against your family. I told her that you can be trained." Her upper lip curled into a snarl. "Which so far ain't goin' too well, is it?"

"We suck at this," Reid said.

Em stared at each of us so hard that I almost thought we'd burst into flames. "You'll get better. Now. Let's try basic levitation. Circle up." She pointed to a small leather-bound book on a glossy coffee table. "I want you to lift that book all together."

"Can I say, 'Light as a feather, stiff as a board'?" Sera said.

I cackled.

"Oh, me too!" Reid said.

I laughed even harder.

"Do you want to die?" Em asked.

My laughter faltered. "No, of course not. It's just…we joke. A lot. Even about serious things. Haven't you figured that out yet?"

Em clicked her fingernails together. "This is grave, a level beyond serious. You'll never master this until you take it seriously."

I shook my arms and legs and said to my sisters, "Y'all. Someone has died. Are we ready?"

They nodded.

"Then let's witch it up."

Em threw me a questioning look, but she didn't say anything. I wasn't exactly poking fun, but I wasn't exactly not, either.

I closed my eyes and focused on lifting the book. I imagined seeing it in the air, high above our heads, floating about the room. We must have been at it maybe five minutes before Em said anything. Honestly I was bummed. I mean, if we couldn't lift a little bit of paper and ink, there was no way we'd be able to protect ourselves against the witch who wanted us dead.

Correction: me dead.

Em's voice quivered. "Okay," she said tentatively. "Open your eyes—but do it slow. Ever so slow, and don't be afraid when you see."

My heart leaped with glee. Sweet! We'd done it. We'd lifted that little book. Readying myself for high fives all around, I cracked open an eye.

Holy crapola.

The book, the one we were supposed to lift, sat on the table, which was still attached to the floor. But the couch in front of it hovered several inches in the air, as did the clothing racks around it, the cash register, the chairs, the coffeemaker, and everything else that wasn't bolted down. Every single thing in my shop floated on some sort of invisible current. Everything except the one thing that we'd been focusing on.

"See? I told you we weren't any good at this," Reid said.

Em swallowed. "I want y'all to focus on lowerin' the book."

"But the book hasn't moved," Sera said.

Em blinked at her as if Sera were an idiot. "Wasn't that your target?"

"Yes," she said.

Em gave a curt nod. "Then lower that book."

I knew what she meant. If we focused on lowering the entire room, that might not work. But if we singled out the book, that should (hopefully) do the trick. We closed our eyes again and a minute later...

"Good grief, y'all," Em said. She slumped onto the couch. For her, it was slumping, anyway. I don't think Queen Witches go about slumping and slumming like the rest of us. But she appeared withered, uncertain, and a bit deflated.

"How'd we do that?" Sera whispered.

"I don't know," I said. "How did we do that, Em?"

Em massaged her forehead. "Y'all focused, right?"

We nodded.

"It don't make sense," she said more to herself than us. "You made everything else levitate except what you were supposed to. Never, not once in my life have I seen that happen," she mumbled.

"You have the ability but not the buildin' blocks."

"What?" I said.

She shook her head. "You have ability but no focus."

I gestured to the three of us. "We focused. All of us."

Em stared at the floor. "I don't know. I can't explain it." She glanced up, catching my gaze. "But if the two of you can levitate an entire room, what else are you capable of?"

***

I can't say I didn't go home confused and disappointed. Determined to get this spelling thing down pat, I said to my sisters as we walked in the door, "As soon as Nan and Grandma are asleep, we're going to practice."

"Okay, but if the house lifts off its foundation, I'm blaming you," Sera said.

I stuck my tongue out at her. Yes, I'm aware that it's childish, but I don't care. Several hours later we sat in a circle in the living room.

Sera narrowed her eyes at Reid. "Why are you wearing all black?"

My youngest sister wore a long-sleeved black tee and black sweatpants. "These are my comfy clothes. Besides, it's chilly in here with the air on."

"Oh. I thought you were trying to be all witchy," Sera said.

I arched an eyebrow. "Witchy?"

"You know what I mean."

"I'm not sure I do," I said. "Explain it to me."

Sera huffed. "You know, all pointy hats and stuff. Like a caricature of a witch."

"Right. Because we know so many witches," I said.

"Don't me smart," she growled.

I shrugged. "I'm not. But with this stuff we don't know our armpits from our buttholes. Even if Reid was trying to invoke some sort of witchy thing, I doubt it would hurt."

"Whatever," she said.

"Girlets or chicklets or chicklin's," Reid said, honeying up her Southern accent. "If you're done bickering, I'd like to start."

I giggled. "Best Queen Witch impersonation. Ever."

Reid performed a half bow. "Thank you. I've worked on it all day."

"All day?" Sera said.

"In my head, of course."

I placed a tissue in the center of our circle. "I think we may have gone wrong today because the book was too heavy."

"Right, and a couch is light," Sera said.

I clicked my tongue. "In one of our minds it might have been. So we're going to try this. Let's close our eyes and concentrate."

As we focused, a wave of energy spilled over my body. It encircled me, flooding every cell. It was electric and alive. Though it resembled feeling as if I'd sat on a live wire, I knew better. This was magic, pure and simple. It swirled and danced, lifting my hair and energizing me. My skin tingled, my heart raced and my stomach flitted. I cracked one eye, wanting to see how high the tissue was.

But it sat in a limp heap on the floor. It hadn't even twitched.

Nan yelled from her bedroom. "What the heck is going on?"

Sera and Reid's eyes opened.

"Oh no," I whispered.

"Oh sweet Lord," Sera said.

We dashed to Nan's room. I burst through the door, deciding that when someone yelled like she had, barging in seemed like the best thing to do.

Nan floated above her bed, her arms and legs tangled in the sheets. She thrashed about. Fear shone in her eyes.

"It's okay, Nan," I said. "We'll get you down."

"You'd better," she hissed. "I don't appreciate you girls levitating me."

What?

I climbed on the bed and took her hand. I pulled, expecting her to drift back down. She didn't budge.

I turned to Sera. "She won't move." My heart raged against my chest. I didn't want Nan to be stuck in the air for the rest of her God-given life.

"We need to lower the tissue," Sera said, her voice calm. Thank goodness someone was, because I was about to transform into a crazy hyperventilating lady.

"Okay," I said. We linked hands and focused. I watched Nan while I thought about a tissue dropping to the floor very, very slowly. After a couple of moments her body floated back down, coming to rest in the gentle embrace of the bed.

"You feel okay, Nan?" I asked.

She threw us a sour look. "What in the dickens made you girls decide to float me? You could've broken one of my fragile bones."

"Sorry," Sera said.

"It was Dylan's idea," Reid added.

"Thanks," I said. "Nan, why don't you seem surprised by this?"

She slid her feet into her Tweety Bird slippers and frowned. "Of course I'm not surprised. I know you're witches. I've always known. Why do you think the council sent me to protect your grandmother?"

My jaw dropped. "Well, I don't know. Why did they?"

She rose, stretching her arms over her head. "Anyone want some coffee?"

"Sure," Reid said. "I'll take a cup."

I scowled. "You don't drink coffee."

She gave me a bright smile. "Sometimes I do."

"I suppose this is one of those times."

"You got it."

Sera raised her hand. "Count me in. If I have to listen to them bicker all night, I'd rather have a warm cup of joe to go with it."

"What?" I said. "The only hot drink Reid likes is cocoa."

Sera flipped her hair back. "Not anymore."

"Right," Reid said snidely. "My tastes are allowed to grow up."

I rolled my eyes. "Great. Let's have some coffee and stay up all night chatting."

When the four of us were seated at the kitchen table, Nan started talking. "The council found out about your grandmother because they'd been keeping tabs on her."

"Yeah," I said. "That's what Em told us. That they'd been watching her for years."

"They found out about her condition quickly and sent me in." Nan sipped from her steaming cup. "I'm sorry about that poor Eckhart girl. It's not the first time a human got caught in the crosshairs of a witch's desire, and it won't be the last. Though I have to say some good has come from it. You girls are discovering your talents, and I hear that Queen Witch has been teaching you."

"Word travels fast," I said.

Nan ran her finger over the rim of the cup. "I would have said something, but how was I supposed to bring it up? 'Good morning, girls. I understand you've discovered that you're witches. About time.'"

"What's that supposed to mean?" Reid asked.

Nan sighed. "Your grandmother should have told you long ago." She touched her chest with the flat of her hand. "Now, I'm not a witch. Not at all. I come from a long line of witch protectors."

"Witch protectors?" Sera said.

"That's correct. I know about your kind but don't discuss it with nonwitches. And in case you haven't learned the rules—that's one of them." She wagged a finger at us. "No talking about witchcraft with anyone not in the know. Got it?"

We nodded.

"So as I said, when the council discovered your grandmother could no longer protect herself, they sent me in and of course I informed them that you had no knowledge of your heritage."

I sat back. "Why didn't she tell us?"

Nan shrugged. "There's no way to know. Not unless she snaps out of her state. Which she could."

I saw Sera eye Nan up and down. "So—and I'm not trying to be rude, but—Nan, how are you supposed to protect our grandmother?"

Nan howled with laughter. I understood Sera's question. At nearly sixty and round as a barrel, Nan didn't look like she could protect much of anything. Unless her skills consisted of sitting on a person while they struggled beneath her, that is. Which I wouldn't put past her.

She pushed herself up from the table. "Let me show you." Nan grabbed a broom from the corner and proceeded to do some sort of tae kwon do stuff with the rod. She twirled it over her head and danced a series of moves that had her thrusting, sideswiping, and kicking. Yes, kicking. Sixty-year-old lady with gray hair didn't play.

When the demonstration finished, we all clapped. "Wow," I said. "I'm impressed."

I noticed a small piece of lint floating to the floor behind Nan. I picked it up and inspected it. A tiny golden thread lay in my palm. That was strange. Nan wasn't wearing anything that color, and the bedsheets we'd found her practically cocooned in weren't that hue, either. I shrugged it off and let the thread fall out of my hand.

"That was so cool," Reid said. "Maybe you can teach me some moves."

Nan returned the broom to its spot. "Anytime. Since you don't have any magic, it's not a bad idea for you to learn some self-protection."

Reid crossed her arms. "Great. Even the person without any magic knows I'm magicless."

"I don't think that's a word," Sera said.

Reid threw her a confused look.

"Magicless," Sera explained. "That's not a word."

"What are you, the word fairy?"

Sera shook her head. "No. I'm just pointing it out for future reference. Not a word."

"Thanks, Sherlock," Reid said. "I'll keep that in mind."

"C'mon, kids," I said. "Time to get some sleep. I have a feeling Em's got a lot planned for us tomorrow."

***

The next morning, Nan made us a breakfast big enough to sate the hungriest of lumberjacks. Eggs, pancakes, sausage, hash browns, grits and, to top it off, homemade biscuits and gravy. Awesome. Of course, since the three of us always watched our waistlines, we barely touched it. I nibbled a sausage while Sera and Reid took a couple bites of the pancakes.

I watched as Nan heaped a plateful of goodies and headed for the front door.

"Where are you going with that?" I asked.

She stopped, turned around. "Why, I'm going to feed that nice man out there who's protecting you."

She meant the assassin. "What?" I squawked. "How do you know about him?"

"Dylan, I'm trained in this sort of thing. I know when a house is being staked out. The hairs on the back of my neck tingle."

"That's impressive," Reid said.

I did not want the assassin to have any food. The man didn't even bother introducing himself. He could round up his own pancakes and sausage. "Don't give him breakfast," I said.

Nan fisted a hand on her hip and glared at me. "I most certainly will. He's stayed up all night watching this home to make sure you're safe. He deserves a nice breakfast."

I crossed to her. "Fine. I'll take it to him."

"Ooo, Dylan's got a crush on someone," Reid said.

"I do not," I snapped. "I just want him to know where his breakfast came from." Besides, I wanted to see if he was awake. I had my doubts. He didn't look too trustworthy.

I scooped the stacked plate in my palm and headed out. Warm sunshine assaulted me. We'd stayed up so late the rays blinded me like they tend to do when I'm good and hungover. Not that that's a regular occurrence. I'm only using it as an example.

I approached the dark tinted windows. Roman or Italian or whatever his name was, stared at me. I reached the car and waited. He continued to stare at me. I motioned for him to roll down the glass.

"What's this?" he asked, a slight smile tugging at his lip.

"Thanksgiving dinner. What's it look like?"

"It looks like you're eating crow."

"I have no idea what you're talking about."

He smirked. "I didn't think you wanted anything to do with me."

"I don't."

"You're having something to do with me now. You're standing here."

I shoved the plate toward the door. "Do you want it or not?"

He glared at me before finally taking it. "You forgot the silverware."

I pulled a fork and knife from my back pocket. Nan had handed them to me before I exited the house. If it had been up to me, Roman would've eaten the meal with his hands. But no, Nan demanded civility, and of course I complied. After all, she was my grandmother's sworn protector.

"This looks delicious," he said.

"It is," I admitted. "Nan's a great cook."

His face fell. "Oh."

"What now?"

"Nothing," he said glumly.

"What is it? I'm not walking away until you tell me what it is."

He stabbed a sausage and shoved it in his mouth, all manly and stuff. I looked away. Golly. How could this guy make eating look sexy? I mean, seriously. Was that legal? Something poked out from under the collar of his T-shirt. I peered closer.

"You first," he said.

"What?" I asked, confused.

"You tell me what's got your interest, and I'll tell you what I was thinking."

Easy enough. No need to sell my soul over this. "Is that a tattoo?"

He nodded. "I have one on the left side of my shoulder that goes down to my waist."

My knees jellied. I gulped. It was now fact. King Sexy guarded me. Wait until I told Sera. If she wasn't nursing a broken heart, she might think it droolworthy.

"What's it of?" I asked.

He spoke between mouthfuls. "A dragon."

My knees wobbled. A dragon tattoo branded the plane of Mr. Muscle's skin from bicep to waist? I know it's not cool to swoon, but I might not have a choice.

"Now you," I said.

"I'm disappointed that you didn't make my breakfast."

I burst out laughing. "First of all, I'm not a great cook. If I'd made your breakfast, it would have been jammy toast and coffee. Second, your well-being is not my first priority."

"Wow. Harsh," he said.

I almost felt bad. Almost. But then I remembered he had no manners. Folks with manners bother to tell you they've been hired to guard you. Folks without, didn't.

"Enjoy your breakfast," I said. I stalked back to the house. Rick, our next-door neighbor, was walking to his car. I waved. He winked and smiled. Dang. That boy was hot. Maybe I needed to steal the binoculars from Reid.

Nah. He was too young for me. Which made Roman just right.

Darn it. I did not have time to fall for some guy. I had a witch trying to kill me. Speaking of, Em was probably waiting for us down at the shop. Queen Witch did not like waiting. Of course, how much wrath could we incur in five measly minutes?

EIGHT

When we arrived at Perfect Fit that morning, Em kept her distance. Her eyes slewed from me to Sera as if she were nervous. As if we scared her a little bit. I didn't know what there was to be nervous about. We only levitated the store—and Nan. It's not like we raised the entire town into the sky.

Hmmm. Interesting thought. I wondered if we could do that.

But there was no time to ponder.

"This mornin', chicklets, we're goin' on a hunt."

"For what?" Reid asked.

"Why, for the person who attempted to kill you," Em said.

"Um, isn't that the job of the police?"

Em shook her head, her fiery curls bouncing. Hard to believe she was ninety-eight and a half. She folded her arms, her hands curling over her biceps. "And what do you think the police are gonna find?" she said.

"I don't know. You can ask him yourself because here he comes," I said. Sure enough, Detective Blount strutted up the walk. He opened the door of the shop.

"Good morning, ladies," he said.

We murmured good mornings. He nodded to me. "Do you have a minute?"

"Sure thing." I escorted him to the back office. We entered, and I motioned to the empty coffeepot. "Would you like a cup?"

He hiked up the thighs of his slacks and took a seat. "No thanks. I only have a few questions."

"Go right ahead." I sat behind a small desk I used for storage and miscellaneous tasks. It had belonged to my family for years. Cup-ring stains and nicks marred the surface, but I loved it. It wasn't nice enough to be showcased on the floor, like my other desk was, but it was fine nestled in the back.

"Miss Apel, you said that was your dress, the one Reagan was wearing."

"Right."

A dark expression flashed across his face. An instant later it vanished. "This may sound like a strange question, but do you know anyone who might want to cause you harm? Get even with you for something?"

I planted my elbows on the desk and leaned forward. "No, Detective, I don't. Why do you ask?" Let's see if Miss Prissy Pants aka Queen Witch, was right.

"We're still trying to figure out the substance on the dress, but it appears the fabric was tampered with. It's science fiction, really. Someone coated the inside of the dress with a substance meant to kill on contact. And since the dress is yours, it only stands to reason that someone wanted to harm you."

I leaned back in my chair and exhaled deeply. "I've lived here my entire life. I don't know anyone who would want me dead."

The detective scrubbed a palm over his face. I could tell he didn't like this case, not one bit. He gave me a tired, weary smile.

"If you think of anything, Miss Apel, let me know. Here's my card."

After shoving the small rectangular paper in my pocket, I escorted him out. I turned to my sisters and pointed at Queen Witch. "She's right. The police won't be able to help us on this. We'll have to figure it out for ourselves."

Reid blanched. Sera shrugged.

I glanced at Em. "Okay, we've got a witch to track down. What do we do first?"

***

Ten minutes later we stood outside an old Victorian home. I'd seen the house probably a thousand times but had never thought much of it until now. White paint flaked off the boards while sun-beaten flowers drooped in the first-floor window boxes. Over the driveway a dead vine clutched a trellis arbor, apparently hanging on for dear life.

"Where are we?" I asked Em as she ascended the poured-concrete stairway.

"Can't you guess?"

We shook our heads in unison.

"We're at a registered witch's house."

"Oh," I said. I hadn't realized a witch lived in town. Were there any more?

"By the look of the dead plants, I'm guessing this witch doesn't have a green thumb," Sera said.

I glanced back to the street. A few people strolled down the sidewalk, heading toward the business district. We were so close people could walk downtown to work or shop.

"There's Tim," Sera whispered.

My belly sank. Sure enough, sauntering down the other side of the street came Sera's ex, all six feet of him with his college-boy haircut and blazing blue eyes. He'd be a real looker if he hadn't been a douche bag to my sister.

"Hey, Tim," she said.

He gave a cockeyed smile. "How are y'all today?"

I tugged Sera's elbow, but she didn't budge. "Great," I said. "How's Olivia? You know, the girl you're dating."

His gaze skirted to Sera. "She's good. You doin' okay, Sera?"

Sera gave me a dirty look and then smiled daintily for the

pretty boy. "Doing great."

"Listen, Tim, I'd love to stay and chat, but we've got to go." I yanked Sera, and this time she came with me. "Let's go inside."

"What'd you have to bring her up for?" she seethed.

"Because last I looked, he's dating her. Don't even think about going back to him. The man doesn't even have a job."

"He's independently wealthy," she said.

"Forget him. He's a waste of oxygen."

I pulled Sera to the front door and stopped behind Em and Reid. Em knocked. A minute later a small, hawkish woman answered.

"What do you want?" she demanded.

"Milly Jones, how do you do?" Em's mouth formed a tight grin. Well, well, well, will wonders never cease? A witch who stands up to the queen.

"Hello, Em," Milly said. The small woman squinted at the queen. "Is this an official visit or what?"

"It ain't official."

"Who are these piddly witches with you?"

"Excuse me, but I am not piddly," Reid argued.

Milly stared at her. "You're right. You're not, because you aren't even a witch. Em, what's this all about?"

Em stamped her foot. "Let us inside and I'll give you a good yarn."

Milly grumbled something I couldn't make out. She dropped her hand from the door and turned back inside, leaving it wide open. I guess that was an invitation?

Em entered. The three of us exchanged glances. We were thinking the same thing—wondering if we should follow.

Em popped up behind the door. "Well? What are y'all waitin' for? Come on. She won't bite."

I wasn't convinced, but since we had no other leads, we went inside.

Where the outside of the home looked run-down and neglected, the inside proved immaculate. Antique rugs blanketed the wooden floors, landscape paintings in gilded frames decorated the walls, and a bronze birdcage housing a wooden parrot sat in the corner. Bright, cheery sunlight streamed through the sheer curtains. Milly thumped her cane on the floor as she plodded over to a worn recliner. She motioned for us to sit.

"Tea, anyone?"

Em answered for us. "Yes, thank you, that sounds refreshin'."

A glass pitcher filled to the brim with dark amber tea and ice appeared in midair.

"Holy crap!" Reid said.

I watched wide-eyed as the pitcher tipped—by itself, mind you—and poured the liquid into a tall glass that had also appeared. In total it poured four drinks. Ice clinked as the glasses danced about the room, making their way to each one of us. One stopped in front of me and hovered. Em took hers in hand and sipped. Since she didn't drop dead after a few seconds, I grasped the trunk of my glass and took a long draught.

"Mmm. Delicious," I said.

"Mmm hmmm," Sera mused.

"Thank you," Milly said pointedly. "It was my mother's recipe. You can't be Southern and not know how to make a great pitcher of tea, she always said. I'm apt to agree with her."

"Here, here," Reid said.

"She also used to say, you can't be a Southern witch and not know your tail from your behind. Which, from the looks of you three, is definitely not the truth of it. You're so green you don't know if you're coming or going."

What a nice old lady. So welcoming. "You've got a great bedside manner. Were you a doctor before you retired?" I asked.

Her sharp eyes penetrated me. "It's not good to cross a witch."

"So I've been told," I said.

Em cleared her throat. "Guess the niceties are over." She glared at me. As if it was my fault Milly decided to be rude first. "We need information."

Milly's head swung in Em's direction. She took a sip of tea and crunched a cube of ice for a full two minutes. After smacking her lips, she said, "What kind of information?"

"Someone wants the girls dead."

Milly threw back her head in laughter. I didn't realize my life ending was so funny.

She wiped tears from her eyes. "Of course they do. These girls don't know what they've got. If I were a young witch trying to prove myself, I'd attempt to off one of Hazel's granddaughters as well."

"You know our grandmother?" Sera asked.

"Of course. Would anyone like more tea?"

We shook our heads. Milly waved at the tea, vanishing it. She rose and caned over to a rough-hewn wooden mantle. She picked up a picture and ran her fingers down it. I craned my neck to see the image. Milly pivoted the picture toward us. Two woman stood in black-and-white, their arms around each other in an embrace.

"This is your grandmother fifty years ago. This was taken here, in Silver Springs, where we both grew up. This was right before she took your mother, who was only a girl at the time, to Savannah. Your grandmother and I remained close until…"

I quirked an eyebrow. "Until?"

She threw her free hand into the air. "We disagreed on a few things."

"Like?" Sera said.

"Like how to raise you three. After your parents died in that horrific car crash, your grandmother brought you back here. Dylan…" She paused. "It is Dylan, right?"

I nodded. "Yes, ma'am."

"You and Sera probably remember a little bit before the crash."

"I was ten, so I remember moving here, but I don't recall too much about before then. Sera might remember more. She's only two years younger than me."

On cue Sera shook her head. "Not really. I only know Silver Springs."

Milly frowned. "Anyway. Your grandmother wanted to keep magic a secret from you. I thought it best that you know." She stamped the cane on the floor. "It was your right, damn it. You needed to be able to protect yourselves in case someone tried to kill you. Which now they are." She coughed, wheezing. I rose and helped the old witch back into her chair.

"With all due respect," Sera said. "You don't even know us. Why would you have any say in how we were raised?"

Milly's beady eyes glared at Sera for a moment. She turned away, gazing at the wooden parrot. It squawked.

I flinched. "That's a bit unnerving."

"Easier to take care of that way," Milly explained. "It talks and sings but doesn't poop. Perfect pet."

"It talks, it sings," the parrot screeched.

I rang out my ear with my finger. "Very nice." Not at all.

Em reached her hand toward Milly. "So do you know who might be after them?"

"Of course not, you idiot," Milly said.

I have to say, Em took the insult in stride. Where my jaw slackened, she didn't even wince.

Milly continued, "There are no other registered witches in the area. Anyone stupid enough to register and try to harm the girls would be quickly discovered."

"So you haven't felt any disturbances in the air."

Milly shrugged. "Sure, I've felt some quirks here and there. A few pulses of energy. I'm not dead, you know."

Em smiled tightly. "I know that. You have a lot of power, Milly. If anyone could sense another witch using her magic nearby, it would be you."

Milly chewed on that for a moment. I mean, literally chewed. "How'd they try to off you?" she said to us.

"She spelled a dress?" I said. "I guess that's what it's called."

Em nodded. "The spell burned the poor girl who tried it on to a crisp."

Milly rubbed the wiry hairs on her chin. "Yes, I heard about the Eckhart girl's surprising demise. Sloppy work. In a perfect world, if you had tried on the dress, it would have knocked you out long enough for the witch to skin you alive. A smart witch would have placed a safety on the spell so that if anyone other than the intended victim wore the gown, they wouldn't be harmed. We know there was no safety. Which means we're dealing with a young, inexperienced witch."

"I agree. A smart witch would also have made sure the spell didn't kill."

"That's obvious," Milly spat. "Why'd they make you Queen Witch again?"

"Because you retired, remember?"

Milly smiled faintly. "That's right."

Em clapped her hands against her thighs. "Any idea where we can start lookin' for this witch?"

Milly's eyes narrowed. Her gaze darted over to me, then back to Em. She opened her mouth and started to say something, but stopped. "No idea. Good luck." She rose, signaling that the interview had ended.

"Are you sure?" I asked. "Any information you give us would be a great help."

"Sorry, but I'm old and tired. I can't help you." She practically pushed us out the front door. "Tell your grandmother I said hello." Then she slammed it in our faces.

"What's up her behind?" Reid said.

"Old age," I grumbled.

As Em led us away, I couldn't help but glance back at the house. The curtains were parted in one of the first-floor windows. Milly's gnarled face stared out. A chill waved through my body. That old witch knew more than she was saying, and I needed to find out what it was. After all, it could mean the difference between life and death. My life and my death.

I rubbed my hands together. Time to come up with a plan.

NINE

"We're going back to Milly's," I said.

"But I've put on my pajamas," Reid complained. She tugged at her red and white striped jammie top while extending her legs so I wouldn't miss the matching bottoms.

Sera glanced up from the magazine she was reading. "You look like a candy cane. Those should be illegal." She flipped a glossy page, pulled back the tab of the perfume sample and sniffed. And coughed. "Ugh. Who would wear that?"

"We're going back to Milly's right now."

Reid yawned. "Why so late? Can't it wait until morning?"

"No, it cannot wait until morning. That old lady knows something, and I'm going to find out what."

"Call her up and ask," Reid said. "I'm all comfy."

I fisted a hand on my hip. "Fine. You two can stay here. I'll go figure out what she knows all by myself." I pivoted on my heel and headed for the front door. "But if she turns me into a toad, it's all your fault."

I knew they'd be looking at each other, silently contemplating how true that statement could turn out. I smiled. It was only a matter of seconds now.

I heard the magazine fold. "All right. But if we get in trouble, I'm blaming you," Sera said.

"Great! I'll be out in the car."

"What about our bodyguard?" Reid asked. "Is he coming too?"

Ugh. I forgot about him. "I'll deal with it. Just meet me outside."

I racked my brain, trying to come up with a way in like five seconds for how to convince Roman not to follow us. No good options presented themselves.

Oh well, the truth it would be. I opened the screen door and stepped outside. Humid air clung to me like mist. I glanced up. Clouds obscured the stars. The air felt heavy, as if a downpour was only minutes away.

As I made my way over to the SUV, I opted for a good old-fashioned one on one in lieu of a simple window-roll-down conversation. Stepping to the passenger side, I pulled the handle and opened the door. Roman's eyes widened in surprise. Before he said anything, I slid onto the seat.

Buttery leather welcomed my heinie. The vehicle smelled new, not stale like I expected since the assassin spent most of his time in it.

"What are you doing in here?"

My own reflection greeted me in his sunglasses. "Why do you wear shades at night? Afraid someone will recognize you?"

He tapped the steering wheel with tight, muscular fingers. "No. They make it harder for people to see me. Even through the tinted window."

"You're worried someone will see you?" That was news to me. Seemed to me like he'd want people to see him. They'd know we were protected and wouldn't harm us.

He gave me a long look. I think he was trying to intimidate me. Didn't work. Big guys who wear shades at night made me laugh, not cower.

"I'm trying to catch a witch here."

"You are? I thought you were protecting us?"

He sighed. "I am protecting you. But I'm hoping the witch will show herself and I can catch her and be done with this gig."

My heart pinged. How could he not like us? My family was fun and full of laughter. We're a riot. "You don't like us?"

"I don't like witches."

I leaned back in the seat to get a good look at him. With his star-quarterback build, only a fool would take Roman on in a fight. I didn't think witches scared him, so it must be something else.

"Why don't you like us?"

He stretched his legs, turning his body slightly toward me. My heart fluttered. I touched my chest. It wasn't supposed to do that. Not for some creepy assassin guy who didn't even like what I was.

"Let's just say we've had our run-ins. They're not the nicest of breeds."

"Then why are you here?"

"You sure ask a lot of questions." He regarded me for a moment and chuckled. "Why are you here?"

Oh, that. "Well." I nibbled my fingers, unsure how much to tell him. The screen door slammed shut. Reid and Sera made their way to the car.

"Where are they going?" he mumbled.

"Roll down your window."

He turned the ignition key and pushed down the automatic window. I leaned over. The musky scent of him infiltrated my nose, filling my lungs. The primal aroma beckoned me. Come hither, it seemed to whisper. I very nearly closed my eyes and curled up beside him. Luckily I found my senses.

"Sera! Reid! Over here," I called out. "He's taking us."

"Taking you where?" he asked.

Sera and Reid climbed into the backseat.

I flashed Roman a wicked smile. "On a stakeout."

***

We nosed down Milly's street roughly ten minutes later. It took five minutes to convince Roman to take us. He tried to be a party pooper and demand we stay at the house where he could keep us safe (yawn), but when I told him we were going with or without his help, he changed his mind.

We slowed to a stop.

"Are you sure this is the right house?" Reid said.

"I'm sure," I lied. Ebony shadows slashed across the old Victorian. A single low-wattage bulb buzzed above the front door. Moths and other night insects flitted around its dim light. Though we were parked in roughly the same spot we had been in this morning, the nighttime atmosphere made the house dark and unsettling.

"It's the right house," Sera said. She pointed down the street. "That's where I saw Tim, remember?"

"Don't remind me," I said.

"Who's Tim?" Roman asked.

Why was he suddenly so interested in our lives? Did he have a thing for Sera? Not that it mattered, because I didn't care. I was just wondering. Just for, you know, wondering's sake.

"Her ex," Reid said. "He's a jerk."

"Here, here," I said.

"No, he's not," Sera said.

I whipped my head over the seat and found Sera nose-deep in a tissue. "Yes. He is. Royal jerk, that one. You're much better off without him."

"For what it's worth," Roman said, "I don't know the guy, but any a-hole who would break up with one of you beauties must be an idiot."

Sera blotted her bottom lashes with the tissue. "Thank you." A curtain of glossy hair fell in her face. She tucked the side behind one ear and looked up at Roman and smiled. He grinned back in the rearview mirror.

For some strange, alien reason, my gut twisted. My insides knotted when they smiled at each other. I swear to God I heard thunder or something in the distance, as if kismet itself had deemed this to be the big kapow moment between the two of them. You know, kapow, when two people touch and sparks or some bullcrap ignite, and then the couple know they've got some serious chemistry. The kapow moment generally leads to either a relationship or hot moments under the sheets.

And I swear on my life I'd just witnessed it between the superhot assassin and my little sister. And people wondered why I didn't date. How could I? My sisters took all the guys.

Not that this was a big deal, because it wasn't. Not at all. I loved Sera and supported anything that helped her get over Tim faster, because Tim was a jerk.

"This place looks eerie at night," Reid said. She snapped me back into the moment.

"You can stay here," I said.

"Like heck I am. I want to see what you're going to do."

"Yeah," Roman said. His lips curved into a crooked grin. "I'd like to see this, too."

I stared up at the imposing house and considered the daunting witch inside. What was I going to do? I had no clue, but I couldn't tell them that. I didn't even know what I was looking for. But I knew Milly was hiding something.

"I've been thinking," I said.

"About what?" Sera said.

"I think the reason the levitation didn't work was because the three of us were trying it together. Reid doesn't have any power."

"Thanks," she said.

"You're welcome."

Sera dug her fingers into the back of my seat and leaned forward. "What are you saying?"

I took a deep breath. "I'm going to try it on my own."

"Here?" she asked.

"Here. I'm going to sneak behind the house and levitate."

"And what? Look through her windows?" Roman asked.

"Exactly," I said. Butterflies tangled in my stomach.

Roman pushed the release on his seat belt. "This has trouble written all over it. I'd better follow to make sure you don't kill yourself."

I bristled. "I don't need you to keep me safe."

He gave me a doubtful look and opened his door.

"If he's going, I'm going," Reid said.

"Great. Let's make it a party, shall we?" I said.

Sera grinned. "Yeah, let's see how far we can get before Milly finds you and spells you."

"What? That's a terrible thing to say." I bit my lower lip. "What do you think she'd do to me?"

"You saw how she vanished that tea set. She'll probably send you to another dimension."

I pressed her forehead with my finger. "Very funny. This isn't Superman."

"Good thing. I'd hate for her to replace you with Bizarro Dylan." Sera puffed out her cheeks. "Me Dylan. Me make beautiful dress for you."

"Shut up and come on." I opened the door and stepped into the night. A cool breeze lifted the ends of my hair. I glanced up at the old home, the unsettling house that looked almost nightmarish in the dark. I clenched my hands and, without a word, stalked toward the back.

Everyone followed. "Reid, you and Sera stay here."

Reid kicked a pebble across the road. "But if you fly, I want to see it."

"Me too," Sera said.

Roman yawned.

"Let's go," I said.

We sneaked to the back. Thank goodness no one giggled, though it shocked me that not even Reid snickered. Light shone through the bottom windows. Living room and kitchen, presumably. A single light illuminated the top half of the house. Bedroom. That's what I wanted. That's where I needed to be. If the old witch was hiding anything, it would lay in there.

I glanced at everyone and nodded, signaling it was go time. Closing my eyes, I turned my thoughts toward levitation and being light, about lifting up.

"Will it help if I throw you in the air?" Reid whispered.

"Shut it," I said.

I wrung out my hands and focused on that room on the second floor, about how much I wanted to see what Milly had up there. Less than a second later, I became weightless. Yes! I cracked one eye open, then the other. My feet hovered only a few inches above the air, but it counted. I was officially floating. I smiled widely at Sera and Reid, who smiled back, and at Roman, who scowled at me. Sourpuss. Who cared about him, anyway?

I focused on reaching the window, and in two seconds flat I floated outside it. Sweet! This was a heck of a lot easier than I expected. My chest expanded. I considered floating to the moon, but realized that one, I'd run out of oxygen, and two, I didn't have time for all that crap. I had to get on with this.

After saying a little prayer, I grasped the bottom of the window and pulled. It gave enough for me to wedge my fingers beneath. I inhaled. My ribcage inflated, and with my not so Herculean strength, I cracked it enough to heave my body through.

I heard Roman mumble something about breaking and entering, but I ignored him. The way I figured it, assassins didn't have room to judge.

I landed with a plop atop orange shag carpet. A fine cloud of must puffed up, irritating my sinuses. I coughed up half a lung, mystified that the witch didn't vacuum more. After wiping tears from my face, I peered into the room and came face-to-face with a pair of black orthopedic shoes.

"You're lucky I don't turn you into a toad," Milly said.

I sat back on my haunches. Milly's silver hair stuck out every which way. She looked, shall I say, fearsome. Perhaps this hadn't been a good idea after all. "Are you going to turn me into anything?"

She smacked her lips. "As tempting as it is to get some practice in, I think the important thing is that you've finally unlocked your magic. Call your sisters and that bodyguard of yours and invite them all in."

I rubbed my forehead. "I thought we'd done such a good job sneaking."

Milly cackled, truly a witch-like sound. "First thing you need to learn—you can't sneak up on a powerful witch. Now get them all downstairs and we'll have a little chat without that nosy Queen Witch listening in."

Five minutes later my sisters and I sat in Milly's living room. Roman remained outside, saying he didn't want to be locked in a room with witches. Whatever that meant.

After a round of magicked hot tea—yes, she did the whole vanishing-act thing again—I cut right to the chase.

"You're hiding something."

Her lips curled. "What makes you say that?"

"There was something you almost said today, but didn't. Do you know who wants us dead?"

Milly stirred her drink. "Sometimes when a witch uses her power, I feel the ripple. For instance, when you finally figured out how to fly, I felt that."

"I didn't fly," I corrected. "I floated."

She dismissed the difference with a wave of her liver-spotted hand. "There's no difference. If you can do one, you can do the other."

"Cool," Reid said.

"You have no power," Milly said.

"Ah, poop."

"I have felt something recently," Milly continued. "A ripple near here."

I exchanged confused looks with Sera. "Why didn't you say something when Em was here?"

"I hate the council," Milly snarled. "Those nosy ninnies always want to know everything. They come in, stir up trouble, and then leave the rest of us to clean up the mess."

Sera rested her tea cup atop the saucer with a clink. "Didn't Em say you were queen before her?"

"Yes," Milly said. "That's why I don't like the council, because I used to be one of them. I know how it works, and trust me"—she wagged a finger at us—"you're better off without them."

"If it wasn't for them, we wouldn't even know we're witches," Sera said.

I scowled at Milly. "You knew we were witches, but you didn't come to help us. Em's the first person who bothered teaching us any of this stuff."

Milly clamped her mouth shut so tight deep creases molded the corners. "I told Hazel to teach you. She didn't listen. What was I supposed to do? That's what ruined our friendship, you know." She thumped her fist on the side table. "Our disagreement ran so deep it caused a rift neither one of us wanted to mend."

"Too stubborn to mend, more like," I said.

"Yes, we were both stubborn," Milly grumbled. "What's done is done. I'm not happy about it, but it's the way things are." She stared at the clock on the wall, then vanished our half-finished cups of tea. "If that answers all your questions, I'd like to get some rest. It's eleven o'clock, two hours past my bedtime."

We thanked her for the tea and left. Roman leaned against the SUV, apparently waiting for us.

"Everything go as planned?"

I couldn't tell if he was being sarcastic or not. "Yes. Everything went great. I have a new fairy godmother."

"Good," he said. "I feel better."

"Why's that?"

He waited for Reid and Sera to get in and shut the doors behind them. Roman grasped the handle of the passenger door as if he was going to open it for me. Apparently some assassins had manners. Keeping his voice low, he said, "Because once Em finds out you've done magic that can be witnessed by regular people, you're going to need all the godmothers you can get."

"Oh. Is that wrong?"

He scoffed. "It's a rule of witchcraft. Don't let anyone see you do magic or else you run the risk of a fate worse than death."

"All these blasted rules. I wish someone would just give me a pamphlet with all of them listed and be done with it."

He said nothing. His quiet, assassin-like silence bothered me.

I sighed. "And what could be worse than death?"

He opened the door. As I climbed into the SUV, he whispered in my ear, "Being boiled alive."

Roman shut the door.

TEN

I tried not to think too much about being boiled alive the next morning as I sat down to breakfast with my sisters. Calico Kitchen, a local meat and three, also happened to serve a fantastic biscuits-and-gravy breakfast, which I now stared at on my plate. All of us must've needed food therapy, because our dishes were piled high.

"I tried levitating this morning," Sera said over a heap of pancakes.

I sipped black coffee. "And?"

She shook her head. "I may have raised up an inch at most. I'm really bad at this stuff."

"We're all bad," I said. "We've never had formal training."

"And let's face it, Queen Witch isn't the best teacher," Reid said. She drenched her waffle in syrup and cut it into itty-bitty bites.

"What makes you say that?" I said.

She pointed to both of us with her fork. "Case in point. Both of you are terrible at this stuff."

"Excuse me," I replied. "I am not terrible."

She shoved a bite in her mouth. "Not last night, no. But you were before then, and as far as I know, you still are. It's like she doesn't want you to get any better."

I set my white ceramic coffee mug on the table. "What did

you say?"

"Hey, y'all!"

I tilted my head back and groaned. No. Not now.

Jenny Butts popped into view, her blonde curls extra tight this morning. She wore a white halter top, white skirt and red heels. I'm pretty sure every male head in the diner had pivoted in our direction.

I scooted to the edge of the booth, hoping to discourage Jenny from asking to join us. "Morning," I said. "To what do we owe this honor?"

Jenny swatted my shoulder. "You're so funny, Dylan. 'To what do we owe this honor?'" She snorted. "Well, silly, I'm just stopping by to wish you good morning."

"Sure you are," Reid mumbled.

Jenny's head swiveled in my sister's direction. "It's just that some of us have noticed you've closed your businesses this week since…well, since poor Reagan died."

"We're opening back up in a couple of days," Sera said. "We wanted to give Reagan's family some respect."

"I figured you'd closed the bakery because you'd heard about Tim."

My eyes fused on Jenny. Blood pounded in my ears.

"Heard what about Tim?" Sera asked. So sweet. So innocent. She didn't deserve to have that wretched Jenny break her heart.

I grabbed my purse, shoved past Jenny and hauled Sera out of the seat. "Heard that Tim's gone skiing in the Alps for the rest of the summer."

"Skiing?" Sera asked.

"Yes. It's the newest thing. People ski on the grass. New type of blades someone invented. All the rage." I pulled her toward the door, but she stopped stone still.

"What is it, Dylan? What about Tim?"

I gave her my biggest doe eyes. And lied through my teeth. "Exactly what I said."

She whirled toward Jenny. "What about him? Might as well tell me before I find out from someone else."

Jenny scoffed. "I don't want to be the bearer of bad news—"

"Sure you don't," I said. It wasn't ladylike, but I saw no point in hiding my feelings from the Mouth of the South.

Jenny flashed me a fake smile. "Hon," she said to Sera. "It seems that Tim and Olivia Helm have gotten serious."

Sera swallowed. She pursed her lips and jutted out her chin. "So?"

I grabbed Sera by the elbow. "So nothing. It doesn't mean anything."

Jenny smirked at me. "They're engaged."

I'm very nearly certain that somewhere a whistle blew while smoke launched from my ears. Sera stumbled back. She grasped the edge of the speckled table, gripping it so hard I thought for sure it would crack. I mean, she's not Superman powerful or anything, but let's face it—we are witches. Not that we know how to use our power, but if she wanted to, like, split some wood karate-chop-style, I'm sure she could.

"Son of a—"

At that moment, sure as shinola, Tim strutted past the window. I wanted to slap the smug look from his face. Thirty years old and the guy wore slouchy brown pants worthy of a fraternity house. He must have thought this was college, not real life. Honestly I don't know what Sera saw in that fool. At some point you had to decide to grow up, and wearing adult clothing needed to be part of that journey—not old man pants or lazy pants—actual slacks. Just my two cents.

Sera clenched her fists. She started for the door. I pulled her back.

"He's a jerk. Leave him alone," I whispered through gritted teeth.

Her face softened. "You've been telling me to stay away from him."

I grasped her shoulders and pulled her into a hug. "I know. I didn't want you to get hurt again."

I held Sera until she leaned out of my embrace. She sniffled and swiped a finger under each eye. Tim stood outside talking to a local. I nibbled my finger as I watched my sister, waiting to see what she would do next.

She noticed me staring and laughed. "Don't worry. I'm not going out there."

"You're not?" I asked. This was a surprise. I mean, they'd broken up six months ago after dating for two years, and now the guy was engaged. I figured if anything, she wanted to wring his neck.

Sera shook her head. Her shimmering tendrils swayed from side to side. "No." She threaded her hands together and cracked her knuckles. "In fact, I'm ready to work some magic."

***

"I want to learn fire," Sera said to Em.

Queen Witch snorted. "We'll talk about that later." She fixed her steely gaze on me. Flames burned in her eyes. I dipped my head, hoping they would go away. I glanced up. No luck.

"First, we need to discuss somethin' I apparently forget to mention," Em said in a cold, distant voice.

"What's that?" Reid asked.

"Absolutely, on no condition should you ever, and I mean ever, perform magic where humans can see you."

I gulped. "Oh. That was me. Sorry about that."

"What's she talking about?" Reid asked.

"Me. Levitating last night. Outside."

Oh, she mouthed.

Em tittered. "Sorry? You're sorry?"

Come on. Don't try to punish me for something you didn't say. "Yes. I'm sorry. I won't do it again, but in all fairness, you never told us."

Her face puffed into a red, angry ball. "Take this as your warnin', chicklet. If you ever let a human see your abilities again, you'll face a nasty punishment."

"And what would that be?" I wanted to see if Roman had told me the truth.

"You'll be boiled alive."

"Boiled alive?" Sera said. "That's horrible."

"Ew. Double horrible," Reid agreed.

"That's why you don't break the rules," Em said.

Sera glanced at me. "Did you know that?"

I scratched at my hairline. "Yeah. Roman told me after y'all got in the car last night."

"And you didn't tell us?" Reid said.

"Was I supposed to?"

"It would have been nice," Sera said.

Ready to change the subject, I turned to Em and rested my forehead in my palm. "How'd you find out what I did?"

Em pulled an elastic from her purse and tied back her hair. "I wouldn't be Queen Witch if I didn't know things. Anyway, am I understood?"

I hung my head like a chastised elementary schooler. "Yes."

She smacked her lips. "Good. Now let's get cookin'."

"I want to learn fire," Sera repeated.

Em froze. "You ain't jokin'."

"I'm not joking," Sera said. She stood stock-still, her shoulders back, her jaw and fists clenched. Anger rolled off her. Evidently she wasn't over the whole Tim thing. I took a step back. I feared she might set the entire store on fire. My beautiful dresses.

No. She wouldn't do that. My sister wouldn't turn all Firestarter on me and cause my shop to explode.

She wouldn't.

She couldn't.

Could she?

Em cleared her throat and cast a nervous glance toward me. I shrugged. The girl wanted to learn fire. Who was I to stop her?

"Have you mastered levitation?" Em asked Sera.

Sera exhaled loudly. Her nostrils flared. She tilted down her chin, staring at Em. "I want to learn fire."

"I suggest you teach her fire," Reid said, "before she explodes."

Em rose, clasped her hands together and said, "Link hands."

"No," Sera countered. "No linking hands. We can't work magic that way. Show her, Dyl."

I bit my lower lip. "Maybe now's not the time."

"Show her."

Okay then. I closed my eyes and thought weightless thoughts. A split second later, my feet lifted from the ground.

Em clapped. "Wonderful."

"Fire," Sera said.

Em cleared her throat. "Ahem. Fire. Lift your hand in front of you." Sera did so. "This is easier if you start with a match, but since I ain't got one, we'll have to do this the old-fashioned way. Stare at the tips of your fingers. Focus on the space right above them, and imagine a small flame appearin'. Nothing big, now. Make it small. Manageable."

I did as she said, imagining flame the size of candlelight above my fingers. Nothing came. I knit my brows together, concentrating, focusing. Finally a small wave of orange and red glowed. I pushed harder, forcing the blobby mass to take shape. After several seconds the colors streamed together, creating a shimmering flame. I beamed. Awesome! I could fly and make fire! The world was my oyster. Insert mad scientist laugh here.

Just kidding.

I glanced at Sera. Beads of sweat lined her forehead. She stared at her fingers, every ounce of focus aimed on them.

"Concentrate, Sera," Reid said.

"I am," she snapped.

Reid closed her mouth. She gazed at me. I shrugged. Sera's

bad moods were legendary. Hopefully this one would pass soon.

Sera tipped her head down. A loud whoosh filled the air. My jaw fell. Hovering above her hand sat an orb the size of a softball. It bobbed in the air, its tendrils of flame cracking as if it were waiting to be told what to do.

"Holy cow," Reid said.

I swallowed.

"That's wonderful," Em said, her voice faltering. "What a great job your first try."

"What do I do with it?" Sera asked.

Em regarded her. "Do you want to vanish it?"

Sera shook her head. "No. I want to set something on fire." The ball expanded, growing to the size of a cantaloupe.

Em crossed to Sera, all the while staring at the ball. "Why don't you save that flame for when you need a barbecue lit? Otherwise it's best to make your magic disappear when you ain't got no use for it."

"Okay." The orb grew to the size of a watermelon. Flames licked the air. My cheeks grew hot. I glanced at Reid, who wiped a line of sweat from her upper lip.

I guessed that Sera wanted to burn Tim's house down. Who could blame her? I didn't. See? That's why I didn't date. If you didn't put your heart on the line, it wouldn't get broken. Very sensible. And then you wouldn't do stupid things like make a dangerous fireball.

"Chickadee," Em said. "Think it gone and it will be."

Sera glared at her. "I'm not ready to let it go just yet." The flames shuddered. The orb inflated to the size of a beach ball.

Uh-oh. It bobbed a few inches below the ceiling. Fingers of fire crackled at the plaster.

Are ceilings flammable? Like super easy flammable or only kinda sorta?

"Okay," Em said. She tossed a nervous glance my way. I sighed and took the hint.

I stepped up to bat. "What are you going to do with that

fire?"

"Stare at it until it burns a hole in my retinas."

"That doesn't sound particularly healthy," I said.

"It's not."

"Why don't you do something more constructive with it?"

"Like what?"

I squeezed her arm. "Like vanish it until you really need it. Use it to scare whatever witch wants us dead."

"Hmpf. That doesn't sound like fun."

The ball pushed into the ceiling. A wave of heat engulfed my body. If the fire grew any larger, my shop would be in big trouble. I'd lose my dresses and have to start all over. Totally uncool.

"Burning Tim's house won't give you any satisfaction. You'll regret it later and feel childish."

Sera's chest heaved as she exhaled. She stared at the ball and then back at me. "Okay." With a snap of her fingers, she vanished the flame. Thank goodness. I wiped away the sheen of sweat that covered my face.

Sera bent her knees and deflated to the floor. She tapped her palm on the carpet and looked up at Em. "Well, I guess I've got that mastered. What else can we learn today?"

Em brought a shaking hand to her forehead. "That's all for now. Rest up. We'll start fresh tomorrow."

I stared at the smudge on the ceiling. "When will I be able to open my shop again?"

Em glanced up at me, her eyes filled with surprise. I don't know why; it was a logical question. "You can open your shop in a few days."

Great. That gave me time to fix the fire stain.

***

We broke for the rest of the morning, and I decided, since Milly hadn't been much (or any) help, that I'd visit the police station and see if Detective Blount had any leads. I know. I know. The murderer used magic to kill. Probably the police hadn't or wouldn't discover anything. I still had to see, though. I threw Sera the keys to my car and stalked over to the assassin's vehicle.

I slid into the passenger side. "Don't you ever sleep?"

"What's that?" He removed his sunglasses. My breath hitched when his sea-green eyes met mine. It's okay. I'm cool. He had the big moment with Sera and all. Not that she cared with the emotional state she was in, but they had it. Not him and me.

I cleared the knot from my throat. "I mean, you're always around. Always, um, guarding us."

He smiled. My bones liquified. I think they actually popped and fizzled.

"I sleep a few hours in the early morning, while Em's teaching you."

"Only a few hours?"

"I'm trained to get by on little sleep." As if that explained everything.

"Okay. Got it." We sat in silence.

"Did you want me to take you somewhere?"

Ha. Oh yeah. Green eyes made me forget. "Yes, yes I did. Do. I do want you take me somewhere."

"Okay. Where?"

I tightened the strap of my purse. "The police station."

"The station it is."

For some reason I thought he'd argue the point. That he wouldn't want to go or would question me excessively about it. "That's it? No argument?"

"Darlin'." A shudder ran down my spine. "I'll take you wherever you want to go."

It was official. I had melted onto the seat. Roman would have to scrape me off. I think I nodded. I'm not certain if I replied at all. But first thing I knew, we were parked outside the station. Roman unclasped his seat belt.

"Where are you going?" I asked.

He glanced around. "Is that a trick question? Inside. With you."

"Why?" It came out gruff. I extended my hand and touched his arm. A bolt shocked my skin. I lifted my eyes to his. He smiled. My cheeks burned. "Sorry. I didn't mean to be so harsh. What I meant to say was, you don't have to come in with me."

He smirked. "My job is to keep you safe. Let's go."

"Okay. But do you have to wear that duster?"

He glanced down at his coat. "This? It hides all my weapons."

"It makes you look like an assassin."

He laughed, a deep-bellied baritone. "I haven't been one of those in a long time."

I gulped. Oh my God. He really was an assassin. Sera would die!

"But you're right. I can't take this in. The metal detectors will blare loud enough to bring in the army."

Hey. It wasn't a great reason to lose the duster, but it would work. Roman's shadow swallowed me as we walked toward the municipal building. As tall as a quarterback with the girth of a wide receiver, the man made me feel like a dwarf. But I had to say, I definitely felt protected with him at my side.

He pulled the door. The suction hold released, blowing manufactured air over my body. The cool breeze tickled the hairs on the back of my neck, sending a chill down my spine. I approached the desk officer.

"Is Detective Blount available? I'm Dylan Apel."

He picked up the phone and made a call. Fluorescents buzzed overhead, their totally unflattering light probably making me look sallow and old. Gross. I hated harsh lighting. What girl didn't?

He hung up the receiver. "Follow me."

Roman and I walked past a room of open desks, officers working. It looked like a quiet day in Silver Springs. Except there was a murderer on the loose. Of course, none of these folks had to worry.

They weren't the intended victim. That would be me.

The officer deposited us outside an office rimmed in glass. A stereotypical police office. Dingy beige blinds lined the windows, ready to be yanked closed on a moment's notice, no doubt.

Detective Blount rose. "Miss Apel, good to see you." He crossed to me, extended his hand. He shook mine and moved to Roman. "Detective Blount."

"Roman Bane," he said. Roman Bane? Ohh. I so liked the sound of that. Kinda rolled off the tongue in a nice, lilting way. "I'm a friend of Dylan's."

"You are?" I said. Both men shot me confused looks. Oops. "I mean, he is." I shook my head. "We are. I just haven't seen Roman in a long time." I laughed, trying to hide my nerves. Detective Blount sat back down.

He gestured for us to sit as well. "What can I do for you today?"

"I was checking to see if you had any leads on the case. If there was anything I can help you with?"

The detective rested back and clasped his hands over his lean middle. Half-moons darkened the planes beneath his eyes. He looked tired, worn. "We're still researching the dress." Which meant they hadn't come up with anything on it, I'd bet. And they wouldn't. "Do you know of anyone who would want to harm Miss Eckhart?"

Didn't I? Few people had liked the loudmouthed debutante. But that didn't mean anyone wanted to kill her.

"No. No one that I know had any ill will against her. But that was my dress. I was the one who was supposed to wear it. Not her."

He steepled his fingers beneath his chin. "Just looking at every angle."

Roman cleared his throat. I gave him a worried glance. He was going to speak? In public? He barely even talked to me. "How long have you lived in Silver Springs, Detective?"

"A few months."

"It's a messy crime for a small town."

The detective eyed him. "It is. I came from Atlanta."

"So you were used to this sort of thing there. Murder, I mean."

Blount nodded. "More or less."

Roman's gaze drifted around the office. He took his time, seeming to absorb the sight of the pictures and knickknacks. When he spoke, it was slow, deliberate. "I bet you came here for a break. Wanted to get out of the city. Put in a few years at a small town and then retire."

Blount scrubbed the back of his short dark hair. "That's what I'd hoped."

Roman leaned forward. "Girl burns up in a dress. Not good for the lakeside economy."

"No. Not at all," Blount agreed.

"What if it turns out to be a freak accident? What if your best chemists never find anything? Puts you in a bad spot."

The detective thumped his fingers on the desk. "Mr. Bane, do you know something you want to tell me?"

Roman relaxed, sat back in his chair. "Only that I hope your guys find out what's going on. I'm sure the Eckhart family would like some closure."

We left a few minutes later. As soon as we stepped back into the heat, I said, "What was that all about? Trying to make yourself a suspect?"

Roman laughed. "Not at all. Just planting a little seed in the detective's head."

I slid into the SUV and slammed the door. "What kind of seed? The kind that gets yourself arrested?"

"Not a chance." He started the ignition and turned to me, his elbow sitting on the rest between us. "That detective thought when he left Atlanta, that this would be a cushy job. Perhaps a few hens stolen from a chicken house here, a lost dog there. I want to make sure he's thinking good and hard about the position he's taken."

I shrugged. "He seemed fine to me."

Roman tapped the steering wheel. "See the bags under his eyes?"

"I didn't notice," I lied.

He relaxed, stretched his shoulders back and expanded his chest. "This job isn't what he hoped for, and now it'll never be the retirement job he wanted. What Detective Blount doesn't realize is that he's stepped into a hotbed of action. Things in Silver Springs are about to get a whole lotta weird."

I fished my pink lip gloss from my purse and applied a liberal coat. "What are you talking about?"

"I've lived around witches my entire life. Now that you and your sisters have been outed, people are going to drop like flies."

"What?"

He shifted into drive. "That's the way it is. Witches kill witches. Don't let that Queen Em tell you any differently. They all want the same thing—power. And they'll do anything to get it."

I pressed my back into the buttery leather. "How do you know so much about witches?"

He threw me a sidelong glance as he nosed from the parking space. "Because I was raised by one."

ELEVEN

"A witch raised you?"

"That's right."

I squinted at him as if that would help me read his mind. "Like a real witch?"

He chuckled. "Yes. Like a real witch."

"But you said you don't like us."

He brushed a blond strand from his face. I realized this was the first time I hadn't seen his shoulder-length hair pulled back. It lay beside his brutally sharp cheekbones in loose, sexy waves.

"It's complicated," he said.

I ran a sweaty palm over the smooth leather seat. "I have time."

"It's not a very interesting story."

"Try me."

He chuckled. His skintight T-shirt stretched over his biceps and chest. I zoned in on his muscles, and Roman turned to me. My cheeks flamed. Crap. How embarrassing. He totally caught me checking him out.

"My mother was Queen Witch. There were four of us—three girls and me. Sometimes boys are born with power, but I wasn't, which never bothered me. But life at court is something else."

"Wait. There's a court? Like Medieval Europe–style?"

He gave me an amused smile. The corners of his eyes crinkled in the cutest way. I wanted to reach out and pinch them. "Not exactly, but when you're queen, you live in a community with other witches and councilors."

"Is that an elected position?"

"Yes." He glared at me. "Don't even think about running for it."

"I'm not," I grumbled, looking out the window.

"Seriously. It's definitely not all it's cracked up to be. There's a lot of backstabbing and fighting."

No surprise there. Weren't we dealing with a bunch of women? I'd never been in a roomful of ladies where there wasn't at least one double-faced person.

"Just because there's backstabbing doesn't explain why you don't like us. I mean, I can't help that I'm a witch. Neither can Sera."

"A witch murdered my mother."

Oh. Well, that explained it then.

He rubbed his palm over his chin. The sound of his hand scratching against morning stubble filled the cabin. "But they didn't stop there. They also murdered my sisters in an attempt to eliminate the entire line."

Roman's face darkened. My heart ached for him. I couldn't imagine the pain he'd endured as a little boy. I touched his arm, doing my best to ignore the burning spark that snaked up my skin at our contact. "I'm so sorry. Did they catch the killer?"

He shook his head. "There were some ideas, some leads, but nothing definitive ever came of the investigation. So when I grew up, I became a witch hunter." He turned the air on. A cool current streamed over my flesh. I shivered, more from the subject than the temperature.

I kneaded a patch of goose bumps away. "You hunted witches?"

"For the witch police, not civilians, and I only hunted those who needed a bit of hunting. After that, I became a detective."

Witch police? Why should anything surprise me at this point? "So you hunted bad people?"

"Yes, only the bad ones," he confirmed. "I hoped to be retired at this point, living the good life on a beach somewhere, and drinking piña coladas for the rest of my days, but that didn't happen."

"I don't think all that sugar would have been good for your physique."

He shook his head.

I scrunched up my nose. "Seriously. You wouldn't be able to keep those big muscles if you drank piña coladas all day long."

He leaned over. "Joking. It was a joke."

I grinned. "I know. Can you believe I was joking, too? Oh my gosh, a witch that gets humor. You must be dying."

He laughed—a good hearty sound that made my heart do jumping jacks. And splits. And spread eagles. "I am. I can't believe it."

We stopped at a red light. Roman looked over. I caught his glance and held on. A web of energy tangled around us. I felt myself being pulled into him, drawn to him. My lips started to pucker…and I cleared my throat.

What was I thinking? He liked Sera. Sera. Your sister, remember? The one with the broken heart.

"So you were a detective. Is that why you gave Blount such a hard time?"

Roman's gaze slid from me back to the street. "It is. We're of the same blood. I can't tell him any of that, of course. I'm a retired witch hunter, and that guy's hunting a witch. He's in over his head, with no idea what he's dealing with."

We pulled onto my street. My heart dived down toward my stomach, disappointed that our conversation was ending. "You must like some witches. I mean, you're here helping us."

"Nah," he said. "I made some bad investments and need the money." He glanced over. His lips curled as if he was teasing me, but of course, I couldn't tell if he was or not. I mean, I'd barely had two conversations with the man. "Trust me, I don't like witches."

Apparently, not kidding.

"As long as I know what side of the fence I'm on when it comes to you," I snapped, irritated that he had to be so mean. And irritated that he had to be so good-looking, with those sea-green eyes and dark lashes that looked like a French artist had sketched them with coal and then smudged the edges with his finger.

What? It was irritating.

"I wasn't trying to get under your skin," he said.

I scoffed. "What do you call it then? It doesn't exactly make me feel safe to know that because you don't like what I am—a minor detail that I have no choice in, by the way—you don't like me. How can I trust that you'll keep me or my sisters safe?"

He opened his mouth to reply. A door slammed. I looked toward the house. Reid rushed out, racing toward the SUV. I opened the door and hopped onto the curb, forgetting my conversation with Roman.

Let's be honest, mostly forgetting.

"What's going on?" I asked.

Her brown eyes shone with fright. "Where've you been? We've called you like a thousand times?"

Err. I pulled the phone from my back pocket and pressed the Call button. I'd missed exactly twenty calls from Sera and Reid. "Sorry. It was on mute. Is everything okay?"

She grabbed my arm and dragged me across the street. "No. Everything is not okay."

I locked my knees, forcing her to stop. "Then what is it?" I asked, raising my fingers to my mouth so I could chew off a line of nails. What could it be? Was Sera hurt? Was Nan okay? Had something happened to Grandma?

"It's Grandma."

"Oh no." I spit out a hangnail. "Is she okay?"

"No, she is very much not okay."

"Is she dead?"

"Worse," Reid said, pulling me toward the house. "She's awake."

***

Taking a deep breath, I pushed open the cherry colored front door and stepped inside the cottage. Reid hovered behind me. Standing in the center of the living room, her silver hair puffed out and a delicate gold tiara on her head, stood my grandmother, Hazel.

She'd changed out of her formless pink pants and paisley blouse into a flowing white tunic, a shimmering blue scarf and orange pantaloons. That's right, pantaloons.

Her face, creased and cracked from age, split into a beaming smile. "Dylan! You're home."

"Yeah, Dylan," Sera grumbled from the corner. "You're finally home."

Nan stood by the kitchen. I tried to gather from the perturbed looks on everyone's faces what the heck was going on, but their narrowed brows conveyed only worry.

Uncertain what to do, I decided the best thing was to hug my grandmother who'd been in a frozen state for the past three years. I wrapped my arms around the frail person in front of me, expecting her to return the gesture, but she pushed me back.

Grandma hustled to the front window. She flattened herself against the wall and peered behind the curtain. "Dylan, there's no time for hugs. The witches are approaching the eastern front. We must be ready for battle."

"Um. What?"

A look of frustration washed over her face. "You too?" she said. "I understand how they got to Reid and Sera. They're the simpletons of the three of you—"

"Thanks, Grandma," Sera said.

Grandma ignored her. "But you?" she said to me. "Don't tell me they've brainwashed you as well?"

Okay, I won't. I tiptoed over to her, afraid I'd shatter what little brain she had left. "Afraid who has gotten to me?"

She threw up her hands. "The Witches of the North. The Northern region. We're in the middle of a battle for our very lives."

"We are?"

Sera plopped down in a chair and swung her legs over the arms. "Didn't you know? It's nineteen sixty and we're in the middle of the great Witch War."

Oooh, I mouthed. I turned to Grandma, who clung to the floral curtains for dear life. "Grandma, we're safe from the witches. The war is over."

"The war is never over!"

Well, crap.

"We've been trying to call you," Sera said. "She's been like this for half an hour. It doesn't look like it's going to let up."

"Great," I whispered. "So Grandma's awake and she's crazy."

Reid crossed to us and sank onto the rug. "Simpleton Number Three agrees with you."

I threw Nan a desperate look. "What do we do?"

She shook her head and retreated several steps. "Don't ask me. I've never had to deal with anything like this."

I decided the direct route would be best. "Grandma, the witches have us surrounded. Step away from the curtain."

She shimmied so fast from the window I thought she'd set the floorboards on fire. "Stand back, girls. I'll protect you."

I kicked Sera's foot. "Actually, Grandma, Sera will protect us. She's a class A certified witch."

"Class A certified?" Sera asked.

I shot her a dark look. "Just roll with it."

Grandma raised trembling hands to her lower lip. "But I'm supposed to protect you. You don't know you're witches. I'm your guardian."

Sera yawned, stretched out her arms and rose. She extended her palm. A ball of fire flamed over the surface of her skin.

"Have you been practicing?"

She shrugged. "Maybe."

Grandma's face darkened. "Who told you?" She whirled toward me. "Who corrupted you? You weren't supposed to know!"

"Good job, Sis," Sera said. "Now she's really in a tizzy."

Grandma spread her arms wide. Rays of light exploded from her hands, pointing toward the ceiling. Anger twisted her face. "Who are you and what have you done with my granddaughters?"

I shrank, furiously trying to think of a way out of this. I glanced at Sera and Reid. Both stared at Grandma, lines of fear etched on their faces.

The rays beaming from Grandma's palms intensified. The building shook. Pictures fell from shelves. Glass splintered across the floor. The walls rumbled, threatening to cave in. I covered my head, knowing this was it. It wasn't going to be another witch that killed me. It would be my own grandmother, who'd gone crazy Carrie-style.

The light from her hands blinded me. I closed my eyes, waiting for my inevitable demise.

The front door slammed open, and a wash of blue swept over the room. "For God's sake, Hazel, stop trying to kill everybody. Don't you know these are your own grown granddaughters?"

I peeked out from under my arm. Milly stood in the center of the frame, her gray hair sticking out like wires. With hands fisted on her hips and legs spread wide, the small five-foot-something-or-other woman glared a look of death at my grandmother.

Grandma pointed to the sky. "The Witch War!"

"Come off it, Hazel," Milly spat. "The war's been done for a long time. Take a chill pill and calm down. You've been asleep for a while. There's a lot for you to catch up on."

Grandma's eyes widened with worry. "Asleep?"

Milly extended her cane, knocking it against the wood floor. She stepped inside. The door shut softly behind her. With a twirl of her hand, the broken frames and shattered glass mended themselves. Dumped flowerpots righted, and the air settled as a layer of dust floated to the floor. Milly sauntered to the middle of the room. "Yes. You've been asleep. 'Bout time you woke up, you old biddy. Your girls are in trouble."

Grandma's weepy eyes fixed on us. "Trouble?"

Milly bent over and yanked at her knee-high nude-colored hose. "Yeah, trouble. Some crazy witch is trying to kill them."

"Is it you?" Grandma asked.

"Hells bells no. Why would I want to kill them? They're half mine, remember?"

Half hers? But that would mean…I clutched the back of the couch. Could it be?

"You're our father's mother?"

Milly winked at me. "You got it, toots. Now let's learn some serious magic."

TWELVE

I wasn't sure what to think, or even say. The fact that I had another living grandmother amazed me, elated me. But when I considered that she'd been kept a secret, anger burned in my gut. Or maybe that was an ulcer.

It took all of five minutes for my Grandma Hazel to calm down once Milly arrived. Let's just say Milly seemed to have a magical touch when it came to soothing my grandma. And goodness knows I was thankful she did. If she hadn't shown up, there's no telling what would have happened to us.

Reid handed Milly a glass of iced tea. "Why didn't we know about any of this?"

"Thank you," Milly said. She nodded toward Hazel. "You want to tell them?"

My grandmother smoothed the edges of her hair. Her fingers glided over the metal tiara. She frowned and pulled the combs through her steel-wool tresses, and then tossed the thing on the table. "Because I didn't want you to know, among other reasons. Magic isn't something to be trifled with, and the way I saw it, there were enough witches in the world. We didn't need three more."

"Good theory." I twisted a paper napkin between my fingers. "But the reality is our abilities were always going to get out into the public. If we'd known, we never would have done the interview in the newspaper."

Grandma clutched her throat in dramatic fashion. "You did a newspaper interview?"

"To get our businesses some exposure," Sera said.

"You have witchcraft businesses?" Grandma said.

"I'm a dressmaker and Sera's a baker," I explained, trying to be ever so patient with a woman who'd been asleep for three years. Well, not really asleep. Catatonic. And it might be bad, but the thought occurred to me that it would have been easier if Grandma had stayed that way.

"You have to shut them down," Grandma said. "Your lives are in danger."

I pressed the heels of my hands into my eyes. "Now you tell us. Grandma, we're not shutting down our stores. You have to teach us how to be witches."

"I don't want you to be witches," she said.

Milly knocked her fist on the table. "Your grandmother had it out with the council. She doesn't like witches, and after your parents died in the car crash, she decided never to tell you the truth of your heritage. And she wouldn't let me, either. That's what ruined our friendship. I respected her wishes, but the fact of the matter is, there's no point in hiding anything from you. You're grown up. If you want to use your power"—she waved her hand—"use it."

"So why didn't we know about you?" Reid asked Milly.

Her lower lip trembled. "Because your father and I didn't get along. He didn't like the man I married after his father, Mr. Apel, died. There was no love between him and Mr. Jones. We never made up."

"So if you lived here, and Grandma and our mom lived in Savannah, how did our parents meet?" I asked.

Milly flapped her lips. The sound reminded me of a lawnmower engine. "Your mother is from Silver Springs. Her early childhood was spent here, before Hazel decided to up and move her to Savannah." She wiped a tear from her eye. "Your parents were friends as children. They never lost touch. I can't say the same for your grandmother and myself."

"But that doesn't explain why you've decided to tell us now," Reid said.

Milly stamped her cane on the floor. "Because you girls need all the help in the world to survive as witches since you've never been trained."

Hazel gnawed at the inside of her cheek. Her mouth worked the flesh hard. I placed a hand on her shoulder. "Grandma, we're witches. We need to learn how to protect ourselves. Will you teach us?"

She leaned back in the chair, letting limp arms fall to her sides. She stared at each of us in turn and finally said, "I only wanted to keep you safe."

Milly folded arthritic hands over the knob of the cane. "You can keep them safe by making them lethal."

"Lethal?" Grandma asked.

"You heard me. By the time I'm finished with these girls, they're going to be the Terminators of the witch world."

"Oh, I like the sound of that," Reid said.

"You don't have any power," Milly replied.

"Dang it."

Grandma regarded us with weepy eyes. "Do you want to learn witchcraft?"

"Yes," Sera confirmed.

"Yes," I said. "But on one condition." She quirked an eyebrow at me. "That you and Milly make up. Become friends again."

Grandma looked at Milly and pressed her lips into a thin, straight line. "Nan!"

Nan popped her head out of the kitchen. "Yes?"

"Better make some sandwiches; we've got a lot of work to do."

***

The next few hours blew past like a spring tornado. We mastered a light spell and an ice spell. Well, perhaps mastered isn't the right word.

"Keep your ice in front of you," Milly hollered when my ice ball whirled out of my hand and splashed against the fireplace, coating the brick in a sheen of crystals.

I cringed. "Sorry."

Sera didn't fare any better. Her light ball whisked around the room like a feral cat, dodging our best attempts to restrain it. It broke the same pictures that Milly had fixed earlier, and even managed to knock down one of the curtain rods, sending it crashing to the floor.

"Oops," Sera said.

"Big oops," Milly snarled.

"See?" Grandma said. "This is why I didn't teach them magic."

Milly snapped her head in Grandma's direction. "If you'd taught them, they'd be much better than this. They'd have mastered these techniques by now."

Grandma only shrugged. "I've been asleep."

"Fine excuse," Milly mumbled.

I sank down to the couch. My hands hurt from trying to hold on to a ball of ice. A ball of ice. Like, what is that even good for? Making snow cones on a hot day? Milly didn't even teach me how to make flavored syrup to go on top. What a waste.

"Maybe there are other spells we can learn. Milly, how do you make a glass of iced tea appear?"

Milly knocked the cane gently on the floor as if it helped her think better. "That is a combination of spells. It includes creating ice, glass and drink. You have to master each one and then combine them."

My head throbbed. So there were no shortcuts. "What are we supposed to do if the killer shows up? Our powers should be increasing, right? The summer solstice is only a week and a half away."

Grandma twitched her finger. The curtain rod sprung from the floor and hung itself back on its brackets. "If the killer shows up, you've only got one chance."

"And that is?" Sera asked.

Granda shook her head. "Run."

"All kidding aside," I said. "We need some help."

Milly swiped a finger over her gnarled nose. "You certainly do." She heaved and hauled her ancient body from the wooden dining chair. It creaked under her weight. "I don't know what that Queen Witch has been teaching you, but her lessons are certainly lacking."

That reminded me. "Yeah, about that—"

Milly pointed to the glass she'd been drinking from. "Dylan, hold out your palm and wish that glass into your hand."

"What?" I said.

She motioned her head toward the sweat-rimmed tea glass. "Imagine it in your hand. Make it so."

I snapped my fingers. "Just like that?"

Grandma folded her hands on the table. "Just like that. You can do it." She spread her hands out in a welcoming gesture. "Just think of sunbeams and mistletoe."

Sera mouthed sunbeams and mistletoe?

I guess Grandma's brain still needed some thawing from its three-year freeze.

"And unicorns," Grandma added. She winked at me. "That's the ticket."

Oh boy. I glanced at the glass and then my hand.

"See yourself holding it," Milly prodded. She tapped her cane to a rhythm that only existed in her head. Tap, tap, tap. Tap, tap, tap.

"Do you mind?" I said.

"What?"

"Can you knock off the cane? I can't concentrate."

"Is that any way to talk to your grandmother?" Milly said.

I stared at the spitfire of a woman. With wiry hair, a knotted nose that hung over her frowning mouth, and a pork barrel body with stick arms, Milly didn't look much like the grandmotherly type.

"Yeah, I'm not going to apologize," I said.

Milly gave me a cunning smile. "Good. Rule one—never apologize to a witch."

"I thought that was never anger a witch," Reid said.

"I thought rule one was don't perform magic in front of humans," Sera added.

Milly's cane thundered against the floor. We jumped. "Just move the glass."

"Okay." With needle-edged focus, I imagined her glass in my hand. I visualized myself holding it. I pursed my lips, furrowed my brow and concentrated. Nothing happened. I shook out my hands, rolled my neck this way and that, and closed my eyes, thinking all the while about having the glass in my hand. I opened them and blinked.

There it sat. In my palm, cool water trickling down the side and onto my skin. "I did it!"

I rushed over to Sera and thrust out my hand. "Look! I did it!" She gave me a warm hug.

"When you're all finished giving each other high fives, Sera can try," Milly said.

"You don't have to be so snarky," I said.

Milly planted her orthopedically shoed feet in the middle of the room. "You're right. I don't have to be."

Which apparently meant that she still would be. I shrugged at Sera and said, "You're on. Let me put the glass on the table."

"No," Milly commanded. "Take it from her hand."

Sera cringed. She looked at me. "Are you okay with that?"

An overwhelming feeling of discomfort gurgled in my gut. I slouched. "I guess?" I didn't know the worst that could happen, but it couldn't be catastrophic, could it? She couldn't magic my hand away, could she?

"Don't amputate her hand, dear," Grandma said in a singsong voice.

Great. So it was possible.

Reid smirked. "Yeah, Sera, don't amputate her hand. Guess there are some advantages to not being a witch. For instance, I can't cause my sisters to bleed out."

Grandma wiggled a chastising finger. "You may get your magic, yet. Don't despair."

"Great," Reid said.

Sera rubbed a spot behind her ear. She circled her arms as if she were loosening up for the big game. "Okay. Don't amputate Dylan's arm. Don't amputate Dylan's arm."

"Saying it doesn't mean it won't happen," Milly said. "You need to focus."

Sera licked her lips. "Okay. Don't move, Dylan."

"I won't."

My sister stared at the glass. She rolled her shoulders back and narrowed her eyes. My heart pounded, and I repeated the mantra in my head—Don't screw up. Don't screw up. Don't screw up. Worth a shot, right?

Half a minute later, the glass vanished from my hand and appeared in Sera's. "Yes," she exclaimed.

"Thank God," I said.

"I knew you could do it," Reid said.

We gave a round of hugs. My grandmother sat at the table, a smile curling her lips. "Good thing she didn't remove your hand. I don't think I have a spare lying around anywhere."

We stopped. We gaped. I opened my mouth to say something. Sera pushed my jaw closed. "Don't. Just don't. I don't think there's anything you can say to that."

"There's something I can say," Milly said.

"What's that?" I asked.

She hobbled over to the couch and sat with a huff. "What the devil has that Queen Witch been teaching you?"

After we explained how Em had been conducting our "studies," Milly and Grandma exchanged glances.

"Well, if you want to teach a ring of monkeys magic, you'll circle them up and make them hold hands, but to teach people, it's individual," Grandma said. "I should know. I taught a circle of monkeys once. Ungrateful primates is what they were. Biting and spitting. I swore I'd never educate any ever again."

A vacant look clouded over Milly's eyes as she listened to Grandma. I couldn't blame her. Grandma had always been a free spirit, but now her brain appeared cryogenically impaired.

Milly rubbed her palm on the head of her cane. "Newer techniques indicate witches should be taught in groups. But the way your grandmother and I were raised, we learned individually." She swatted the air in disgust. "This younger generation is so obsessed with not hurting one another's feelings, they think one-on-one attention leaves others out. Bah. It's silly nonsense, if you ask me. And obviously the strategy doesn't work, because you're awful witches."

"Thank you," I said.

"Don't mention it. But the real thing we need to know is who's trying to kill you. They only have a few more days while your power grows toward the solstice. They'll make another move soon."

Sera tugged at the tips of her bob. "As far as I know, we're all out of ideas on that front."

"We never had any to begin with," I said.

"Good point."

A thought hit me. I turned to Milly. "How did you get here so quickly?"

She smacked her lips. "A birdie told me."

"What birdie?" I asked.

"Me." The voice came from the front door. I leaped to my feet, ready to do some witch combat that involved moving a glass from the table to my hand so I could throw it at whoever had broken into my house. But after my eyes adjusted to the light streaming in from the front windows, I realized it was only the assassin.

"You can walk in at any time," I said.

"Dylan," Sera hissed.

"What?"

"Be nice."

I shrugged. Roman stood in the doorway, his expression blank. "When witches wake up from a freeze, they're often a little cranky."

I stared at Grandma. "This is common?"

She fluffed her head of curls. "It can be."

"And no one told us? Where's Nan? Did she know?"

Grandma tightened the scarf around her throat. "I believe she's stepped out."

I turned to Roman, annoyed that I had to be agreeable. "It was nice of you to go get Milly. Thank you."

"Don't thank me yet."

"Why's that?"

He lowered his sunglasses. His gaze seared me. "Because Queen Witch is marching up the walkway, and she's pissed."

"How do you know?" I asked.

"The flames sparking from her fingertips tipped me off."

Uh-oh. We were in deep doo-doo.

THIRTEEN

Em stormed in. With eyes blazing and fists clenched at her sides, she entered like a WWF wrestler hell-bent on destruction. I shrank back. I couldn't help it.

"What's going on in here?" she demanded.

Milly placed the cane between her legs and rested her hands on it. "Did our little ripple get your attention?"

Em shot her a dark look. She ruffled her curly hair. Her bangles tinkled and clinked. Em smiled. "That wasn't no ripple. That was a tidal wave." She glanced around the room until her gaze rested on Grandma. Her eyes widened. "You're awake."

"It looks that way," Grandma said. "Though part of me thinks this is a bad dream—one where my granddaughters have been sucked into the dangerous world of witches. Do I have you to thank for that?"

Em sniffed. "You have them to thank. They announced themselves to the world. I'm only tryin' to help keep your girls safe."

Milly rocked her cane back and forth. "Not the best teaching methods I've ever seen."

Em whirled on her. "Excuse me? They've been instructed by the Queen herself. How many witches can say that?"

"Apparently not many," Reid said.

I elbowed her. She rolled her eyes as if to say, Well, it's true.

"Anyway, I don't think the girls will need your instruction anymore," Milly said.

Em lifted her chin. She took a moment to stare at each of us in turn. I fought the urge to squirm under her scrutinizing glare. "Fine. If you don't need me, then good luck." She snapped her fingers, and in less than a blink, Em had vanished.

"Good luck not burning that bridge," Sera said.

"Yeah," I murmured. "I don't think you made her happy."

Milly plugged her ear with a finger and scratched away. "Bah. Who cares? It's only the queen. She's the minority of witches, in case you hadn't guessed."

"What about the council?" I asked, really having no idea about the importance of the council. But I figured since they existed, they might have some weight.

"The council is a bunch of nincompoops," Grandma said. "They don't know their eyeholes from their eyeholes."

"Okaaay," Reid said. "That made sense. Didn't you mean to compare eyeholes to a different hole?"

Grandma shook her head. "No. Of course not."

"Of course not," I said. "Everything here makes absolute sense, didn't you know?"

Sera grimaced. "Right. So how are we going to learn about spelling, or whatever?"

Milly cleared her throat. It was a soothing sound, one that involved lots of hacking and snarling. "We're going to teach you."

"Great idea," I said, unconvinced. Though they were better than Em, I still figured someone would end up getting hurt. I looked from our coven (was that the right word for it?) to Roman. "What about you? Are you outta here now that Em is gone?"

He slid his sunglasses back over his eyes. "I've been paid through the solstice, so I'll stay."

How comforting to know that payment was his reason for staying—not that he wanted to be, you know, ethical or anything.

I clapped my hands together. "Great. So we have a

bodyguard."

"Yeah. Great," Reid said with a twinkle in her eye.

My stomach rumbled. "As great as this has been, I think I'm ready for some dinner. Can we call it a day?"

Milly rose, her knees popping. "I've got things to do. Girls, come by anytime and I'll teach you some more magic."

"I've got a lot to do before I open my store back up in a couple of days. We'll try to stop by."

Milly shrugged. "Whatever. I don't care. I'm not the one someone's trying to kill."

"What a cheery disposition you have," I said. "How is it we never met before now?"

Milly eyeballed me. "Because I didn't want to."

And with a twitch of the nose, Milly vanished.

"Mr. Bodyguard," Grandma said.

"You can call me Roman."

"Roman," my grandmother said in her most aristocratic voice. "Would you like to have supper with us?"

"He doesn't like witches," I said with a sharp tone.

"Perhaps you should consider a new line of work," Grandma said.

I swear a tinge of pink smeared his cheeks. Who knew assassins could blush? He ignored me and said, "I would be honored to stay."

"Nan!" Grandma called out.

Nan popped her head out of the kitchen door. "Yes?"

I stretched my arms over my head. Magic apparently put a lot of cricks in my back. "I thought Grandma said you were out."

"Oh. Well. I wasn't too far away," she said.

Right. Just didn't want to be near us witches, I'm sure.

Grandma waved a hand at her. "There'll be one more at dinner."

"Great. About to heat up the jar of pasta sauce now."

And there you have it. Cooking at its finest.

***

Roman sat beside me at dinner. I don't know why. Perhaps he wanted a better look at Sera across the table. His entire presence distracted me—from the husky scent wafting off him to the constant brush of his sculpted thigh against my leg. Honestly, how was a girl supposed to keep her focus on staying alive with all this testosterone around?

"How is everything?" Nan asked expectantly. She gave Roman a wide grin. Her blue eyes shone as she nodded her head in his direction. "Does it taste okay?"

Yeah, it tasted like a Michelin-starred French chef opened a can of Boyardee and microwaved it.

Roman lifted his fork and did the best bite and smile I'd ever seen. "It's great. Thanks for having me."

Whoa. Not the answer I expected from a hardened man such as himself.

"Are you dating anyone?" Grandma asked.

"Grandma," Sera said.

Grandma split her bread roll and buttered one side. "What?"

Sera rested her elbows on the table. "You haven't even asked if we're dating anyone. You've been asleep for three years. Don't you think you need to do some catching up?"

Grandma laughed. "None of you are dating anyone. I may have been frozen, but I could still hear." She wagged her finger at me. "Dylan, of course, hasn't dated since that Colten boy popped her cherry and dumped her. Of course, he didn't tell her he dumped her—he simply didn't show up the night of prom."

I nearly threw my fork at her. "Grandma!"

She ignored me. "And Tim, that worthless toad, broke up with you, my darling Seraphina, six months ago. Good riddance. And Reid—"

"I think we've heard enough," I said, trying to cut her off.

"And Reid talks about bedding boys but wouldn't know what

to do if one ended up in her lap."

"True that," Reid said.

Roman chuckled.

"What are you laughing at?" I said.

He swiped the napkin over his mouth. "I can't help it. This is the best family dinner I've been at in a long time." His eyes crinkled in amusement, making his lashes look extra smudgy.

"I haven't even gotten to you," Grandma said.

"You don't know him," Sera said.

Grandma wiggled her hand in a so-so gesture. "I don't have to know him to tell his story."

"Grandma," I warned.

Roman rested back in his chair. "No, by all means. I'm up for grabs. I'm available for embarrassment."

Nan sucked a noodle through her puckered lips. "Be careful what you wish for."

Grandma closed her eyes and placed both palms on the table. She hummed. I quirked an eyebrow at Sera, who shrugged. She had no idea what the woman was doing either.

After several minutes of humming, she spoke. "Roman's had his heart broken before." She opened one eye and squinted at him. "She lost her life because of your work."

Alarm bells blared in my head. This was a bad idea. A terrible idea, in fact. Grandma had gone from being up close and personal with Roman to giving him a virtual prostate exam in less than five seconds. Though I had to admit, I was intrigued. His girlfriend lost her life because of his work? Tell me more. Must have been the Jenny Butts in me.

He scratched his brow with the back of his thumb. "More or less."

Grandma's other eye creaked open. "You blame yourself."

I bit my lower lip and sneaked a glance at Roman. The blood had drained from his lips. His jaw twitched, and a cold stoniness had replaced the warmth that played in his eyes only moments earlier. He gripped the edge of the table and stared at the linen cloth that covered it.

Grandma needed to stop. I leaned over, clasped her hand. Her head jerked in my direction. She blinked several times. "Okay, Grandma, I think we've punished Roman enough. He's here to help us out, remember?"

She turned back to him, totally ignoring me, because apparently dredging up someone's past was more important than listening to common sense. "It wasn't your fault, son. No matter what you did, she would have died. You couldn't have stopped it, couldn't have prevented it."

Roman's face darkened.

I jumped up. "Who wants dessert? I think we have ice cream. Right, Nan?"

"And brownies. I made some this morning," Sera said. She picked up her plate and Reid's.

"Hey! I'm not finished."

"Yes, you are."

Roman dropped his napkin on the table. "Thanks, but no thanks. I'm full. No dessert for me." He shoved back his chair and rose. "I'd better get back to my post. I've got some guarding to do."

"You can stay inside and watch, if you'd like," Grandma said.

But Roman was already at the front door. He turned back, gave a curt nod and said, "No thanks." He opened the door and, in less than a blink, was gone.

After the door shut behind him, Sera said, "Something tells me he won't be coming to any more of our dinners."

"Something tells me you're right," I said. "Grandma, why'd you do that?"

She looked at me blankly. "Do what?"

"Say all that to Roman?"

"Yeah," Reid said, "and how'd you know all that stuff?"

She folded her napkin on the table. "Everyone knows that about him. It's all in his dossier."

I stopped cleaning up. "Dossier? What are you talking about?"

A worn manila file folder appeared in her hand. The edges were ragged, the spine of it soft, as if it had been opened hundreds of times. "This." She thumbed it open and started sifting through the contents. "It's everything the witch police have on your bodyguard. It's his official file."

We stared at her. She stared at us, and then a lightbulb or a forest fire went off in her brain. "You think I made all that up? Heck's bells no. I read his file years ago and just recalled the information."

What I wouldn't do to get my fingers on that folder. I confess. I wanted to snoop. I thrust out my hand. "Let me see that."

"No. That's official witch police business."

"Witch police?" Sera asked.

"There's a witch police." I sighed. "As if all this witch business couldn't get any crazier."

"Interesting," Reid replied.

"Anyway," I said to Grandma. "Let me see the folder."

She vanished it. My hopes to find out more about the assassin and that story disappeared with it. "You're not allowed."

"You're not the witch police," I said. "You're not allowed either."

Grandma splayed her hand against her chest. "I'm old. That entitles me to lots of things."

Whatever.

***

I tried to put the fiasco of dinner behind me by helping Nan wash the dishes. Barely ten minutes later and that job complete, I wiped my hands on a kitchen towel and swung it over my shoulder. Grandma sat in the recliner reading a gardening magazine.

"So, Grandma," I said. She pulled her nose from the glossy

page and blinked in my direction. "Would you like to explain why you never told us about our power?"

She shrugged. "I thought we'd already gone over this."

"All we've gotten are cursory answers. I want the truth. The nitty-gritty truth."

Reid entered the room and sat on the footstool at Grandma's feet. "You knew we were witches."

Grandma gave her a sympathetic smile. "Not you, dear."

"Okay. Well, you knew Sera and Dylan have power."

Sera leaned against the wall, arms crossed, a curtain of hair slashing over her face. "That's a question I'd like the answer to as well."

Grandma sighed like it was a great favor she was doing us. She folded the magazine over on a page advertising some newfangled spade and placed it on her lap. "Being a witch, as you have no doubt already discovered, is very difficult. Not only do others covet what you have, but the magical world is a dangerous one. It got your parents killed."

"What?" I said. "They died in a car accident."

She lifted her index finger. Her eyes sparkled with intelligence. "An accident I believe was intentional. Your parents worked undercover for the witch police. Your mother said they'd unearthed something big, but wouldn't say what it was. Barely two days later, they were both dead."

Reid rubbed her chin. "Do you have any idea what it was?"

Grandma shook her head. "No. The witch police will have the old case files, but that's not a thing to concern yourselves with now. At this moment you need to stay alive."

Sera drummed her fingers on her arm. "That doesn't explain why you didn't tell us about Milly."

"Bah," Grandma said. "Milly was too busy being Queen Witch to have granddaughters. Besides, your father thought one witch for a grandmother was plenty." Grandma leaned forward and whispered, "It isn't polite to speak ill of the dead, but what she told you was right—they didn't get along."

"Surprise, surprise," I said.

Grandma glared at me. "She's rough-and-tumble, to be sure. But that woman is good and will help you however she can."

Lucidity had descended on Grandma. This was the most sense she'd made since I'd been home. Perhaps her brain was thawing out.

She placed a wrinkled hand to her breast. "I owe that woman my life. Milly once saved me from a horde of flying monkeys."

Or maybe not.

"Girls, it pains me that your lives are in danger. But I can help."

My ears perked up at that. "How?"

Her gaze shifted from side to side. "Circle around. Witch's secrets aren't meant to be heard by nonwitches."

"You mean Nan?" Sera asked. "She's your bodyguard. The council sent her after you went into your coma."

She wiggled a jeweled hand at us. Grandma did like her rhinestones. Three ropes of pearls dangled from her neck while a ring sparkled on each finger, including her thumbs. "Yes yes yes. I know the council sent her, but still. These are secrets."

We huddled up. I wondered who was going to run the ball down the field. I almost voiced it aloud but didn't have to.

Reid smiled. "Seventy-nine, thirteen, twelve. Hut-hut."

"Reid, shut it," Sera said.

She put on her best teenage pouty frown. "Just trying to lighten the mood."

Grandma leaned back and closed her eyes as if she were about to meditate. A low buzz sounded from her nose.

"Is she asleep?" Sera asked.

"I don't know. Poke her," I suggested.

"You poke her."

"No, you do it."

Grandma's eyes popped open. "I am not asleep. I am

thinking. I have to remember how to work it, but there is a way for you to discover who's trying to kill you."

I twisted the ends of my hair. My dark, boring hair. Nothing as interesting as the blond hair the assassin had been born with. I bet in the summertime the sun bleached it even blonder, giving him natural highlights. Not that a stud like him would care whether or not he had highlights, but it was kinda cool.

"How?" Sera said. "How can you help us find the killer?"

My mind snapped from thoughts of Roman running shirtless down a sandy shore back to our cramped bungalow. "How can we find out?" I said. "We need to know. The police need to make an arrest."

Grandma raised a sharp eyebrow. "Don't ever leave witch business to civilian police. They can't help."

"Let's stay on track here. How do we do it? How do we find out?"

My grandmother straightened her back and proclaimed, "Concentrate on who wants to kill you and they'll appear."

We waited. She didn't say anything else.

"Is that all?" I asked.

She clasped her hands together, the metal rings jangling. "That's it. Focus and they will come."

Reid rolled her eyes. "Like in that stupid baseball movie?"

Sera slapped her arm. "Hey. I like that movie. And I like this idea. If we think it, they will come."

Okay, let's calm down. "How will they come, Grandma? Like in a dream?"

"Of course not. They'll show up wherever you are." She tapped her nose. "Focus and they'll appear. Works every time."

"She doesn't know us, does she?" Sera mumbled.

"Okay. We can do that," I said.

"Did you do that when you were frozen?" Reid asked.

I smirked. "No one did that to her."

Sera tilted her head. Her bob haircut sashayed back and forth.

"Yeah, it just happened."

At that, Grandma laughed. All heads turned to her. "Frozen states can occur for a number of reasons. For instance, they can happen because the witch is undergoing a growth of power."

"Huh?" Reid said.

She patted Reid's cheek as if she were dumb. "Like a caterpillar in a cocoon. The caterpillar goes into stasis, which it must if it's going to become a butterfly. A frozen state does the same thing. So if a young witch receives a surge of magical ability, she will often freeze for a while, until her body has adjusted to the new power. Otherwise…"

"Otherwise?" I asked.

Grandma shrugged. "She might explode. I've seen it before. Not a pretty sight. Gore and body parts everywhere. Yuck."

"Yeah, yuck," Reid said.

"So then why did you freeze? Is that what happened to you?" Sera asked.

Grandma laughed. "No, of course not. I'm too old to undergo a surge of ability like that. No. My chrysalis occurred for a different reason entirely."

"And what was that?" I asked.

"I was experiencing a power drain. Quite the opposite. I needed to conserve and regenerate what I had."

"A power drain?" I said. "How does that happen?"

"There is a finite amount of magic in the universe. Magic is physics based, from what I understand. It can't be created or destroyed, only transferred into something else. It's possible there was a witch vampire trying to drain my power, or that I simply needed to reenergize. I'm not the first person this has happened to. I'm sorry I couldn't tell you about it, but I knew at some point I would awaken. Or at least I hoped so." She stood up in a whirl of fabric and pearls. The powdery smell of her wafted up my nose, reminding me of the comfort she'd given me my whole life. "But that's enough talk for tonight. Now it's time for bed."

"Grandma," Reid said, "did you put yourself into the cocoon?"

Grandma tittered again. "Of course not. I couldn't do that. It's very dangerous, and only someone I trust could put me under."

"Well, who did it then?" I asked.

"Some nice young witch who was new in town. Said she could help me out."

"What?" I asked. "I thought you said only someone you trusted could do it?"

Grandma shrugged. "She seemed trustworthy."

"She might have been the person draining you. Where was Milly?" I asked.

Grandma sighed. "I don't know. We were in a fight at the time."

"So you let someone you didn't know, and haven't seen since, put you under?"

"Of course."

Of course. Like it was the most natural thing in the world. And so were hordes of flying monkeys. I rubbed my nose. A burning thought tugged at the back of my mind.

Grandma tee-la-la'd off to bed, leaving the three of us alone.

"You thinking what I'm thinking?" Sera said.

"Yep." I clenched my jaw. "We find the person who put her under, and we've got our killer."

FOURTEEN

The next day was filled with fixing the fireball stain on the ceiling of my shop and catching up on work I'd ignored for the past week. I also called Carrie and reminded her we'd be opening tomorrow.

"I've been so bored this week," she whined. "I'll be in after I get my doughnut and coffee from Sera's."

"See you then." I scrolled down my phone, glancing at the mountain of calls that had been transferred from the store phone to mine. So many people had been disappointed that we'd closed during the week, and between attempting spells, I'd had to call and apologize to folks, promising a free pair of panties when they came back in.

Don't judge. Panties were cheaper than shirts. I couldn't exactly afford to give away my best stuff, but some underwear I could part with.

I yawned, stretched my arms and settled into bed. My mind churned with thoughts. To settle it, I flexed my witch muscles by moving a pen from my nightstand into my open palm. After a few minutes of that, I was tired enough to fall into a dreamless sleep.

***

I, too, liked to grab a coffee from Sera before opening. So the next morning I showered and got ready. I kissed Grandma on the way out and managed to avoid getting sucked into a conversation about winged monkeys.

The first thing I noticed was that Roman's car was gone. I'm sure that was thanks to Grandma's off-the-rails behavior at dinner the other night. When I thought about, I didn't remember seeing him the day before, but I'd been distracted with phone calls and paint.

My gut twisted. Next time we met, I needed to apologize. I didn't think the assassin would be particularly forgiving, but you never knew. According to my grandmother, monkeys could fly, so nothing seemed out of the realm of possibility.

Sera and Reid had taken my car, so I walked into town. It took less than twenty minutes to reach the center of Main Street. I stepped inside an empty Sinless Confections.

Reid wiped down the counter with a pink towel.

"Morning," I said. "Where's Sera?"

Reid pointed out the window. "Talking to the assassin."

I glanced over, and sure enough, Sera sat in Roman's car. They looked to be in deep discussion. My heart sank. So that was that. I don't know why it hurt my feelings. I was happy for my sister. She deserved to be in a healthy, good relationship with anyone other than Tim. Heck, even a slug would have been a step in the right direction.

A few minutes later Sera returned. She kept her head down, as if she was embarrassed about talking to Roman. It's not like I cared, because I didn't.

"Hey," I said. "Since we have a few minutes, do you want to try that thing that Grandma told us about? Imagine the killer and they'll show up?"

Sera hooked a red apron over her neck and tied the back. "Sure. Let's do it. The early morning rush is over. I've got a few minutes before the next wave pops in."

So we closed our eyes and concentrated. "Reid, this is just me and Sera."

Reid raised her hands in surrender. "I wasn't doing anything. I wasn't going to screw it up."

"Good," I said.

She stuck her tongue out at me.

"Mature."

I closed my eyes and focused. A current of air sprang up beside me. The magic tilted and pivoted, funneling around my body. My hair rose; my clothes lifted. My head swam in the energy of the thing. It pushed and pulled, sending my stomach rolling. The urge to vomit crept up my throat. Right as I felt I needed to break from the spell, or whatever it was, the wind stopped dead.

I cracked one eye. "Did we do it?"

Sera shrugged. "I guess we'll find out."

I turned to my youngest sister. "Reid, did you see that tornado?"

"What tornado?"

"Didn't you feel the wind?" I asked.

She wiped down the cash register. "Nope. I just saw you two standing in the room like a couple of dopes."

"Thanks," Sera said. She tugged on the end of her short ponytail. "Do you think our growing power caused it?"

I walked behind the counter and poured myself a cup of coffee. "No clue. Hey, do you have any chocolate I can put in this?"

Sera pointed to a bowl. "I keep some shaved right there."

I opened the lid and forked out several pieces, swirling them in my cup. Nothing like a little bit of cocoa in my java. I sipped. "Yum. Perfect."

Reid settled her chin in her palm. "Don't mention it."

"You didn't do anything," I said.

She gave me a smug grin. "I know. I just like to take credit for things."

"Good morning!" a voice boomed from the doorway.

I held my breath. This was it. This was the person we'd been waiting for, the one who wanted to kill me and presumably my sisters. I pursed my lips and pivoted toward the door.

Carrie waved. "What's wrong with y'all? Look like you've seen a ghost."

My heart deflated. My magic-making abilities were so hit or miss. Float to the sky—hit. Try to see a killer—miss.

"Morning, Carrie," I said.

She frowned. Her eyebrows knit together in worry. "I told you I'd stop by here first to get my coffee. Was I supposed to be at the store already?"

I shook my head. "No. Why?"

"Because you're looking at me like I'm in trouble."

I shouldered my purse and tugged on the end of my high ponytail. "No, you're fine. I'm just feeling a little weird. You know, opening the store when a girl was killed in it, and all."

Carrie peered over the counter. "Can I have a donkey tail and a to-go coffee?"

Reid pulled a sheet of paper from the dispenser and bagged the sugary treat.

"I know. It's so awful. And just think, I almost touched that dress. It's a good thing my nails still needed some curing."

I glanced at the pink polished beauties. "Nice color choice."

She beamed. "Thanks."

I fished the keys from my purse and handed them to her. "Go ahead and open up. I'll be there in a sec. There's something I need to discuss with Sera."

"I have to make more coffee for you anyway, Carrie. I'll send it over with Dylan," Sera said.

Carrie tossed her locks over one shoulder. "Okay. See you in a bit."

When she'd gone, I slid onto one of the red bar stools at the counter. "Well, I guess that didn't work."

Sera trashed the old grounds from the coffeemaker and got it ready to make another pot. After pouring coffee and water in the contraption, she hit the Start button. "Maybe it'll be the next person who walks in."

I shook my head. "No. I don't think it worked." I sighed. "I don't know that I've got what it takes to make it in this witch business."

She stared at me as if I were crazy. "Grandma woke up from a deep freeze batty as ever, and Milly's got a personality like a cheese shredder. And you don't think we're up to this? You can take that bad attitude right out of here."

I slapped my knee. "You're right. If those two have survived this long, there's no reason why I can't."

The industrial coffee machine finished, and Sera filled a to-go cup. She set it in front of me and placed a reassuring hand on my shoulder. "Don't worry about it. We'll get the hang of this. Hey, we've survived a week since Reagan's death. Surely we can last a few more days till the solstice."

"I guess," I grumbled.

The bell above her door tinkled. We glanced to see who it was. My lifted spirits crashed and burned in a fire fueled by gossip and slander. Jenny Butts, her Marilyn Monroe curls extra tight this morning, sauntered in.

She did that arm-pump thing she does when there's extra-exciting news to talk about. "Y'all. Y'all. Y'all."

I rose. "Hey, Jenny. Bye, Jenny."

She scowled at me. "Where are you off to in such a hurry, Dylan Apel?"

"Uh. Work. You know, that thing most of us do Monday through Friday?"

Jenny rested her weight on one hip. "Very funny. I know all about work. I do it nearly every day."

"So I see," I said.

She beamed at me. I tried to smile back, but it came out queasy and phony. I hoped she'd take the hint that I wasn't interested in anything she had to say. But she didn't. Instead Jenny took mine and Sera's hands and formed a circle. What was this—ring-around-the-rosy?

"I hope you're excited about being honorary guests for the solstice."

Crap. I'd forgotten all about that. My dress for the occasion had been used as a weapon to kill someone, and now I was being honored at the dinner? With all the other craziness going on, that made perfect sense.

"Jenny, that is so nice of you," I lied, "but I don't even know if I'll be going."

She splayed a perfectly manicured hand over her heart. "Of course you'll be going. You're my honored guests."

"Jenny," I said. "The dress I designed for the banquet is the one Reagan died in. I'm not exactly feeling up to attending."

She brought her hands to her cheeks. "Oh no! It was?"

"Good going," Sera murmured.

"Yeah. Now the entire town will know," Reid said.

I shot Reid a look that said shut it.

"Well, they will."

The mechanics in Jenny's brain spun so fast she didn't even notice we'd been talking about her. "What? That's the dress she died in? No one said anything about that." She grabbed my wrist. "Dylan, you have to tell me everything."

I flipped my wrist and glanced at my watch. "Oh dear. Look at the time. I must be going. The store's about to open, and I'm afraid it's going to be absolutely swamped today." I skirted toward the door, my sandals clicking on the tile. "Thanks so much for the invite, but I don't think I'll be going to the banquet this year. Toodle-oo!" I waved and ran off.

Of course, Sera had warned me months ago that she was helping with some of the catering, so I had to attend. However, with the way things were playing out, I was banking on the fact that she'd take pity on me and let me off the hook. Since the banquet was the night of the solstice, and the next most likely night that someone would try to kill one of us, I figured a huge crowd that I could be lost in was the last place I needed to be. Wouldn't it be better for me to stay at home, all by myself, with Grandma and Nan for company?

On second thought, maybe I would go.

I stepped onto Main. The turquoise awning of Sinless Confections shielded me from the already scorching June sun. Good thing I only had a couple of steps to my store. Summer in Alabama was not fun, to say the least. I had already put the Mouth of the South (aka Jenny Butts) behind me and was ready for a fabulous day at Perfect Fit when I heard—

"You! You killed her!"

My heart flopped to my feet. I stopped and turned toward the voice. Harry Shaw teetered down the sidewalk. A ten o'clock shadow sprouted from his chin. I know it's normally a five o'clock shadow, but this beard had been left to weed for a week too long. Purple circles ringed his eyes, and his clothes looked like they'd been thrown to the ground, stomped on, and then put back on.

I knew it was futile, but I gazed around to see if possibly, by some slim chance, Harry meant someone else had killed Reagan. Since I was the only person within fifty yards, all guesses were on me.

He pointed at me. Well, that solved that mystery. "You killed her." He clutched a whiskey bottle. The fat glass looked like a pretty useful weapon for him to use, given the circumstances.

I backed up, raised my hands. "I didn't do it, Harry. I would never hurt Reagan. You were going to be married last Saturday."

"You killed her!"

Doors creaked open. People stepped into the street. I expected someone to intervene before he whacked me over the head with the bottle, but all they did was stare. Was this high noon at the O.K. Corral? What was wrong with people? I was a freakin' damsel in distress. Didn't anyone want to be a hero?

Then I realized—I can vanish the bottle. But that meant doing magic in front of people. I'd be boiled alive if the council caught me. "Harry, you need to calm down. Listen to me. I didn't hurt Reagan."

134

"Why haven't they arrested you? You said so yourself; you and she were mortal enemies."

Uh-oh. I had said that, hadn't I? Well, it had been true in high school, at least.

As Harry plodded forward, I retreated. For every one step I backed up, he stumbled forward two. In three seconds flat he towered over me. The stink of his sour breath caused the ends of my hair to frizz.

Kidding.

He raised the glass. My heart thundered against my ribs. I had no choice. I had to do something. I needed that bottle out of his hand.

"You killed her and you have to pay!"

I scrunched up my face and imagined the bottle in my hand. I focused hard, giving it all I had.

The whiskey slipped from his fingers. It fell to the ground in a mess of shattered slivers.

"Huh?" he said, staring at it. "I don't need it anyway."

Then he lunged. For me.

I crouched down, ready for the impact. The lone card in my hand had been played. I was out of options.

Crack! I opened my eyes. Harry lay flat on his back. Roman stood over him, his fist red. A black shadow smeared his face.

"Next time you try to hurt Dylan, you'll get a lot worse than a busted lip."

Sitting at Roman's feet, I felt I was looking up at a god. Wind rippled through his yellow-streaked hair, while his black T-shirt strained to contain his muscles. Honestly I wouldn't have been surprised if they ripped right on through. And I wanted them to. All Roman needed was a cape and a hammer and oh my God, he'd look like Thor. I almost died.

He held out his hand to me and smiled. I floated away to la-la land, forgetting my own name.

"Are you okay?"

"Yes?"

"Did he hurt you?"

I shook my head. I was drifting in a dream, having been saved by a green-eyed god.

A frown of concern crossed his face. "Did you hit your head?"

What's my name again? "I don't think so."

I grabbed his hand, and he pulled me up like I was nothing more than a feather. Roman gazed into my eyes. I thought he might kiss me. After all, he'd just saved me from a potential murderer.

Roman thumbed my eyelids up.

"Ow." I swatted him away. "Why're you doing that?"

"Making sure your eyes dilate."

"Why?"

"I'm not convinced you don't have a concussion."

I wrestled from his steel arms and placed a fist on my hip. "I didn't hit my head, and I don't have a concussion. Thanks anyway."

"Hey, anytime." He gave me a crooked grin.

From the concrete, Harry groaned and rolled to one side. "What happened?"

Before either one of us answered, a police car bleeped its siren and came to a screeching halt in front of us.

"Looks like they're here to arrest you, Harry," I said.

"For what?" he moaned.

I smacked my lips. "My first guess is public intoxication. The second would be attempted assault. But I'm no expert."

Detective Blount exited the vehicle along with another officer. He walked over to us, his hands in his pockets, his head low. "We heard there was a commotion out here."

I nodded to Roman. "There was, but he stopped it."

"How's the investigation going, Detective?" Roman asked. I didn't understand why he continued to pick at the detective about the case.

Blount threw Roman a tight smile. "Great. Small-town

murder is always fun, especially when the victim's fiancé spouts off that Dylan's the murderer."

I fanned myself. "Whew. Is it hot out here or what?"

The detective jingled some coins in his pocket. "Dylan, I'm afraid I have to bring you in."

"Why?" I asked, leaning toward Roman, hoping he would protect me from this.

"As I said, I've got a man who just accused you of murder."

I pointed at Harry, flabbergasted that they would believe him. "But he's drunk. He's riddled with grief."

Blount took my elbow in a gentle hold. "Dylan, I need you to come with me down to the station."

Seriously? Could things get any worse?

FIFTEEN

"Where are you holding my granddaughter, you big buffoons?" Grandma's voice assaulted me all the way across the station, to the confines of Blount's office, where I was being interviewed. "If anyone lays a hand on Dylan's head, I'll sick a flock of fire-eating piglets on the lot of you."

Good ole Grandma. Making me look more innocent by the second.

Blount stuck his head out of the office. "Send her on back. We're wrapping up in here."

Grandma cussed the whole way. "In my day we didn't have all these uniforms. No one knew an officer from a regular person."

Blount glanced at me. I circled my finger around my ear, making the universal sign for crazy. "Sorry. This is how she is."

Roman, in the seat beside me and confirmed it. "She's a little off, that's for sure."

Which reminded me, I needed to apologize to him for her rude behavior.

"Dylan, where are you?" Grandma called.

"She's back here," Blount called out.

"Finally, someone who speaks English."

I shrugged. There was just no way to win with this woman. I rose. "Perhaps it would be better if I met her out there. Do you have any more questions for me?"

He shook his head. "No. You're free to go."

I drummed my fingers on the back of the chair. "You do realize that the entire town is going to think I'm guilty?"

He rested his hands on his hips. "It's a small-town murder. What can I say?"

"Say country life isn't all it's cracked up to be," Roman prodded.

I elbowed him. "Be nice."

Grandma burst through the doorway, practically knocking the detective down. Her triangle head of hair jutted out like a silver halo. Her orange pants looked fit for a clown, and a white linen scarf choked her neck like Amelia Earhart preflight. "This place is a madhouse."

I looked into the bull pen. A few officers sat, working quietly. I rubbed my thighs. "Yep, regular old crazy house in here. Thanks for the chat, Detective. Let me know when I can be a town spectacle again for you."

Blount frowned but said nothing. I threw him a cheery smile.

We left his office. "Talk about me picking at him," Roman said in a low, husky voice.

"The difference is I'm not insulting his ability or interest in doing his job," I said.

He took my elbow, guiding me toward the front door. "That's not what I'm doing."

"What did they want?" Grandma shouted.

"Nothing, just to go over what happened that morning one more time. Hey. How did you get here?" I pushed through the glass doors that led outside. The suction hold released, and with a swoosh we were standing in sunshine. My skin prickled in the heat.

Reid waved from the lot. She did a Vanna White gesture over my car. "Well, at least she didn't wreck it."

"What are you talking about?" Grandma said. "I drove."

I now had a blossoming headache. I escorted Grandma to the

car. "Reid, drive Grandma home and stay there with her. I don't need her wandering the streets of Silver Springs."

Reid pouted, no doubt disappointed that she wouldn't get to hot rod my car around town. "Where are you going?"

I clapped Roman on the arm. It was like touching rock. "Roman's going to drive me back to the shop."

Reid sulked her way into the car. Grandma hugged me. "Thank goodness you're all right."

This post-freeze craziness had about worn on my last nerve. "Thanks, Grandma. See you at home."

I slid into the SUV and leaned my head back. "Calgon, take me away."

He started the ignition. The car hummed, softly vibrating my seat. "Where would you like to go?"

"How about Paris?"

"We could be there by tomorrow morning."

I squinted at him. Was he kidding? He was kidding. Wasn't he? But the stone look on his face reflected only a quiet intent.

I threaded my fingers through my ponytail and snagged a tangle. Sexy. "So what was that about? Why did Blount haul me in only to ask me the same questions?"

"He needs people to see that he's doing something because he doesn't have any leads."

"How can you be so sure?"

Roman glanced at the gear shift, his long lashes practically brushing his cheek. He looked up and smiled, the dark edges of his eyes smudging. They willed me to nibble on them. I bit my finger and stared out the window.

"I was a witch cop, remember? Whenever my cases crossed into the regular world, cops were always befuddled."

"Befuddled?"

He nosed the vehicle into the street. "Don't make fun. Anyway, I'm right. Blount came here to retire. Now that you and your sisters are out as witches, his life is about to be even more complicated than it was in Atlanta. I'm trying to make him realize this isn't the job for him."

"Why? What's it to you?" He didn't answer. "Listen, I'm sorry about Grandma the other night. It was inexcusable for her to pry like that."

He shrugged. "It's okay. I know she didn't mean anything by it."

"Still," I said. "I wanted to apologize."

"Nothing to be sorry for."

"Can you at least accept my apology?"

"Is that what I'm supposed to do?"

"That's what a gentleman would do."

"What makes you think I'm a gentleman?" he said with a twinkle in his eye.

Sand filled my mouth. Was he flirting? He was definitely flirting. But he liked Sera. I saw them talking together. "Um. Well, you took a job to protect a couple of witches, a subgroup you've repeatedly said you don't like. Doesn't that make you somewhat of a gentleman?"

He shrugged. "That's debatable. But for now, let's say yes." He turned the car down Main and parked in front of my store. "Good job dropping that bottle out of Harry's hand this morning."

"Oh, that." I rubbed the lines that formed on my forehead. "Yeah, I broke a cardinal rule, I know, but what other choice did I have? Do you think I'll be boiled alive?" Please, please don't let that happen to me.

"Nah. The witch police'll probably throw you in jail, is all."

I pulled my ponytail. "What? I have a business to run."

He smiled. "I'm kidding."

I placed a hand on my chest. "Thank goodness."

Roman laughed. The sound soothed my soul. I felt like curling up next to him and purring. "No, they won't throw you in jail. It was for your own protection. If you don't bring it up, perhaps the council won't know."

He put the car in park, and I unfastened my seat belt. I glanced toward the store. Em stood in the window, a dark scowl on her face as she glared at me.

I shrank down. "Something tells me they already know."

***

Em ruffled her silky crimson and cinnamon curls when I walked through the door. "We need to chitchat."

"Just us," I said.

"No. Your sister too."

I nodded toward Carrie, who sat behind the desk. "Is there anyone waiting on me?"

She finished filing down a nail and said, "No. No one's here."

"Great. Do you mind taking an early lunch and bringing something back for me?"

She beamed. "Sure. There's a delicious hunk at that new brick-oven pizza place."

Uh-oh. That delicious hunk would be Rick, our next door neighbor and the guy Reid regularly used the binoculars to spy on.

"Want me to bring back a slice?"

"That would be great. Thanks!"

She swung a wristlet over her hand and said, "Dylan, don't forget your promise about the banquet."

"I haven't." I had. "Can you remind me what that was, again?"

Carrie splayed her fingers over a jutting hip. "That I can pick out whatever dress I want to wear."

I swatted the air. "Of course I haven't forgotten that." I had. "Just let me know what you choose."

After she left, I called Sera and told her to come over. Barely a minute later she walked through the door, brushing flour off her apron. "What's going on?" She saw Em sitting in a wingback chair. "You could have warned me," Sera mumbled to me.

"Sorry."

Em steepled her fingers under her chin. The bangles on her arms tinkled prettily. "I may not have made some of the rules clear."

"No, you did," I said. "Rule one—don't anger a witch. Which it seems has been broken."

She exhaled, did a slow blink and said, "There's an even more important rule than that. Can you remember what it is?"

I grimaced. In the smallest voice possible, I said, "Don't do magic in front of regular people?"

"Correct."

Sera gaped at me. "You did magic in front of someone?"

I gestured with my thumb and forefinger. "Only a teensy bit." I sat across from Em in another boutique chair. "Harry Shaw had a weapon raised to hurt me. What was I supposed to do?"

She gave me a blank stare. "Run."

"That's not very good advice," I said.

"I didn't say it was." She tousled her perfect Queen Witch locks. Her gaze settled on Sera and then back at me.

"How did you even know I'd done any magic? I thought you were long gone."

A smear of pink blazed over her cheeks. "I ain't your teacher no more, but I'm still keepin' an eye on you. Magical ripples are easy to sense if you know what you're lookin' for. When you use your power, I feel it."

I looked at Sera. Her eyes narrowed with suspicion. We were thinking the same thing—why was she so interested in us?

"Why are you spying on us?" Sera asked.

Em scoffed. "I ain't spyin' on you. Queen Witches don't spy. I was being mindful of your presence."

"From where? Across the street at the diner?" I asked. I figured you couldn't feel a ripple of magic from a thousand miles away, so she had to be close.

The pink on her cheeks deepened. Seriously? She was spying on us from Gus's Diner, home of the deep-fried burger?

She rose. "I don't answer to you. This works the other way around. I only came to remind you—don't work magic in front of nonmagics."

"Then I suppose next time a drunk lunatic is trying to kill me, I'll just let him."

"Yeah," Sera said. "You can't expect her not to use magic in a life-threatening situation."

"Thank you," I said.

"You're welcome."

Em raised her hands. "Would both of you please shut up?"

"Yes," I squeaked, having been properly chastised.

"Now, stop bein' so darn childish," Em snapped. "Next time, don't use magic. And if you find yourself in a situation like that again, use a small amount of power and try to trip the person instead."

"Trip them? I don't know how to do that."

"It's not hard. Imagine and make it happen."

"Oh yes," Sera said. "Magic is so easy for someone who's been around a hundred years. To the rest of us peons, it's a bit more complicated."

Em clapped her hands together. "Y'all have to practice, that's all." She slinked like a cat to the door. She placed a hand on the knob and glanced over her shoulder. "Been keepin' up your protection spell?"

I rubbed a kink from the back of my neck. "No. I've been busy."

"I recommend you do one. Need to keep yourselves safe."

After she left, I cupped my head in my hands. "There are too many rules to this whole witching business. Seems like it should be easier."

Sera rolled her eyes. "Okay. You tell Em that. Let me know how it goes." Her eyes drifted to the window, she stared for a moment and then her lips pressed into a hard line. I followed her gaze and saw Tim fiddling with his yellow environmentally friendly bicycle.

I took her hand and squeezed. "He's a loser."

"And a jerk," she said.

"You're better off without him."

Her lips curled into a whimsical smile. I did not like that look. Not at all. "Sera? What are you doing?"

She ignored me and kept watching him. "Look," she said.

I peered out the window right as Tim's shorts fell. His yellow T-shirt barely covered his little-boy-style tighty-whities. A laugh exploded from my mouth. "Oh my God. Are those Superman Underoos?"

Sera held her sides, trying to contain her own laughter. "I think so."

"And no playing tricks on people." Em's disembodied voice boomed overhead.

I shrank. "All right. We get it. Don't do anything to save our lives and no having fun." Em didn't reply. Guessing she was gone, I said, "But that was definitely worth it."

"I'd better get back to work," Sera said. She reached for the door as Reid burst in, apron strings flying.

"What's wrong?" I asked, not wanting to know.

Reid pulled the apron off her head. "Nan called. Milly's in the hospital. She's been attacked by a witch."

Holy crapola.

SIXTEEN

When we arrived at the hospital, Milly was in rare form. She could be heard from halfway down the hall. "Don't you poke me with that. I'm fine. Why do I have all these wires and things in me? Get them out!"

People stared in the direction of her room. I turned to Sera. "Do we really need to be here?"

"She's our grandmother."

I lifted my finger. "But we only just found that out. A couple of days ago this wouldn't have concerned us."

She tugged my elbow. "Come on. Let's see how she's doing."

Sera led me and Reid into the room. An IV line ran from Milly's arm to a hanging bag of saline. A black screen bleeped as it flashed her heart rate, blood pressure and whatever else those things showed. The room had the distinct smell of old people, which was fitting seeing as Grandma and Nan had arrived before us.

Milly swatted an exhausted-looking nurse away from her. "I don't need anything. I'm fine. Just look at all those numbers on the screen there. Everything says I'm fine."

The nurse offered Milly a patient but stern smile. "The doctor will make the final call on that."

"Then send him in. What are you waiting for?"

Another tight, reserved, I-really-want-to-kick-you-in-the-heinie smile and the nurse said, "I'll see if I can reach him."

"You do that."

"Hi, Milly," Sera said.

Milly shifted her beady eyes in our direction. She glanced at Grandma and Nan, who sat in one corner of the cramped room, and then over to us. "Great. So everybody had to come and see me at my lowest."

I knew this was a bad idea. "No," I said quickly. "We wanted to make sure you were okay."

"A witch gets knocked out and everyone thinks she's lost her touch," Milly grumbled. "Could have happened to anyone." She pointed a bony finger at me. "You could have been up and killed. No one would have thought you'd lost your touch."

"We didn't know we were witches at that time," I corrected.

"Tomato, potato."

Reid frowned. "Um, isn't that tomato, tomah—"

I kicked her.

She rubbed her leg. "Ow."

"What happened?" I asked.

"I'd gone outside to weed some plants. Had my back to the street, which is not something I normally do. Next thing I know, I'm here."

"So you could have blacked out," I said. "Maybe your blood pressure dropped or something, and you fainted."

Milly glared at me hard enough to burn a third eye through my forehead. "I did not pass out. I was attacked. I could still smell the magic on me when I woke up."

"You can smell magic?" Reid asked.

Grandma nodded. "You most certainly can. Life doesn't always smell like raindrops and kittens. Sometimes it has a lemony scent."

"Lemony?" Sera said.

Milly nodded. "Magic can smell like citrus. It's a common

occurrence."

"I haven't noticed that," I said.

Grandma fluffed her gossamer scarf. "You don't have a particularly good sniffer. Remember that time you stepped in dog doo and the rest of us had to tell you?"

"Right. Not a good sniffer," I said.

"I've noticed something," Reid said. "But I can't say it's lemons."

"Whatever," I said, knowing I'd have a massive headache by the time I got home. "So you think it's the killer?"

Milly slammed her fist down on the bed tray. "Of course it's the killer. She's getting bold. Brazen."

"So why aren't you dead?" I asked. Everyone looked at me like it was the rudest question in the world. I shrugged. "What? If the witch knocked you out, how did you end up here?"

"One of my neighbors saw me and called the hospital."

"So did they see anyone else?" I asked.

"No."

We stared at her.

"But the stink of magic was on me." She shoved her fist in the air. "I know when I've been attacked, and I was, without a doubt, assaulted with magic."

The room quieted, and a soft knock came from the door. A middle-aged man wearing a white lab coat entered.

"Milly, I haven't visited you in years, but I had to come once Hazel told me what happened," he said.

She sniffed. "I haven't needed a witch doctor for a long time, and I wouldn't need one now if I'd been standing the right way."

Witch doctor? Oh, this was rich. Seriously? How had I lived for twenty-eight years and been oblivious to all this? Witches and witch doctors and magic?

Sera flashed me a what-the-bejesus look. I shook my head. I give up.

Said witch doctor's expensive Italian loafers clicked as he

walked across the peel-and-stick hospital tile. His peppery hair was clipped short on the sides with a sweeping pompadour on top. Fine vertical lines streaked his tan face, and he took a moment to smile at each of us in turn.

"Afternoon," he said, his white teeth nearly blinding me. "I'm Dr. Spencer Burns."

I had to admit, this dude was handsome. Witch doctor or not, he looked professional, classy and totally competent in his abilities. Pretty much the exact opposite of me with my powers, aside from the few times I managed to transfer something into my hand. That, I was good at, except under pressure, of course, à la Harry Shaw and his drunken craziness. Em had said that as the solstice neared, our abilities would heighten and we'd get much better at casting spells, or whatever it was that we were doing—moving energy. Or watching butterflies grow. That's probably how Grandma in all her sane glory would put it.

"Check me out and tell them I was attacked by magic," Milly insisted.

Dr. Burns pulled an otoscope from his lab-coat pocket. He leaned over Milly. "Let me see your eyes."

With a triumphant humpf in my direction, she tilted her face toward him. The doc flashed the tiny light in each of her eyes, then her ears and finally her nose. "Open your mouth and say ah."

Milly licked her lips and belted out an "Ah" so hideous, if peace-loving woodland animals had heard it, they would have raced to a nearby river to see who could commit suicide first. I plugged my ear and wiggled the canal so it would stop ringing.

Dr. Burns sounded a series of "hmms" and "that's interesting" before stepping to the end of the bed and flipping through the chart that hung there. The seconds ticked past as he read line by line. Finally he looked at Milly and said, "You've been attacked by magic."

"See!" Milly said, "I told you. I told you all. But you snotty girls didn't want to believe me."

I rolled my eyes. "It's not that we didn't want to believe you; it's that the attack happened in broad daylight with no witnesses."

"I can understand that," Dr. Burns said. "But there's evidence on Milly." He pulled a pair of tweezers from a different pocket and walked back to her. "Milly, turn your head away from me." She did, and he placed the tweezers next to her left ear. "Almost have it. Don't move. Aha!" He lifted the tweezers in the air and said, "Come here, let me show you."

I pulled my purse tight against my chest, not because I was afraid he would do anything, but simply out of habit, and crossed to him. Sera, Reid, and I formed a semicircle around the doc. I squinted at the tweezers. Trapped in their tines hung what appeared to be a blue string. But the string didn't hang limply. It coiled and wriggled like a tiny worm.

Reid wrinkled her nose. "What's that?"

Doctor Burns flashed his thousand-watt smile. "That is magic. And more importantly, that was the magic used on your grandmother."

"It doesn't look like magic," Reid said.

"Oh, it is," Grandma said.

"How can you be so sure?" Sera asked.

Milly flapped her palms on the bed. "Because if that Queen Witch had taught you anything, the first thing she would have told you was that every witch leaves a mark when you work a spell. It's a very small thread, nearly imperceptible. You have to know what you're looking for."

"It's just a thread," Reid said. "Couldn't it have come from anywhere? Couldn't it be Milly's?"

The witch doctor chuckled. "Let me guess, you haven't been doing this for very long."

"Is it that obvious?" I asked.

The doc scratched his chin. Even under the fluorescents his perfect tan skin appeared smooth and bronzed. "It's obvious after you've seen your first thread. No two are ever alike—some are hairy, some sleek, some multicolored and some, like this one, are only one color. But the key, the most important thing to know is that you'll never leave a trace of your own magic on yourself." He pulled a small glass specimen bottle from another pocket in his coat, unscrewed the top and dropped the thread in. "I'll deliver this to the witch police. They'll run it and see if there's a match."

I remembered something. "I have seen a thread before."

"You have?" Sera said.

I nodded. "Yeah. The night we made Nan levitate. One fell off her when she was demonstrating her ninja moves. It must have been our magic." The image of the gold thread stuck in my head. So that's what it had been.

"Probably so." Grandma rolled up her sleeves. "When you make magic, you create threads, but they disappear if you're only doing the spell on yourself. They only appear if you perform a spell on someone else." She flicked her wrist, and a rain cloud appeared above Reid's head. A fine mist sprayed down on her burgundy curls.

"Hey!" She yanked the collar of her T-shirt over her head, shielding herself from the shower. "What's the big deal?"

Grandma lowered her hands. "The big deal is this point." The rain stopped.

Dr. Burns extended his hand for Reid to take. She slid her palm over his, and he proceeded to inspect her with his otoscope. "It's difficult to see magical remnants with the naked eye. This tool shoots out infrared light, making it much easier to find the threads." He picked through Reid's hair with the tweezers like a chimpanzee looking for fleas to eat. "And there's one!" He waved me and Sera over. The doc nodded at the small thing in the fabric. The squiggly rainbow noodle of a thread curled in the grasp of the metal tines.

"Ew. That was in my hair?" Reid said.

"Of course it was," Grandma said. "It's the physical form of my magic."

Doctor Burns patted the pocket where he'd placed his specimen bottle. "Every spell leaves one behind. If the police find a match, we'll have our culprit. The threads don't last forever, though; they eventually disappear. We should have a good twenty-four hours before this one vanishes, plenty of time to find a mate."

"But Em said that more than likely the witch isn't registered."

The doctor shrugged. "Not being registered and not having a criminal record are two very different things."

I tucked a strand of hair behind my ear. "So you're saying the witch might not be registered but have a record, so the police may be able to track the thread."

The doc pointed his finger in the air with a flourish. "Exactly."

"But wouldn't someone who's got a criminal record automatically be registered?" Sera asked.

Milly threw the blanket off her body. "Only witches in good standing are on the official registry. Criminals aren't. They're simply criminals."

"Well, that's smart," I said sarcastically.

Milly ignored me. "This only means that magic was used; it doesn't tell us who did it." She swung her legs over the edge of the bed and rose.

"Where do you think you're going?" Nan asked.

Milly yanked the lines from her vein, and with a nod of the head, bandages magically appeared on her arms to stop the bleeding. "I think I'm going home. Since we know I was attacked magically, there's no reason for me to stay here. Right, Doc?" Her tone held an undercurrent of warning that would have made anyone hesitate to argue with her.

"You seem okay. Here's your discharge papers." He handed her a paper that hadn't existed a moment before. Impressive. That was such a fancy trick I wondered if I could master something like that. Don't have a hundred dollars for dinner? Voila! Suddenly I've got a wad of cash in my pocket. Hmmm. I'd have to ask Grandma.

Wait. Better ask Milly when she got in a better mood.

***

When we got home, I sat on the couch and thought. "So let's go over what we know," I said to Sera, Reid, Grandma and Nan, who popped in every once in a while from the kitchen. "Reagan was murdered by a dress that I wore. We know it was magic even though we don't have a thread."

"Definitely not spontaneous combustion," Reid said.

Grandma tapped a ringed finger on the table. "Though it could have been spontaneous combustion. I've seen that done with magic."

I shot Reid a dark look for getting Grandma on a tangent. "It was not, I repeat, not spontaneous combustion. We also know mostly women do magic."

"Except for that doctor," Sera said. "He could do magic. How is that, Grandma?"

She shrugged. "Probably born from two witches. Men aren't always given abilities, but they sometimes are."

"But we believe this to be a woman," I said. "We also know that three years ago, Grandma let a witch put her into a coma."

Grandma nodded. "That's right."

"But before that, Grandma, your power was being drained," I said.

She fluffed the coarse curls of her triangle-shaped haircut. "Drained or I was just overly tired, one of the two. Could've had a thyroid problem at the time and the deep sleep took care of it."

"Right," Sera said. "A thyroid problem. Sounds like something being made into a Popsicle will solve."

"Does so every time," Reid said.

"Focus," I said. I glanced around the room. My gaze rested on the comfortable clutter of the space. Overstuffed couches, family photos, antique side tables, all surrounded by yellow walls and framed with cherry-red curtains. It was a cheerful room, one that I loved with every inch of my being. I wanted to keep it safe. Wanted to keep the women inside safe.

"So, Grandma, you believe your power was being drained,

but now you aren't so sure."

She took a walnut from a candy dish, suspended it in the air, and I watched as it split apart with a crack. That might have been more impressive than the papers appearing in the doc's hands.

"Grandma, how did you manage not to do magic in front of us while we were growing up?" Reid asked.

She threw a walnut half in her mouth and chewed. "Sometimes I did it, but then I went back and made sure I erased your memory."

All our jaws fell. "You erased our memories?" Sera said, dumbfounded. "Is that ethical?"

"Probably not," she said, unperturbed. "But I had to keep you from knowing, and it was the easiest way to do so."

A blanket of silence fell on the room. Oh well, nothing we could do about Grandma's ethics now. "Since we know Grandma doesn't have any scruples, let's get back to piecing together the killer."

Sera dragged her eyes from Grandma to me and nodded.

I drummed my fingers on the arm of the couch. "So anyway, the freeze happened three years ago. I'm going out on a crazy hunch here, but I think the person who committed the freeze and the killer are the same. That means the killer would have arrived in town around that time." Reid raised her hand. "Yes?"

"But then why wouldn't that person have killed one of us then? I mean, Grandma was out of the way. Why wait until now? Even better than that, our powers were only recently—well yours and Sera's—were only recently fully released. The murder happened before that. There's something we're missing."

My gaze drifted around the room. I took in all their faces and folded my hands over my chest. "That's what we need to find out, and I have a good idea of who to start with."

Nan made an appearance, a wooden spoon filled with a red sauce in her hand. "Even I want to hear this. Who do you think can help you? Milly?"

I shook my head. "No. To go back three years and find out

what was going on in town at that time, I need an expert."

Sera squeezed the bridge of her nose, something she did when annoyed. "And who would that be?"

"Why, the Mouth of the South herself—Jenny Butts."

***

I climbed into the SUV. Roman gave me a stern look. "Where would you like to go?"

Confused by the expression on his face, I said, "You act as if you aren't happy to see me."

"I'm not really excited to be a chauffeur, no. I'm here to protect you."

"Yeah, about that," I said. "How exactly do you do that?"

An amused twinkle sparkled in his eyes. "Want to find out?"

An uncomfortable feeling washed over me. It could have been his green eyes, the closeness of our bodies, the musky scent of his cologne—or just the fact that a hot guy was winking and nodding in my direction. I'm pretty sure a few moths flew out of my belfry, if you know what I mean.

"Um, sure?" I said.

Without one word, he peeled the SUV out of park. That was hot, right? Driving dangerously? I thought so.

Within a few minutes we were outside the town square and on a backwoods road. "Where are you taking me?" I asked, trying not to sound too nervous.

"There's a shooting range out here."

"Oh. Are we going to be shooting?"

"Yes, you are."

"Excuse me?"

"Kidding. I'm going to show you what I do."

"Which is?"

He glanced at me from the corner of his eye. "You tell me."

"I don't know. You have a very interesting résumé. You

worked for the witch police, have admitted to being an assassin, and now you're a for-hire bodyguard. I have no idea. Do have nun chucks in your pocket?"

He parked the car, and we got out. He pulled something from an inside pocket of his black duster. "No. But I do have these." He brandished a pair of throwing stars. "Want me to show you how to throw them?"

"Are you flirting?"

He placed one hand on his lean hip. "If I am, this is the strangest date I've ever been on."

Okay. Well, that answered that. "Sure. Show me how to throw them."

We walked from the SUV to a grassy patch of trees. He sidled up next to me. Yes, sidled. Roman then tucked the cross-shaped star into my palm and raised my hand until it was parallel with the ground.

"Aim for that tree."

"Okay. Aim for it and then what?"

"Are you always so difficult?"

"Yes. You haven't figured that out yet?"

"I mean, I guess I had, but I was holding on to some sort of hope that it wouldn't be so."

I lowered the star. "Well, it is so."

He raised my arm, tucked his body into mine. Did I mention how good he smelled? Seriously. It was like nature and animal merged, becoming one sort of frontier-man scent. It was awesome.

"When you throw, do so with your entire body, but only let the follow-through happen with your arm."

"What?"

"Feel the swing, but don't overcompensate."

"You know, I make dresses for a living."

He sighed, his soft breath blowing on the back of my neck. A tingle raced down my spine. "I realize that, but you can do this. I don't expect you to be assassin perfect, but I think you'll be able to put a dent in that tree over there."

I stared at the forest before us. "You mean the one three feet away?"

"That's the one."

"Thanks," I griped. "I'm so glad you have confidence in me."

He chuckled. His arms around me tightened. Heat blossomed across my chest, and I was, for once, relieved that I couldn't look into his perfectly sculpted face.

"I have a load of confidence in you. It's just I want to start slow. Make sure you can hit the target."

I pressed my arms back. "If you'd get your hands off me, I could."

"Don't you want to learn proper technique?" he whispered in my ear.

My bones jellied. "Sure," I said, not remembering what I was agreeing to.

"Okay. Hold the star eye level."

"Eye level," I repeated, holding some cross-shaped bit of metal to my face.

"Use the energy of your body to throw, but only move your arm."

Oh, that seemed simple. Sort of like, whisper to the wind, but only use half your voice. Of course, that didn't make any sense either. Not wanting to think it through any farther, I aimed, pulled back my arm and fired off the star. It hit the tree with a thud, then bounced off.

Roman gave me a chaste clap on the shoulder. "Good first try." He retrieved the star and pocketed it.

"You don't want me to try again?" I asked, mildly disappointed.

"Nah. I need to keep them sharp in case I actually need one. Besides, you get the idea of what I do."

I do?

"So you find a bad guy and throw stars at them?"

Roman nodded. "More or less."

"So it's more." I held out my palm and bent my fingers toward me in a come-on gesture. "Fess up. How else will you protect us?"

He threaded his fingers through his silky hair. "See the duster?"

Oh, that. "How can I miss it?"

"It holds about ten pistols," he said sheepishly.

"What?" Surely I hadn't heard him correctly.

"I'm packing a lot of heat."

I mean, I figured he was packing some heat, but ten guns? "So it is an assassin jacket."

"It's a bodyguard jacket. And don't you want your body guarded?"

Oh boy, did I ever. "Well, if that's what needs to happen, of course."

He grinned. "It's what needs to happen if you're to stay safe." He leaned toward me, his hulking body blocking the light. I felt so small before him, so insignificant. That reminded me—what about Sera? They'd been talking. I knew he had to like her.

"If I'm to stay safe as well as my sister," I corrected.

He glanced away. "Right. All of you."

"Don't you think we should be heading into town?"

"Why?"

"Because I've got an errand to run, and you need to get back to protecting all of us, including Sera."

He didn't say anything. I wasn't sure how to take that. Had I said the wrong thing? Roman escorted me back to the SUV. Opened the door. He motioned for me to climb in, so I did.

"Thank you," I said.

"Don't mention it."

"I mean, I'm a witch and all, so I probably should mention it."

He shut my door, walked around the vehicle and got in. He

pulled off his sunglasses. The heat from his body billowed off him, practically paralyzing me in my seat. "Why do you feel the need to constantly mention that I don't like witches?"

So that I remember not to fall for you. "So that you keep it straight in your head."

He leaned forward. The intensity in his eyes made me want to pitch forward, press my lips against his, taste his mouth.

Whoa. Wait. What was I thinking?

"What if I don't want to remember that? What if I like being around you?"

I fastened my seat belt, wedging myself into the side of the SUV. I'd spent so much time throwing myself into my work, ignoring men, that when one expressed his feelings, I felt like a schoolgirl— unsure of what to say and do. But he meant as a friend, right? Yes. Definitely. Liked me as a friend.

I cleared my throat for a good thirty seconds. "If you, um, like being around me? Well, that's nice and all, but um, perhaps we should focus on the job at hand."

He looked away. His jaw muscle flexed and tightened. Oops. I guess I said the wrong thing. "Well, since I've got some protecting to do, where can I take you?"

"You can take me to the Mouth of the South. I've got some sleuthing to do."

SEVENTEEN

I found Jenny Butts sitting behind her desk at Rustic Touch and Travel. She was hard at work filing her nails down to the quick. She leaned way back in her chair when Roman entered. His bulk didn't intimidate me anymore, but I could see where the wide receiver of a man could frighten others.

Jenny raised a questioning brow. Okay, let's call it what it was, a nosy brow. "Why, Dylan Apel, what are you doing here? Want me to book you a trip to Hawaii? Or perhaps you want some of my copper-wire balls—they're perfect for any living room."

Tempting. "No, I had a few questions for you." I slid into a chair in front of her desk while Roman wandered around the room.

Jenny eyed Roman like a tiger surveyed her prey. "Aren't you going to introduce me to your friend?" she cooed.

"Roman, meet Jenny. Jenny, Roman."

Jenny batted her fake eyelashes in his direction. "Nice to meet you."

Roman grunted. I suppressed a laugh. Jenny wove a finger through her Marilyn curls. "What can I do for you, Dylan?"

"I need some information."

Her ruby lips split into a smile. "You've come to the right place—or person, I should say." She settled back into her seat and returned to filing her nails. "What kind of info you looking for?"

160

"Did anyone new move into town about three years ago?"

She tapped the file against her cheek. "Now let me think back. Three years ago was when that little Ashlyn Sawyer was born with webbed fingers. Terrible tragedy, though the doctors were able to snip the webbing and give her normal-looking hands. Thank goodness, because otherwise she would have had to join a carnival in order to live a normal life."

Roman coughed into his hand. I ignored him. "Other than Ashlyn and the fingers, do you remember if anyone new moved into town, or if something strange happened?"

She narrowed her eyes. "Strange? Like what?"

I shrugged. "I don't know. Just anything."

She stopped filing and studied me. I suddenly felt like a giant mole had sprouted on the tip of my nose. "Is this about what happened to Reagan?"

"Do I have to answer that?"

She smirked. "No. It's not like I'm going to tell everybody or anything."

Right. It was definitely not like that at all. "I'm only looking for anything you remember."

"I heard they released Harry from jail. Are you pressing charges?"

I'd forgotten all about that. Detective Blount had left a message on my voice mail. I needed to call him. "No, I don't think so. Harry was drunk. A night in jail should have been lesson enough."

She sawed the file back and forth. "I mean, it's not as if you had anything to do with it. Some sort of freak accident, if you ask me. I figure she spontaneously combusted, and that's it."

Yeah, let's go with that. "So does that mean you don't remember anything?"

She caught Roman glancing at a poster of Italy. "Rome's half off right now," she said. "Trip for two will cost you only a sliver of what it normally does, but you have to book now."

"Thanks, but no thanks. I'm busy as it is."

Interest glimmered in her eyes. "Oh? How's that?"

"I'm actually about to change jobs."

She placed her elbows on the desk and pitched forward, letting her cleavage spill out the top of her blouse. Roman didn't even blink toward them. A small tinge of victory swelled in my core. I don't know why; it wasn't as if he was my boyfriend.

"Oh? What are you about to do?" she asked.

I turned toward him. "Yeah. What's your new job going to be?"

He shrugged. "Nothing's worked out right now." He crossed his arms and turned his back to us. Conversation, over. But I wanted to find out more about this. I'd have to pick his brain later.

"The only thing I remember of any consequence is that redheaded woman you've been spending time with."

Em? "How do you know about her?"

"Please, Dylan. I notice things. I've seen her in your shop."

Fair enough. "So then, what about her?"

"It'll cost you twenty."

"What?"

She scrunched up her nose and smacked my arm. "Just kidding. I always wanted to say that to someone. But really, I remember her from a few years ago. I can't say it was exactly three." She stopped, thought about it. "Yes, it was. It was after Ashlyn's birth, because I was hitting the prayer group at that time. We met a lot at Java House. There's nothing better than coffee and prayer, I always say." She snorted. "One Saturday that woman walked right on in, that red hair all the way down to her heinie. Who could forget that fiery color?"

"She's very striking," I agreed.

Jenny frowned. "I wouldn't necessarily say beautiful. But striking, yes."

Was someone feeling a bit jealous? "Okay, but you're sure you saw her."

Jenny flashed me an oh-please look. "Do you think I'd forget something like that?"

"Jenny," I said, cinching my purse strap, "I doubt there's much of anything you forget."

I walked to Perfect Fit after that. Roman returned to his normal post of sitting in the SUV and watching from a distance. After thinking about it, was that really the most efficient way of keeping us safe? I'd have to ask him about that.

The scent of lavender filled the air when I entered. "Carrie, are you wearing some new perfume?"

She laughed. "No. It's the latest thing—scented nail polish." She wiggled purple fingers toward me. "Do you like it?"

"Yeah, it's interesting," I lied. Gag. It wasn't the lavender that bothered me, just the overwhelming scent of it. "Do me a favor and open some windows, okay?"

She left her post and crossed the room. "You think it's a bit much?"

I pinched my nose, desperately trying not to sneeze. "A touch. Let's air the store out before any more customers come in." I grabbed a small fan from my office, set it on the desk and got it going. Immediately the scent diminished. "Was anyone annoyed that we were closed last week?"

Carrie shrugged. "Not that I could tell. The woman who came in was just so happy to be here, she didn't care."

"Did she buy anything?"

"Oh yes, two hundred dollars' worth of shirts and pants."

"High five!" We slapped hands, and I topped it off with a fist pump. "Great! I hope the rest of the day turns out as awesome. Want the afternoon off?"

Carrie's eyes widened. "Definitely! I've got to find shoes and a purse to match the dress I've chosen."

"What are you going to wear to the banquet?"

Carrie waltzed over to a baby-pink chiffon dress with a scoop neck. "This," she gushed. "I absolutely love it!"

I smiled. "It's one of my faves. Do you want to take it with you?"

She shook her head. "No, I'm afraid it'll wrinkle. I'll keep it here a few more days and take it home on Friday." Carrie pushed the door open with her backside. "See you tomorrow."

"See you later." Honestly I was glad to be rid of her. Maybe the smell would clear out now. I walked to the desk and called next door.

"Sinless Confessions," Sera said.

"Close for a few minutes and come on over."

"Excuse me, I can't just close the bakery. Someone might need a brownie."

"Then don't close. But that means you'll have to wait until dinnertime to find out what I learned."

"We'll be right over." Click.

That's what I thought. Less than thirty seconds later Reid and Sera tumbled through the door. "What'd you find out?" Sera asked, pushing Reid out of the way so she could get inside first.

I relayed everything Jenny had told me, minus the part about the webbed fingers.

"But how could Jenny be sure?" Reid asked.

Okay, so I had to fill them in on the webbed fingers as well.

Sera nestled into a chair and stretched her legs on a pleather footstool. "So you think it's Em?"

I shrugged. "I really don't know, but it sort of makes sense. I mean, she wanted to teach us magic, but the method she used ensured we couldn't use our power to the best of our abilities."

"Hmm. But then why didn't she go ahead and knock you both out already? She's had plenty of opportunity, if you ask me," Reid said.

"Because of the assassin, dummy," Sera said. "She couldn't exactly off us with him around. And we can obviously clear him of any wrongdoing. Dylan's been with him plenty of times."

"I've seen you in that SUV talking to him, too," I said, trying not to sound defensive but failing epically at it.

Sera blushed. "I had a few things to ask him."

None of my business, but her evading gaze said it all. She liked him, so I couldn't. That was fine with me. I wasn't attracted to tall, hot, emotionally detached men anyway.

"So if it is Em, what are we going to do about it?" Reid asked.

"There's only one thing to do," I said.

"What's that?" Sera asked.

I stared at them both for a long moment. "We set a trap."

EIGHTEEN

Milly pulled the wooden parrot from its cage and dusted it off before setting it back on the perch.

"Thank you," it squawked.

"You're welcome," Milly cooed. She turned to us. "What is it you want me to do again?"

I sipped sweet iced tea from a glass that had appeared moments before. Reid and Sera also sipped on tea, the three of us looking very Southern as we sat on her Victorian furniture drinking our refreshments.

"I'm not exactly sure. I need you to help us come up with a plan."

She snapped the wire door shut and waddled over to the recliner, cruising from one piece of furniture to the next without the use of her cane. "Let me get this straight." Milly wiped a line of sweat from the glass on the side table. "You want me to request the Queen Witch's presence and con her into doing a bit of magic that will make her create a thread."

"Right. Then we can match that thread with the one the witch doctor pulled from your ear."

She hummed a note, then stretched out her fingers and kneaded them into the plush armrests. "This is serious business. We're not playing games anymore. You start trying to bring down the

Queen Witch, you'll have a whole host of problems you can't even imagine."

I gulped. Okay, perhaps I needed to rethink this whole thing.

"You want us to back down?" Sera said.

Milly gummed her lips. "I want you to be sure of what you're doing. This isn't something to trifle with."

"Neither are our lives," I said. "It's not like I'm singling Em out."

Milly glared at me.

"All right, I am. But it's for good reason. I have an eyewitness who remembers her from three years ago, around the same time Grandma went into her freeze."

"The council had to make sure Hazel remained safe. That's their job." Milly snorted. "So of course Em would have been around during that time."

Reid tapped her fingers against the tea glass. "What about her shoddy teaching skills?"

Milly rubbed her chin. "That's the one point worth investigating, and gives me pause. I know she wasn't taught witchcraft that way, so for her to nearly sabotage your learning makes me question her motives." She stared around her room as if taking a mental photograph. "We need to have the witch police on call. If she is indeed the killer, we won't be able to contain Em. They'll need to be ready to capture her. Dylan, can you handle that?"

Sure. I was best friends with the witch police. Had them over for dinner every night. "I'll see what I can do."

"Now"—Milly grasped her cane—"when are we going to do this, and what's the plan?"

Sera gave me a wary glance. "We need to do it before the solstice."

"Well of course we need to! If we do it after, you'll be dead."

"Thanks for the vote of confidence," I said.

"It's the truth," she said. "And we'll need your grandmother there."

A tidal wave of panic rushed up my chest. "What? Why? She might do something like cast a spell for winged monkeys to show up."

She slammed the cane on the floor. "This is a witch dinner. Hazel must be there."

I sank back into the couch. "No problem. She'll be there. We'll do it Friday night. The night before the solstice."

"Whoa. Wait," Sera said. "I've got a ton of baking to do Friday for the banquet on Saturday."

"And that's my problem?" Milly asked. "Do you want to catch a killer, or do you want to make cupcakes?"

Reid set her tea on a side table. "Actually…"

"It was a rhetorical question!"

"Milly," I said. "I speak for us all when I say, we want to catch a killer."

"Then we'll have dinner at your place, six o'clock sharp, Friday night. I'll get Em there. You do the cooking." She leaned over, a glimmer of mischief in her eyes. "Now. Tell me your plan."

***

Since I had been deemed the witch police consort, I needed to use the one and only contact I had for them. Since this was a delicate issue, I felt a gentle hand had to be used.

I knocked on room 304 of the Magnolia Inn. Seconds passed before it opened. Roman stood sopping wet, a cheap motel towel knotted around his waist. Beads of water dripped off his chin, and his muscles glistened with a sheen that made my mouth fill with saliva.

He shifted to one side, and I made out the tattoo he'd told me about days earlier. Inked in black, the curling dragon, clearly influenced by Asian artistry, coiled down his shoulder and onto his rib cage. I nearly fainted.

Then I noticed the glare of molten lava he was giving me. "How'd you know where to find me?"

Was that a trick question? "There's only one motel in town. It didn't take much to figure it out."

He shuffled forward, glanced around to make sure no one was with me, and dragged me inside. Steam poured from the bathroom, the scents of soap and aftershave wafting about the room.

He shut the door behind him. "What's going on? I'm assuming this isn't a social visit."

"Actually it is. Want to grab some dinner?"

He cocked his head. "What are you up to? Trying to get me drunk?"

"Ha, ha. No. Just thought you might like a bite of Mexican. Nothing fancy."

"Let me guess. You need a favor."

How did he know that? "No. I don't need any favors. Just thought you might like a little company for once—outside of your truck."

He watched me as if waiting for me to cave in and tell him the truth. When I didn't, he crossed to the doorless closet. "I'll be outside in five minutes."

Okay then. I left and waited outside.

***

"Want a margarita?" I figured he was a straight tequila guy, but I felt it polite to ask.

He flipped the laminated menu over. "No. I don't drink when I'm working."

"Me either," I said.

He quirked an eyebrow. "Are you working?"

"Maybe."

We ordered, and I sank back into the booth. A mariachi band played in one corner, entertaining the families and couples who'd shown up for some food and fun.

"Want to dance?"

I looked around to see who had spoken.

"Dylan?" Roman said.

"Yes?"

"Would you like to dance?"

I stared into his brilliant eyes. Roman was looking at me. Roman had asked me. Oh my God! Roman was asking me to dance! I pitched to the side, catching the table with one hand before I fell out of the booth.

"Are you okay?"

"Yes. Fine. I'm fine." I placed a hand on my temple. "Just a head rush, that's all." I smiled. "I'm okay."

"Does that mean you don't want to dance?"

"Yes!" Wait. "No. No. Yes."

"Breathe."

I did so. "There's not a lot of space to dance."

He shrugged. "We'll make some space."

"Um..."

"If you don't want to dance with me, just say so."

Oh God. No. Yes! I wanted to dance with him. Unable to trust my mouth to say the right thing, I nodded.

Roman gave me a warm smile. Was that a dimple? He extended his hand. I slid my palm in his. A shudder rippled down my spine. I tried not to think about it. About him. About dancing. About vomiting up the contents of my stomach all over his feet. You know, I tried to keep my mind blank.

He escorted me over to the band. I felt every eye in the cozy restaurant single in on me. My lower lip trembled, and I stopped.

Roman gave me a questioning look.

"There really isn't anyplace to dance," I whispered.

He leaned over and nestled his mouth to my ear. "We'll make one. In five minutes I promise we won't be the only ones dancing."

I slid a sweaty palm down my side. "Promise?" I whispered.

He placed a hand on my hip. I squealed. He squeezed and said, "Promise. Just keep walking."

I forced my feet to move, and we slinked past a couple of tables and secured a spot a little distance from the band. Roman pulled me to him. With one hand on my hip and the other chastely holding my hand, we started to sway.

It felt amazeballs, as Reid would say.

He released my hip, raised my hand and spun me around. I giggled. "So," he said. "What sort of business did you want to discuss?"

He pulled me to him. I rushed forward. My body crushed against his solid chest. "What made you think I wanted to discuss business?"

"Don't play. I've lived long enough to know these things. You need a favor."

"Maybe I do."

We swayed to the music. From the back of the restaurant, I noticed a young couple leave their booth. They threaded through the tables and booths and came to stand a few feet from us.

"See?" he said.

"You win."

His head tipped back to his shoulders in defeat. "But we didn't bet anything, so there's nothing for me to win."

I giggled. "What would you have bet?"

He shook his head. "Some other time."

"Must be something embarrassing if you won't tell," I teased.

He twirled me around. "What did you want to discuss with me?"

Now I really wanted to know what he would have bet. Here was the big bad assassin being evasive. "If I tell you, will you tell me?"

"Dip," he said. He squeezed me close and dropped me back. I was down and up so quick I forgot what we were talking about.

Kidding.

"Maybe. It depends on what you need."

I pressed my body against his and stood on my tiptoes to

reach his ear. He instinctively bent toward me.

"I need the witch police on standby." He straightened. Deep lines creased his forehead, and the frown he wore made me question whether I should have asked him or not. "You're the only person I know who can contact them. Otherwise I wouldn't be bothering you."

He glared at me. "Why do you need the witch police?"

I winced. "Just 'cause?"

"Not a good answer." I didn't know how much to tell him—how loyal he was to Em. I mean, here was a guy who didn't like witches, yet he was dancing with one. Talk about mixed signals.

"I think I've got a lead on who tried to kill me."

He pulled me close, swayed me to the music. "And who would that be?"

"You only wanted to know what I wanted. You didn't say you needed all the gory details."

He slid a hand down my arm and entwined his fingers in mine. He raised my hand and kicked to the beat of the music. Who was this man? He could dance, throw stars, probably kill a bear with his bare hands—he gave me surprise after surprise.

"I need all the gory details if I'm going to involve them."

"Don't you have a good relationship with the police?"

"Let's just say they don't like guys of my type."

"You mean a killer? Weren't they the ones who hired you?"

The song ended, and we stopped dancing. The crowd erupted in applause, a few catcalling us. I blushed. Roman nodded to them. He wrapped his hand around my waist and nuzzled his mouth to my ear. "Smile for your fans. They love you."

I think I purred.

We returned to our table. The stern look on his face clued me in that his cheery mood had now soured. "I've never needed anyone's approval to be who I am. I have no regrets."

Whoa. I lowered my voice. "Do you think I'm judging you? I don't care what you do, who you've been. You've done what you needed to survive. I can't imagine what you went through as a child, and quite honestly, I don't want to. Your family was taken from you."

"So were yours."

"Yeah, but in an accident." He shrugged. "Oh, so you know the rumors, too—that they were murdered." I flattened my hands on the table. "I don't have any proof of that, and until there is some, I have no reason to believe it. Besides, I have bigger fish to fry. Someone wants to kill me, and they want to do it before the solstice. I need the police ready to make an arrest in two days' time—Friday night. I need you to do this for me. You're my protector."

He crossed his massive arms against his chest and exhaled. "I'm your bodyguard." He stared around the room and then folded his hands on the table.

I reached across and squeezed his arm. An electric current ran from his skin to mine. I shivered. Focus. "Yes, you're my bodyguard. I need you to help me. I think I know who's doing this, and I need the police ready to make an official arrest."

The waiter arrived with our food. I released Roman and nestled back to my side of the booth. He forked a wedge of burrito into his mouth. "You can have the police there, but there'll be one problem."

I pushed my refried beans and rice together, making a glob of food. I shoveled it onto my fork and then nibbled it off. "What's that?"

He wiped his mouth with a paper napkin. "They'll arrest me."

NINETEEN

I dropped my fork. "They'll arrest you for what?"

He sighed. "I'm a private person. My past is not something I like talking about."

I rolled my eyes. "Let me guess? And you really don't like discussing it with"—I glanced around to make sure no one was listening—"a witch?"

He smirked. "Why do you need to remind me of that all the time?"

I shrugged. "Maybe it hurt my feelings when you said it. We've spent time together talking, and for some weird reason you danced with me, yet you don't like me."

"What kind of crazy talk is this? Darlin', if I didn't like you, we wouldn't be talking at all."

A piece of bang fell in my eyes. I raised my hand to brush it away, but Roman's fingers slid to the strand and tucked it behind my ear. I glanced at him. The fire in his gaze sent my eyes drifting back over the rest of the room.

I scratched the back of my neck for half a millennium to get the image of his intense expression out of my mind and said, "So tell me why you'll be arrested."

"It goes back to what your grandmother was talking about the other night. Years ago, after I gave up being a witch hunter, I became an undercover agent with the police. My partner and I were investigating a rumor we'd heard that some witches were manufacturing magic."

"Wait. Making magic? How can you do that?"

He looked at his plate and said, "Maybe we should take this conversation somewhere else."

I wasn't hungry anyway. He paid and we left. He glanced around. We stood in a square off Main. Several shops with brightly colored awnings surrounded us. "How about a Popsicle?"

I spied the corrugated-steel-topped building with a sign that read SILVER POPS and said, "Sounds great. They have a watermelon that's fantastic."

So like two teenagers on a date, minus the county fair and a big stuffed animal my beau had won for me throwing balls into baskets, we got two Popsicles and settled on a bench overlooking the town's one and only koi pond/fountain. It performed double duty—you could enjoy the fish and make a wish.

"How do witches sell magic?"

He sucked the edge of his banana-flavored Popsicle and said, "They strip it off themselves. It's complicated and can be messy, from what I hear, but also a very lucrative business. Any witch caught doing it is automatically put to death."

"Yikes," I said.

"Regular folks aren't allowed to know about magic. So if the council discovers a witch has been selling secrets, she dies. It's part of the rules. Didn't Em tell you?"

"No, not really."

"She's sort of scatterbrained for a Queen Witch. Most witches are. Your grandmother isn't an exception; she's more like the rule. You'll find out as you meet more of them."

I licked the bottom of my dripping treat. "Meet more of them? I don't want to meet more of them."

He chuckled, flashing me a grin that made my heart melt. "You have no choice. They'll be coming out of the woodwork wanting to meet you; just you wait."

I toed off my sandals and dipped my feet in the cool water. Golden koi scattered. "Anyway. Back to your story."

"Right. I was dating a woman at the time; her name was Sheila. She wasn't a witch, so she knew nothing about my real life— or my hidden life, as I prefer to call it—and I loved that. I wanted to keep things that way. After what I'd gone through with my family, I wanted to be with someone who didn't know about magic and wasn't tainted by it."

My heart sank. Roman didn't want to be with anyone related to magic. He didn't want to be with me; he was only being nice.

I jutted out my chin and put on my big-girl pants. That was fine, because I didn't have time for a boyfriend anyway. I had a shop to run. Wasn't I forgetting someone? Like my sister? Didn't she have a claim to him anyway?

He rubbed the back of his neck. "One night we received an anonymous tip. It was the first solid lead we'd had in months, and of course I jumped on it. I wanted to go right in, guns blazing. My partner, on the other hand, wanted to take some time, scope it out. We compromised." Roman stopped. He stared at the fish and took a deep breath. I placed a reassuring hand on his shoulder. He tilted his head toward me and smiled. I smiled back. A rush of energy buzzed between us, holding me in his mesmerizing gaze. He leaned back, took my hand from his shoulder and held it in his.

My heart flipped. It flopped. It rumbled in my chest, pounding my ribs to bursting.

"In the time we took to create a solid plan, the witch or witches found Sheila. They killed her as a warning to me."

My breath hitched. Dear God, that was tragic. "I'm so sorry. I had no idea."

A sad smile crossed his face. "There are a lot of reasons why I'm not crazy about witches, to say the least. They have a nasty habit of killing people I care about."

"It seems they do," I murmured. "So did you catch them?

Did you find the people who killed her?"

He glanced over the green. Kids giggled as they played on the swing set and grappled with giant Lego blocks that the town had shipped in for its children's playground portion of the square. Their laughter filled my heart. As sad as Roman's story was, they reminded me of hope and of joy.

"I found one of them."

"What'd you do?"

"The witch was already dead when I found her. Unfortunately for me, I was alone when I made the discovery. The witch police showed up minutes later and arrested me for the murder." His steel gaze hardened as he stared off. "But I didn't do it."

I exhaled. Thank goodness.

"Since I'd eliminated rogue witches in the past, it was just assumed that I'd killed her. But I didn't. They threw me in jail and were going to execute me, so I escaped. I have a price on my head."

"But then why is Em using you?" I said.

"Because she's the one person who believed in my innocence. That is, her and my old partner." Roman finished his Popsicle and tossed it in the trash can beside us.

I squeezed his hand. "If you can't help, I understand."

"If I'm going to contact the police, I need to know who you suspect."

I took a deep breath and told him.

"You're wrong," he said.

"How do you know?" I bristled. I slid my hand from his and took a long, hard suck of my frozen watermelon treat.

"Because it doesn't make sense. If she'd wanted to do it, she would have offed all of you by now."

So I, being the Miss Smarty-pants that I am, explained my hypothesis.

"That's nothing, darlin'. Not a foot to stand on. The council won't like you accusing a Queen Witch without proof."

"That's what I intend to get at the dinner. Proof. Look, I

won't need the police if she's innocent, but if I can match those threads, then it's for sure her, and I'll need the police to make the arrest."

He dug his hands into his pockets and shook his head. "If you think it's her, I'll make the call to get them on standby." He rose, extended his hand to help me up. "You realize, though, I can't be anywhere near there at the time. If something goes wrong…"

I grinned. "Nothing will go wrong. There'll be four other witches there."

He pointed the key chain at the SUV and pressed a button. A short bleep filled the backside of Main. "That's what I'm afraid of."

When I got home, Grandma was standing in the middle of the room flapping her arms. "And they squawked like this: squaaaawwwk! Squaaaawwwk!"

I walked over to Sera. "Like to explain what this is about?"

She brushed a parcel of hair from her eyes. "She said no one ever believed her when she talked about the winged monkeys. Said we all thought she was crazy, so she's doing a demonstration. Grandma! I didn't hear you. Can you do it again?"

"Squaaaawwwk!"

I plugged my ears to drown out Grandma's screeching. "That's enough! We hear you. I believe you, Grandma. There are lots of flying monkeys out there, ready to attack at any moment."

She gave a satisfactory nod and sat on our ancient recliner. The darn thing had a bottom cushion that was more bent springs than foam. It was lumpy as all get-out. "About time someone believed me. If I have to summon a monkey to prove it, you won't like it, believe you me. Those are nasty little creatures." She bent her hands to resemble claws. "They scratch and bite. Sometimes they even spit."

"Sounds horrible," I said.

"Yeah," Reid added. "Definitely doesn't sound like something I want to find under my pillow."

"Well, heavens no! I'd have that Tooth Fairy hauled into court for delivering one of those." She wagged her knotted finger at Reid. "You tell me if she does something like that. I'll have her license taken away."

Reid saluted her. "You're the first person I'll call."

"Make sure of it."

"I will."

"So exactly what's going on?" I asked Sera.

Sera shook her head. "Don't even ask. She got on a tirade, and that's been the end of it."

I laid my purse on the table. "Does she know about dinner tomorrow night?"

"She knows."

A buzz sounded from Sera's pocket. She pushed off the wall she'd been leaning on and dug out her phone. After looking at the number, she frowned and pressed a button to silence it.

"Who was that?" I asked.

"No one."

Right. "Tim trying to explain why he got engaged to Olivia?"

She shot a wad of buckshot from her eyes to mine. Nice. Loved getting hate looks from my sister as soon as I got home. "It's nothing," she said.

Fine. "I've got everything all set. The police will be on standby. All we need to do is make sure Em arrives tomorrow."

Sera nodded. "Milly said she's got everything all set. I called her today to follow up."

"Called? Like on a phone?"

"Yeah. She gave me her number in case we ever needed help."

I stroked my chin. My fingers glided over a zit that I'd probably need to pop in the morning. "I suppose I'll have to help you get ready for the banquet on top of everything else."

"I'm counting on it."

I glanced at Grandma, who was looking around the room as

if waiting for monkeys to descend on her. "You gonna take care of that?" I joked.

She clapped me on the shoulder. "No. You are. Good luck getting her to bed. I'll see you in the morning."

Panicking, I said, "Where's Nan?"

"She took the night off."

Great. This should be epic. I approached Grandma slowly, like I was trying to wrangle a wild horse.

"Grandma? You ready to go to bed?"

She turned a beady-eyed stare my way. "I am not. I'm angry at you."

"For what?"

She picked up an apple from the fruit bowl on the dining table and shook it at me. "For not telling me you plan on entrapping the queen."

"Sorry. I didn't know I was supposed to tell you."

"It's impossible to keep things from me. I can hear better than most hawks."

"I thought their gift was sight."

She waved her hand. "Whatever. Anyway, I'm looking forward to this. It'll be the most fun I've seen in years." She took a bite of apple and said, "So. When do we catch the witch?"

TWENTY

Fittings filled most of my Friday. Three brides showed up, all wanting original designs for themselves and their bridal parties. I kept my measuring tape around my shoulders all day, ready to whip it off and size this or that body part. By the time the sun reached its apex, I was beat.

I fell into a chair. "Whew. I hope we're done for the day," I said to Carrie, who was busy straightening the clothes on the racks.

"Yeah, that was fun," she said. "Made the morning fly by."

"It certainly did." I glanced out the window and watched as Roman's black SUV pulled up. He got out and walked toward the store. I sat up. He'd only been in the shop one other time. Was everything okay? Did he have to leave? Was he mad at me?

"Carrie, why don't you take lunch? Take an extra hour if you need it to get ready. In fact, since the banquet is tomorrow, why don't you go ahead and clock out for the day?"

Her eyes widened. "Are you sure?"

"Do we have any more bookings for the afternoon?"

Carrie checked the appointment book on the slender front desk and said, "Nope. Not a one."

I waved her off. "Then go and relax. Get a pedicure. Give yourself a manicure."

She glanced down at her perfect nails. "They do need some

touching up. Thanks, Dylan. See you at the banquet tomorrow."

"Bye!"

She walked out right as Roman entered. "You got a second?" he asked.

I motioned to the matching chair across from me. "Have a seat."

He shook his head. "That won't be necessary."

Okay, then don't.

He studied the sea of dresses. "I called my old partner and explained the situation. They'll be ready for you." He handed me a black circular object with a red button protruding from it. "Press this and someone will come."

I studied the smooth object. About the size of a silver dollar, it didn't look impressive. "Does it display a W in the sky? You know, like in 'witch police'?"

He smiled. "No, it doesn't work like a superhero signal. Commissioner Gordon isn't going to appear."

"I was hoping more along the lines of Batman."

"No Batman. Only the witch police."

I slid a finger over the shiny red surface. Seemed normal enough. "I know this is a stupid question, but how does it work?"

"Press the button and an officer will arrive."

"Will it be your partner?"

He shook his head. "No. He's out of the country on a case. It'll be someone else."

I knew what he meant. Someone who thought he was guilty of murder. I held the device carefully, not wanting to set it off. "What if I accidentally press it?"

"It won't be activated until tomorrow."

"Phew. That's good to know. I didn't want to set it off while you're around and have something happen."

"You mean, like my arrest?"

"Exactly."

He smiled. "Glad to know you care."

I met his gaze and that weird, uncomfortable feeling crept over me. The one where I wasn't certain what to do. Do I keep staring? Do I look away?

So I smacked my lips. "Are you going to the solstice banquet tomorrow?"

"If Em's the killer and you prove it tonight, I'll be gone by then."

My heart battered my ribs. "You'll be gone? Why?"

"My job here will be over, remember? I was only hired to guard you until the killer was caught."

"But what about others?" I sputtered. "You've said so yourself, that the witches will be coming out of the woodwork to kill us." Way to play it cool, Dylan. I should've jumped in his arms and told him I couldn't live without him. Which I could. I didn't need to date any men. I didn't need to date anyone. I was perfectly happy all by myself, with my sisters and Grandma for company.

Maybe I should jump in his arms.

"I think you'll find a way to stay safe, Dylan. You strike me as the type of woman who knows how to protect herself."

Speaking of, I needed to do that protection spell again. I'd forgotten all about that, what with Milly being in the hospital, and the sting on Em coming up.

The front door slammed open. Grandma stood in the center of the room, her arms spread wide. "I'm here to have you make my dress for the banquet." Her eyes swept Roman from head to foot. "You here for that, too?"

Roman chuckled. "No, ma'am. I'm on my way out the door." He nodded toward me. "See you later."

Before I had a chance to ask him a gazillion questions, he left. Dang it. I turned to Grandma. "How'd you get here?"

"You think I can't get a ride from Nan to come into town? Ha. That woman's ready to get out of the cottage every chance she gets."

I crossed to the window and peered through the blinds.

"Where is she?"

"Next door having some hot chocolate and a brownie. Says it's delicious. I say it sounds like suicide by chocolate."

"Of course it does."

"Listen, girlie, I need a dress for the banquet tomorrow."

"Only if you show me the file on Roman. The one you had the other night at dinner."

"Who?"

My chest deflated with an exhale. "The bodyguard."

"Oh." She shook her head. "No. I don't know. Maybe."

"That's definitive."

She sauntered toward the racks. "Help me with the dress and I might change my tune."

I gestured toward the mass of gowns. "Let me show you some."

Now I've yet to have a client who didn't agree with my selection for them, but when I showed my grandmother a cream-colored suit dress, she shook her head. The same thing happened when I presented an aqua pantsuit and even a pale blue chiffon gown.

"I don't see anything I like. I guess you'll have to make me something."

Okay, since I had nothing to do—no killers to catch and no baking to help Sera with. Since my plate was completely clean for the next twenty-four hours, I could definitely sit down and sew Grandma a dress.

"Grandma, I don't have time to make you a banquet gown."

She threw her hands up. "Of course you do! You're a witch, aren't you?"

"That's still up for debate."

She rubbed her spotted hands together and, with weepy eyes, took in my shop. "This is where we can get a little Mary Poppins."

"I don't follow."

She grasped me by the shoulders and said, "Let your magic

make the dress. Think Cinderella and the mice."

That cleared up any confusion. I'd just conjure some Disney cartoon characters and get them to make the outfit. "You might have to guide me on this one."

"Dim the shades," she commanded.

I turned my blinds so no one could see in.

"Put up the CLOSED sign."

I frowned. "How about the BE RIGHT BACK one?"

She fluffed the ends of her silver curls. "That will do."

It would have to. I didn't need to lose any more business than I already had since the murder.

"Now," she said. "For the banquet, I want a shimmering black tunic dress with silver thread."

I arched my eyebrow. "Black? For a summer dress?"

"It will be made of linen."

I rolled my eyes. "Much better."

She stared at me as if expecting me to do something. "Well? Get started."

I laughed at the absurdity. "I don't know how."

Grandma rolled up the sleeves of her orange linen jacket. Yes, the woman was a sucker for linen, and orange, apparently, since she always seemed to be wearing it. "First thing's first. Pull the fabric and the thread from storage. Do you have both the black and silver?"

I shrugged. "I guess so."

She thrust out her hands, palms up and open. "Then command them to come!"

I gave her a questioning look.

"Command them!"

Afraid I'd be cursed to the depths of hell—or at least some sort of unicorn purgatory—I imagined the black linen and said, "Come forth," unsure of what the heck would happen. Two seconds later, no lie, a bolt of ebony fabric floated in from the storage room.

I reached behind me, gripping for the armrest of the chair.

"Ha," Grandma said. "Witchcraft still scare you?"

"No," I lied.

"This is nothing, chick. You need to get with the program. If this scares you, there's no telling what a herd of talking humpback baboons will do to you."

"No telling," I murmured.

She instructed me to call the thread, which I did. And then she said, "Now, make the tunic with your mind. Cut the fabric, sew it together."

"Don't I need measurements?"

She raised her arms over her head. "If you must."

I took a few quick measurements and thought, what the heck? I focused on every dressmaking scene from Disney cartoons I could remember, and told the objects what to do. And you know what? They did.

Scissors cut wedges of fabric. Silver thread unwound, and the shears cut several strips. Slips of thread poked through the eyes of several needles, and faster than I could even push the fabric through a sewing machine, each needle and thread created a hem, lining, even drew an embellished design on the front of the tunic. It was a better oiled machine than I was. I stood back, orchestrating the entire thing with my mind like a conductor on the opening night of Carnegie Hall's season.

"Keep going," Grandma hummed. "You've got it."

I told this thread to sew the arms, told that thread to finish the sides and brought forth rhinestones and sequins to add shimmer and shine. I pushed myself to do more, juggle harder, add another layer until one entire wall of the room was a mass of thread and fabric, needles and scissors, cutting and constructing. This was my symphony. I harnessed all my energy to keep everything going, to continue the steady pace. A melody sounded in my head as I gathered each and every working cog and moved them to finish Grandma's gown.

"It's working," she said. "You're doing it. Focus."

Someone knocked on the door. I panicked, dropping

concentration. Thread I didn't need unwound from the spool. Scissors cut it. The silvery strip floated to the floor as more thread unwound.

"Rein it in," Grandma said.

I tried. I pushed my focus on the thread to make it stop, but now the knocking came harder.

"Stop the dress," Grandma hissed.

I told everything to stop. Saw the image in my mind, but nothing happened. In fact, cutting increased, sewing sped up. The knocking came harder, more aggressive. The doorknob jiggled. I panicked. I could not let anyone see this. I'd be stripped of my power, boiled by the council, or by the Queen Witch herself in a bloody, horrible death.

The door pushed open.

"Stop!" I cried.

I hunched down, not wanting to see the catastrophe of cloth and thread before me. I imagined silver shears still cutting, silver thread still unspooling.

Silence.

I glanced at the door. Detective Blount stood there, a worried expression etched on his face. "Stop what? Is everything okay?"

Think quick. "Yes. Grandma kept pinching me, so I yelled at her?" My heart shattered against my ribs. I held my breath, knowing my face must have turned a deep shade of crimson.

He nodded as if everything was fine.

In the slowest of slo-mo, I pivoted back to the dress. Everything lay perfectly on a back table I used for construction. There wasn't one shred of evidence that, only moments before, the entire contents had been suspended in the air, moving about as if God himself had breathed life in them.

His gaze swept the room. "Thought I heard a commotion in here."

"No," I tittered. "Nothing in here but us chickens. Right, Grandma?" He threw me a confused look. Come on. "You know, that's that old-time joke."

Grandma glared at me as if I had three heads. "It was originally a song. But that's neither here nor there. What sort of commotion are you talking about, Detective? You're not suggesting some sort of drug-infused party, are you?"

Blount's face reddened. "No. Of course not. I was walking by, heard a noise and wanted to make sure Miss Apel was all right. You are, aren't you?"

"Of course. Fine." I coiled the tip of my ponytail around my index finger. Nothing to see here. "How's the investigation going?"

He glanced back toward the street. "Just fine." The detective coughed into his fist. "Following up on some leads. I'll be gone week after next. I'm taking a vacation."

"Oh? To where?" Grandma asked.

"Atlanta," he said.

"Isn't that where you came from?" I asked.

"Yes," he said.

I had the distinct feeling it wasn't a vacation the detective was after, but I said nothing. "We'll, we're fine in here."

He pressed his lips into a thin line. "That man you're always with is outside in a black SUV keeping an eye on the place."

I gulped. "Is he?" Perhaps playing dumb would help me in this situation.

He thumbed his hand toward the street. "I'm aware you know he's out there. Is there some reason why you feel the need to have him around?"

"The mafia," Grandma said.

Both of us snapped our necks in her direction. "The mafia," Blount repeated.

"There's a little known sect of them that steal dresses." She leaned forward, lowered her voice to a whisper. "From what I hear, there's a mafia queen who likes a five-finger discount on designer clothing."

"You don't say," he said.

"Yes, I do. Detective, you carry an awful lot of tension in your shoulders." Grandma placed a hand on his bicep and tiptoed behind him. She grasped both his shoulders and started kneading. "Yes, a lot of tension. In fact, I haven't seen this much since my husband was dealing with our daughter's teenage years." Her head appeared beside his neck. "Do you have one?"

"What's that?"

"A teenager."

He chuckled. "No. My kids are grown." He moaned. "Does that feel good."

"It does. I know it does."

He closed his eyes and smiled. "Boy, this is heaven."

"No, it's not," she said. "There aren't enough angels."

I groaned. Sheesh. Could the woman have one conversation that was normal?

"If you keep this up, I'll fall asleep."

She rubbed her hands down his arms and clapped them against his shirt. "We don't need that, do we? There are enough police officers in doughnut shops. No reason to add one more."

He squinted at me through a slit in one eye. "Um, sure." The detective straightened his back and adjusted his tie as if embarrassed that he'd let an old woman massage him. "Thank you. I needed that."

Grandma gave him a whimsical smile. Was she flirting? Gross. "You're welcome."

He placed his hands on his hips and tapped his fingers. "If you come across anything that might aid the investigation, let me know."

"You'll be the first I call, Detective," I said.

He perused the shop one more time before reaching for the door. "Ladies. Have a pleasant afternoon."

I waved. "You too, Detective."

Once he was gone, Grandma turned to me. "About time you got rid of him. I thought he'd never leave."

"What? You were the one massaging him. If you'd wanted

him to go, you probably shouldn't have started in with the whole do-you-have-a-teenager bit."

She walked over to the tunic dress and lifted one arm. "What was I supposed to do? Kick him out? He's the police, Dylan. They matter in this part of the world."

"This part of the world?"

She pressed a finger to the middle of her lips. "As opposed to the other part of the world—that of witches and creatures."

"Right. The winged monkeys and unicorns," I said with zero enthusiasm.

"I know none of you believe me, but they exist. Now"—she lifted the dress to the light—"let's see what we have here." After several seconds she said, "It's absolutely gorgeous, Dylan. One of your finest pieces. All I need is a belt and it'll be perfect for tomorrow night." She folded it and set it inside a canvas bag that had appeared on the table. "You know, it's funny how inanimate objects sometimes have minds of their own."

What was this craziness? "Pardon?"

"That's why they wouldn't stop when you commanded them. They didn't want to." She clenched her fist and shook it. "Had a little taste of freedom and wanted more."

"Huh?"

"That's why I had to erase their memories. That's how I stopped them before that tense detective walked in."

I cocked my head so far over, my cheek nearly touched my shoulder. "Are you saying what I think you're saying?"

She zipped the bag shut. "That depends. If what you think I'm saying is that a group of scissors and such didn't want to stop creating because they enjoyed it, and the only way to stop them was to wipe their memories, then yes, that's what I'm saying?"

I closed my eyes and squeezed the bridge of my nose. "I can't. I just can't. Grandma, objects don't have memories."

She clutched the bag to her chest in surprise. "Of course they do. Objects remember."

I raised my hands in surrender. "Fine. They remember. So am I going to have to wipe their memories every time?"

She relaxed the bag and puckered her lips in thought. "Maybe. I don't know. Did you like making a dress that way?"

I had to admit I did. The surge of magic flowing through me had made my veins zing with life. I felt focused, on target, like I could create a thousand more the exact same way. "Yes."

She shouldered the bag. "Aha! I knew it. When we get home, I'll teach you how to wipe a memory clean."

I went to the windows and opened the blinds. "We can't do that tonight, Grandma."

She stared at me. "Why ever not?"

"Because," I sighed, "we have a witch to catch."

"And do you know the best way to catch them?" she said.

"No."

"Set out a glue trap. They'll walk right into it."

I rubbed my forehead. Was this going to be a long night. I glanced at my watch. Less than five hours before Em showed up for dinner.

"All right," Grandma sneered. "Let's get this witch."

TWENTY-ONE

"If you so much as sniff one of those petit fours, I will cut you," Sera said. She brandished the most lethal-looking icing spreader I'd ever seen. Light glimmered off one end—the cutting end, I assumed, or what Sera would make the cutting end. Reid, iced confection closing in on her mouth, inched back a step.

She stared at Sera as if she'd never seen her before. To do the situation justice, this may have been the first time Sera had threatened her with the promise of bodily harm.

Sera spoke through an iron hard jaw. "Put. It. Down."

With a dainty touch Reid laid the miniature cake back in its plastic container. "I thought you said I could try one."

"At the banquet. You can try one there. Right now we have five hundred to make, dinner to conjure, a witch to catch and beauty sleep to get. There isn't time to stand around and taste the wares."

Reid's face fell. "Oh."

Grandma swept into the room. "Don't worry about dinner. Nan and I will have it whisked up in no time. You just keep doing what you're doing."

Something about the idea of Grandma cooking dinner made my stomach sour. We'd probably be eating bananas picked by bonobos in some sort of mango chutney sauce, or unicorn greens. You know, something random and embarrassing.

Nan entered the kitchen and pulled an apron over her head. "So you and Grandma are making dinner?" I asked in my most cheerful voice.

Nan's lips trembled as if she was about to laugh. She pinched them together, suppressing any hint of amusement. "Yes. Your grandmother wants to make parmesan-stuffed artichokes." She opened the refrigerator and pulled several of the green leafy vegetables from the bin.

Okay, so it wasn't unicorn food or monkey meat. We were starting off in the right direction. But would we veer off course to crash and burn? "That sounds delicious. What else are you making?"

"Bacon-wrapped green beans and strawberry salad," Grandma said. "Does that meet with your approval?"

"In fact, yes it does." I glanced at my watch. It was nearly seven. Looking at the mountain of unwashed and uncooked vegetables, a knot of anxiety clumped in my throat. "Sera, didn't you tell Em to be here at seven?"

"Yes. Why?"

"Because it's almost time." I shot a look to Nan. "How long will dinner take?"

Grandma pushed me out of the kitchen. "Five minutes. I'm a witch, remember? I know how to use magic."

I gripped the sides of the door frame. She pressed her hands into my back, trying to force me out. I held fast and glanced over my shoulder. "That's what I'm afraid of."

Five minutes later the doorbell rang. I twisted my fingers together. A tornado of butterflies whirled in my stomach. I wanted to back out. To hell with it. Who did I think I was, trying to capture a witch queen? She'd probably rip me to shreds before I even had a chance to hit the button in my pocket, a button that pressed lightly against my thigh, a constant reminder that this wasn't a game we were playing.

I held my breath and opened the door. I smiled, ready to

welcome Em, and for some reason was surprised when Milly slewed me out of the way with her cane. "Is everything ready?" she demanded.

I scoped out the street and noticed Roman's SUV was nowhere in sight. Good. He didn't need to be nearby when I called the police. I didn't want him to wind up in jail, or worse, on my account.

Sera walked into the room licking pink icing from her fingers. "It's all set. Grandma! Are you ready?"

Grandma floated in, a gauzy white chiffon scarf wafting behind her. "Of course I'm ready. I used to hunt bad witches for a living, remember?"

This was news. "You did?" I asked.

"Of course. How else do you think I know about the flying monkeys?"

Reid scrubbed a hand over her forehead. "Dear Lord, not again."

Grandma raised a threatening finger. "One day, girls. One day you will all see and understand."

"Let's hope that day never comes," I whispered.

"What was that?" she asked.

Ding-dong. Saved by the doorbell. "I'll get it," I said, praying it was Em so we could get this whole thing over with.

I opened the door. Tim Harper thrust out a bouquet of roses. "What the heck is this?" I asked.

He thumbed his nose. "Sorry. They're not for you."

I glared at him, doing my best to look intimidating. "Darn right they're not for me."

He gave me an embarrassed grin. "They're for Sera."

"Listen, Tim, haven't you broken my sister's heart enough?"

He brushed his junior-high bangs out of his eyes. "Don't you think that's for her to decide?"

Steam poured from my ears. I fisted my hand, readying to punch his nose across the other side of the Mississippi, when Sera walked up.

"Tim, what are you doing here?"

"Who is it?" Milly said. "Is it Em?"

"It's no one," I said.

"I think I'm a little more than no one," Tim said stiffly.

"Not really," I said. I backed up from the door.

"Sera, I came to apologize."

"There's nothing for you to say."

Grandma gestured toward Tim. "For goodness' sake, either come in or go out. You're letting flies inside by keeping the door open."

Sera took a step forward, blocking Tim's path from entering. "I think it's best if you—"

"Oh, I didn't know this was goin' to be such a big dinner, or else I would've worn a better dress."

Crap. Em walked into the frame, right behind Tim. Sera flashed me a desperate look. I stepped up. "Em, thanks for coming on such short notice. Tim, I'm afraid you're going to have to excuse us for dinner."

"I won't. I have important things to discuss with Sera."

"For the last time, shut that door," Grandma shouted.

Southern hospitality dictated that no matter how awful the circumstance, I couldn't just kick Tim away like an unwanted dog. So there was only one choice.

I grabbed him by the collar of his button-down shirt and pulled him in. "You want to talk to Sera, you can do it over dinner."

She gasped, and I put my mouth to her ear. "Keep him busy in your corner of the table." I flashed a smile to the queen. "Em, welcome to our humble abode."

***

I had to admit, the artichokes were delicious. I had no idea that with a little witchcraft, Grandma could make a meal soar. I knew

195

she'd only been frozen for three years, but even before then she'd never made anything as exotic or tasty.

"Love the artichokes," Em said.

"Yes ma'am," Tim added. "It's wonderful. And I have to thank you again for letting me join your dinner on such short notice."

"What notice?" I mumbled. Sera kicked my leg. For the life of me, I couldn't understand what she saw in Tim. Here was a guy who dressed like he didn't want to grow up—and he acted like it, too.

"How's the engagement to Olivia going?" I asked.

He tugged at his collar. "Well. Um. It's not. We broke it off."

I narrowed my gaze at him. "We? Or she?"

He pushed a bundle of green beans across his plate. "Delicious food. Did I say that?"

Grandma wiped her mouth with a peach-colored cloth napkin. Weren't we high eighties fashion? "This is what I serve all my honored guests."

Em raised a glass of wine. "Thank y'all. I'm honored to be here."

"Speaking of honored," Milly spat. "Aren't you girls supposed to be the belles of the banquet tomorrow night?"

I swallowed a mouthful of red wine. It burned my throat as it made its way down. I inhaled to soothe it and ended up coughing all over the table. "Yes," I croaked. "We're the guests, thanks to that newspaper article."

"What article?" Tim asked.

Reid dropped her fork on her plate. "The article in the Birmingham News, dummy. The one that came out right before Reagan was killed."

"Oh," he said weakly. "That." He straightened his back and puffed out his chest. "Bet it sure made Sera look great."

"Oh yes," Milly said. "Made her brownies famous. They're calling in from Paris, France, for orders."

I shot her a nasty look. Milly shrugged. That old woman didn't care one lick what anyone else thought.

"When I served this meal to the unicorn king, he complimented the wonders of cheese," Grandma said.

Every mouth dropped. Tim leaned over to Sera. "Did she say what I think she said?"

Sera tittered. "Oh, Grandma. Don't make up stories in front of Tim."

She fluffed the ends of her wiry hair. "Who's making up stories? It's not like the king showed up here or anything. We had a nice dinner in a pasture."

Sera circled her finger around her ear so that Tim could see.

"You'll meet him someday," she added.

"So," I boomed, "anyone have any new information to discuss? Anything of interest?" I gave Milly the eye, hoping she could steer Grandma away from talking about mystical creatures.

Milly folded her hands and rested her elbows on the table. She picked a rather rude piece of artichoke out from her teeth and set it on the plate. "I was going through some old books of mine the other day."

Em glanced up from her plate. "Really? What kind of books?"

Milly wiggled her fingers. "You know the kind."

"I should invite him to come right now. Prove the truth to all of you," Grandma said.

"Don't you dare," I hissed.

Milly continued. "There was a very interesting story about a woman who could appear to be anyone else."

Em shrugged. "That's not all that interestin'."

A sparkle of mischief sprang into Milly's eyes. "There are very few people who can do such a thing. You know, even in the storybooks."

Tim watched the conversation with interest. Sera murmured something in his ear, but he remained focused on Milly and Em. Reid bull's-eyed in on them as well, nibbling a roll as she leaned her ear ever closer to their tête-à-tête.

"I'll show you," Grandma said from the end of the table. I

paid her no attention. This was the moment we'd been waiting for.

Milly buttered some bread and took a bite. She spoke as crumbs toppled from her mouth. "I once heard a story that a certain young girl made herself look like an elder councilwoman so she could sneak into the library."

Em giggled. "I heard somethin' like that, too."

Tim craned his neck toward them. "I didn't. I haven't read that story."

"Tim, let me tell you something," Sera said, tugging his ear toward her.

"What is it?" he asked, a sloppy grin on his face. She whispered something to him, keeping him busy so that Milly could hook Em into our plan.

Milly placed her knife on her plate with a clink. "I wonder if that person could do it again."

Em tossed a bundle of saffron curls over one shoulder. "Of course. It's not like it's hard."

Milly poked at her green beans. "It's also not as if it's easy. Most of the ones I know can't do it at all."

Grandma's voice wafted in. "He would love to come. He'd show all of you."

Em sipped her wine. "They ain't tried. Not that this is the time or place for such a thing. Another time and maybe another place."

I kicked Sera. Her eyes widened as she realized what needed to be done. She yanked Tim's napkin from his lap. "Listen, I think you need to go."

"What?" he asked, glancing around the room. "Why? I want to hear how the story ends."

Sera wrapped a hand around his arm and pulled Tim to his feet. "It ends with you leaving."

"Why now? Can't it wait a few minutes?"

"I'm afraid not."

Tim pried her hand from his arm. "But I haven't even had

dessert."

Milly sloshed the red wine around her glass. "Of course, only someone who can't do it would suggest this isn't the right time."

Em's eyes tightened into angry little slits. I hid a smile. The Queen Witch owned pride in gallon-sized buckets. How far would she go to keep it?

"I didn't say it because I'm a coward. I said it because of you know who."

Grandma yelled, "Who? The unicorn king?"

"No, Grandma," I whispered. "No one's talking about him." I gazed at Sera and jerked my head toward the door. Tim needed to get the heck out of here. His presence could ruin everything.

Sera yanked him across the room. "Tim, come on."

"But we still haven't talked."

"There isn't anything to say."

You go, girl! That's what I wanted to hear—Sera giving Tim his permanent walking papers. And with that, she ushered him out of the house and, hopefully, out of our lives forever.

Milly cracked her knuckles together. "I bet you couldn't make me look like Councilwoman Gladiolas."

Em shuffled her seat a few inches from the table. "Why should I? I'm certain you're powerful enough to create that."

Milly tilted her head back and forth. "I'm not. I don't know many witches who are. It's one thing to make objects appear, move them around, that sort of thing, it's another entirely to shift molecules and atoms to rearrange the way someone's face and body look. You know that; you studied witch theory at all the good schools."

Em's eyes slid from one side of the table to another. "It isn't exactly good dinner etiquette to transform a guest to look like someone else."

"It might not be etiquette, but it would certainly be cool," Reid said. "I don't have any power, so I'll never be able to do anything neat like that. I'd love to see."

Em threaded her fingers through her loose curls, breaking

them apart at the ends. "Would y'all really like to see that?"

"Sure," I said. "I don't know who this councilwoman is. Whoever she is, the woman's got to be prettier than Milly."

That won me a nasty glare from my paternal grandmother. Em laughed. Grandma Hazel went on about the unicorn king. "And I could have him here right now," she said to no one.

"Very well," Em said. She cleared her throat and looked at me and Sera. "The way to do a glamour, whether you're performin' it on yourself or someone else, is to have an image of the person you want the intended to become fresh in your mind. You must concentrate solely on that. Not a lot of people can do this well. It takes practice and focus." She rose and gestured for Milly to do the same. "Ready?"

Milly snorted. "I'm ready."

"I could have the king here any second," Grandma said.

Sick and tired of hearing my grandmother spout off, I said (without thinking, mind you), "No one believes in that stupid unicorn king!"

Grandma gasped at me. Em raised her hand. Milly stood stock-still. Like a conductor, Queen Witch motioned with her hands. My fingers flew to my mouth, and I bit my nails with a zeal I hadn't found before.

The door opened. "I forgot my keys." Tim!

Milly's body shimmered like heat wafting over asphalt in the summer. In a blink, she became a young woman with long blonde hair. Even her clothes had transformed. She no longer wore brown old-lady clothes that reminded me of a bag of potatoes. Now a skintight black evening gown hugged her curves. Which no longer sagged, I noticed.

"What the…?" I heard Tim say.

A light flashed. I shielded my eyes and heard a sound that made my heart stop. A whinny. A loud, over-the-top neigh erupted from the center of my living room.

Tim screamed. I always knew he was a pansy.

I opened my eyes. An ivory unicorn stood in my house,

pawing the floor.

"It wasn't there, and then it was!" Tim said.

Sera ran interference. "Tim, calm down."

He pointed at it. "It appeared. That thing came out of nowhere! And she," he directed toward Milly, "was Milly Jones only two seconds ago."

The unicorn swiveled its head toward Tim. "Excuse me, but I am not a thing. I am Titus, King of the Unicorns."

Sera screamed.

Reid screamed.

Tim screamed.

Grandma crossed her arms over her chest. "See? I told y'all I'd make him appear."

Em waved her hands over Milly, and in a snap she returned to her normal self.

Tim screamed again.

"Sera, deal with that," I said.

"No need," Em said. "I can help." She walked over to Tim. I didn't know what she was going to do, but it couldn't be any worse than the situation we were already in.

I rushed over to Milly and pulled a miniature flashlight from my pocket. With magic, Milly had tweaked it to be able to see threads. With Em's back turned, this was my one chance to find the thread. I turned it on and waved it over the back of her head, keeping an eye on Em to make sure she wasn't looking in my direction.

"The ear," Milly whispered. "Look in there."

Though I knew lightning wouldn't strike twice in the same place, I shined the light in those tiny canals anyway, and voila! With a pair of tweezers I pulled out a small, wiggly blue thread that looked exactly like the one from the hospital. I pulled the button from my pocket and pressed it.

The front door banged open. "What's going on in here? Is everything all right?" Roman stood in the room, concern plastered all over his face. "I heard screams."

He surveyed the scene. Em waved her hands over a frightened Tim, a massive unicorn finished what was left of Grandma's artichoke while she stroked its mane, and I held a pair of tweezers with a blue squiggly pinned between the tines. All in all, it was a pretty normal day.

Poof!

A ball of smoke appeared. The scent of cool fog filled my lungs. I coughed, waving away the smoke. A small man wearing a bowler hat and cape—he must've come from the same era Grandma pulled the unicorn from—stepped forward.

"Inspector Pearbottom with the witch police. Who called?"

I jumped in front of him, hoping to shield his view of Roman. "I did." I pointed to Em. "Arrest that woman. I have proof that she's trying to kill me and my sister."

Em gaped at me. "What are you talkin' about?" She motioned her hand over Tim, and he fell unconscious. Sera caught him as he dropped to the floor and eased him down the rest of the way.

Feeling very amateur-sleuth smart, I raised the blue thread. "This was found on Milly after she was attacked in her front yard." I pointed at Em. "It's you—you've been trying to kill us and steal our powers."

Pearbottom—really? Who comes up with these names?—surveyed Em. "But that's Queen Witch."

"Jonathan, I didn't do it," Em scoffed. "You know me."

The inspector frowned, appearing uncertain of what to do. "I have to bring you in for questioning at least." He glanced at me. "Where's the proof?"

I held out the thread. "Here it is."

His face darkened as he turned to Em. "I'm afraid I have to do it. Em, come with—Roman Bane!"

Every eye in the room swiveled to Roman, who stood with jaw clenched as he faced down the inspector. Pearbottom, clearly shaken, fumbled with a pair of handcuffs on his back pocket. After wiggling and yanking at them, he finally got them free from their place on his belt.

He took a timid step forward. "R-r-roman B-b-bane, you're under arrest for m-m-murder. You will come w-with me at once to the c-c-c-council for p-punishment." He sighed, appearing relieved at finally getting the sentence out.

I didn't blame him. Roman was intimidating on a good day, and downright scary on a bad one. Roman stepped forward. He held out his arms as if resigned to take his punishment.

No! I couldn't stand and watch as Roman was arrested, ready to be sent to his death. He might not like me, but I cared for him.

What?

Cared for him? When did that happen?

I threw myself in the path of the inspector. "You can't take him. Whatever he did, it was for a good reason. Leave him alone."

Pearbottom glared at me. "Step aside, miss. This is witch police business. You called me here. This man is a criminal."

Roman placed a hand on my shoulder. "Dylan, it's for the best."

"No."

He cupped my face in his hands and smiled. "I knew the risk. Let him take me."

"No," I whispered as tears blurred my vision.

Roman reached out his arms. The inspector, tight-lipped and probably tight-bottomed, snapped the cuffs on Roman's wrists. The air crackled, and sparks flew from the metal restraints.

Roman flashed me a smile.

Then he vanished.

TWENTY-TWO

"Where'd he go?" I demanded. I grabbed the inspector by his cape. "What have you done with him?"

Pearbottom retreated. "I didn't do anything." He whirled on the roomful of women and one unicorn. "Which one of you transported him away?" All the witches wore blank stares. "I will ask only one more time. Which one of you did that?"

Milly stepped forward. "It wasn't any of us, so why don't you do what you're supposed to and take this woman in for questioning?" She pointed at Em, who thrust out her chest.

"Yes, take me in so that I can prove how stupid all of y'all are being. Arrest me, a person who can help catch the killer, while the real murderer is still on the loose."

My stomach churned. Maybe she wasn't the killer. Perhaps I had it all wrong. But I'd come too far to back down now. "Inspector, I summoned you for this woman. Now, I don't know anything about a witch council or even a witch board of directors, if there is such a thing, but I do know that my life is in danger, and I suspect this woman is the culprit. Now, will you take her in? Or will you set her free?" I poked him in the chest. "But know this—if me or my sister dies, our blood will be on your hands."

He smashed his lips together and squeezed his brows until they were practically one. "Fine. Queen Witch, Esmerelda

Pommelton, come with me."

Em crossed to him. She threw me a scathing look and said, "I hope you don't regret this."

"I hope that isn't a threat," I tossed back.

Pearbottom took her by the arm, and a moment later they were gone. I collapsed onto a chair. "Good night."

"Glad that's finished," Sera said.

Milly crossed to Tim and toed his arm. He didn't stir. "It's not over. One of you has to go get Roman."

I jerked. "Where is he?"

She thumbed her finger toward Grandmother. "I don't know. Ask her. She's the one who vanished him."

Grandma stroked the unicorn's mane. "I'll only tell if you give the king the reverence he deserves."

After ten minutes of bows and hand-feeding apples, I turned to Grandma. Yes, it was cool that a unicorn was in my living and managing not to poop on the floor. Yes, it was even cooler that he could talk, but darn it, I wanted to know what happened to Roman.

"All right. Where is he?"

She smiled. "Why, he's in his hotel room, watching television. Where else would he be?"

***

I made it there in five minutes flat. It would have been three, but a black cat dashed in front of my car, forcing me to slam on the brakes. I filled my lungs with several heaving breaths and flattened my forehead to the steering wheel. Cool plastic pressed against my skin, making me feel better. I clutched my shaking hands until they calmed, and drove off.

I knocked firmly on the door. After waiting half a lifetime, it opened. Roman greeted me with a dark, contemptuous glare. "You could have been arrested for obstruction of justice, you know."

I gave him my innocent doe-eyed look. "What do you mean?"

"When you threw yourself at Pearbottom, blocking him from arresting me. Obstruction of justice."

"Well, if you want me to call him back, I will, because that's the rudest thank-you I've ever heard."

He raised his hands. The metal handcuffs were still shackled to him. "If I didn't have these, I might thank you, but seeing as I'm basically under arrest, it's hard to find any gratitude."

My lips curled into a smile. "Come on, grumpy. Let's go find Milly. I'm sure she'll be able to get these things off you."

He scratched the spot right above his eyebrow. "I don't know if she'll be able to help. These are magical."

I grabbed the ingrate by his arm. "I'm aware of that. That's why I'm not calling a blacksmith. We're going to a witch."

"Hey, I know what Milly is."

"Then why are you still standing here? Do you want to be handcuffed for the rest of your life?"

He paused, shifted his weight from one hip to the other. "I don't think I want you to help me."

It was a freakin' dagger to the heart. Pain serrated my chest. Of all the things I expected, I didn't think Roman would say that—to cast me off with such a blatant rebuke.

I dropped his arm and backed up. "I'm only trying to help. Besides, you can't very well protect me like that. What's your plan? To spend the rest of your life shackled?" I smirked. "Doesn't sound like a very fulfilling life if you ask me."

He glanced up at the dingy motel-room ceiling and swore. After shaking his head, he met my gaze. Turbulence filled his green eyes. "All right," he said, deflated. "Let's go find that witch grandmother of yours and see if she can fix this."

When we found Milly, she was saying her good-byes to the unicorn king. He was still here? And he hadn't pooped? Maybe we'd invite him back for tea sometime. I dragged Roman over to her.

"He needs these off."

She stared down her nose at the handcuffs and said, "And

what do you expect me to do about it? I don't have the key."

Fright boiled in my throat. "What do you mean? Can't you get them off?"

Roman sighed. I flashed him a stern look that said, I know you're annoyed, but just zip it. Don't say anything.

"Me? What makes you think I'd be able to do such a thing?"

I nibbled what was left of the nail on my pinky. "Why wouldn't you? You're a powerful witch."

Milly snorted. "Powerful, yes, but even my power has limits. And breaking the witch police's magical cuffs is not on my list of abilities."

I hung my head. What would I do now? I couldn't press the button and ask them to release Roman without Pearbottom taking him into custody. I wanted to go bury myself in a deep, dark hole and not come out for at least five lifetimes.

"It's okay," Roman said. "I'll find a way out of them." He touched my shoulder. I glanced into his face. His green eyes shone brightly, as if he didn't want me to lose hope. What a turnaround from, like, ten minutes ago.

"How?" I asked.

From the other side of the room, Grandma cleared her throat. I was not in the mood to hear how flying monkeys could solve all our flipping problems. I'm sorry, but there are some things even a flying monkey can't do.

Against every bone of better judgment in my body, I cocked my head toward her. "Yes, Grandma? Do you know a way out of this?"

She pointed a jazz hand at her chest. "Moi? Don't be a sillypants. How could I know magic that powerful? I'm not nearly old enough...but perhaps there's someone else in the room who is."

I kneaded my temples with the tips of my fingers. "Who, Grandma? Who could possibly do it?"

She jerked her head toward the unicorn. Figured. The four-footed creature was the only one who could perform the magic required. At least he was housebroken.

I pressed the heels of my hands to my eyes. "King Unicorn?" Was that even right?

"You can call me Your Highness."

Of course I could. I removed my hands and opened my eyes. "Your Highness, would you be so kind as to please remove the handcuffs from my friend?"

The majestic creature pumped his head up and down. "I will on one condition."

Great. Why couldn't anyone do anything without conditions? I mean, how hard was it to do something out of the kindness of your heart? I did all the time. Even for people I didn't like. After all, I'd created Reagan's wedding dress, and I didn't like her. Certainly, she had paid me to do it, but I didn't have to. I could have said no.

"Okay. What's the condition?"

He bowed his head and said, "Come visit me in my world."

That didn't sound too bad. "Sure. I'll be glad to. It's a small price to pay for you to help my friend."

The unicorn looked at Roman. "Extend your hands." Roman reached forward. The unicorn touched the metal with his horn. Light sparked. I shielded my eyes, afraid my retinas would burn out. Y'all, the last thing I needed was to go blind from all this nonsense. When the piercing light finally receded, the cuffs lay on the ground.

Roman had been freed.

After a thousand thank-yous to the unicorn king, he vanished to his home. Everyone hugged and we all sat down for a snack of petit fours and coffee, which Nan was kind enough to serve, and Sera was nice enough to allow us to eat.

I bit into one that consisted of strawberry cake surrounded by vanilla icing. Amazeballs. I moaned with pleasure. "Sera, this is beyond great. The banquet committee is going to be over the moon with these."

She gave me a knowing look. "You mean Jenny Butts."

"But of course," I said. "These may be the best thing that

happened all night." I raised the tiny cake to Roman, who of course had declined the sugar but sat back drinking a cup of black java. "That is, except for the unicorn king's invitation to visit his homeland. That was pretty cool."

Milly chuckled.

Grandma joined her.

Something about that made me very nervous. "What am I missing?"

Milly wiped a tear from her eye. "You might not think that such a welcome invitation."

A line of sweat beaded my brow. I was definitely nervous. "Why not? What's wrong with going there?"

"Well," Grandma said, "his people aren't always the nicest to witches."

"Okaaaay. Can you elaborate?"

Milly scraped the last bit of icing off her plate with the edge of her fork. "They don't like our kind in their territory."

"So?" I shrugged. "I still don't get it. What's the big deal?"

"The big deal," Roman interjected, "is that they kill witches."

I slapped my forehead. Oh no. What had I gotten myself into now?

TWENTY-THREE

By the time Saturday morning hit, I felt pretty good. The witch police had been in contact via some sort of old-school magic mirror, and I knew with confidence that Em wouldn't be released until after the solstice, which meant I wouldn't die.

"I need those petit fours in the hall by two o'clock," Sera said. She laid the small cakes in a plastic tub with great care, making sure each was individually wrapped and protected for transport.

"Aye, aye, captain. I'll have them there by two," I said.

"That gives us three hours to pamper ourselves before the banquet," Sera said.

I rolled my eyes. "Yes, because we both have hot dates for the night. Listen, I'm only going for an hour, tops. A bunch of town elite dancing and looking merry, talking about snobby things, is not my idea of a good time. And you know if Jenny Butts is there, that generally means I'm out anyway. Tonight is an—"

"Exception, I know," Sera said, sighing. "Just get the cakes there, and the rest will take care of itself."

I'd been avoiding bringing this up, but I needed answers. "Sis," I said.

Sera tossed me a curious glance. I never called her Sis, so she must have been suspicious of me. "Yes?"

"That day when you were in Roman's car talking to him," I

said, "do you mind if I ask what you were talking about?"

She stared at the confections in front of her. "It's kind of embarrassing. I was asking him for man advice."

"Man advice?"

"Yeah, stupid old me was asking him about Tim, that idiot."

My heart somersaulted. "So you don't like him?"

"Who, Roman? No, of course not. I mean, he's good-looking and all that, but it's obvious he's interested in someone else."

"Who?"

She rolled her eyes. "You, dummy. He likes you. And after I had to haul Tim home last night and drop him off on his doorstep, I've pretty much decided I'm done with that guy. He needs to grow up."

Yay! She didn't like Tim anymore. That was the best news I'd heard in, like, forever. I still wasn't convinced Roman had feelings for me, but I had other things to think about—like a banquet.

***

By three o'clock I was soaking in a tub, waiting for that heifer Calgon to take my troubles away. Unfortunately it didn't work. Even though Em was in custody and I felt safe, my heart sank every time I thought of Roman. For one thing, he'd be leaving; for another, I sensed he was angry at me for getting him involved in a plot that almost got him captured. I could have been wrong, but the idea nagged at me. So I soaked in the tub for an extra-long period of time, hoping the milky water would dissolve all my problems. But in reality all it did was let me sit in my own sloughed-off dried skin and dirt. Ew and double ew.

At five o'clock the five of us ladies—myself, Sera, Reid, Grandma, and Nan—left for the banquet. The fine arts building, an ode to ancient Roman architecture with its columns and triangular arch, was lit up like Christmas in July. White lights twinkled from the magnolia trees that lined the walkway, and the yellow bellies of lightning bugs glowed in time, adding to the ambiance.

Inside was a mass of crepe paper and even more white lights. It was romantic and, if I say so myself, quite lovely. Jenny Butts and the banquet committee had outdone themselves. Sera's petit fours lined a table that sat off to the side. People strolled by it, commenting on how delicious they looked and how tempted they were to go ahead and dive into dessert, skipping dinner altogether.

Jenny Butts waved from across the room. "Oh no," I whispered to Sera.

"Well? We're the honored guests. You knew we'd have to deal with her," she said.

"I know. Hey! Maybe we can get Reid to be the single honored guest?" I asked hopefully.

Sera shook her head. "Good try."

Jenny did that arm-pumping thing she does with every word she says. "Y'all. Y'all. Y'all. I've got a table in the front all ready for you. Dylan, you look beautiful, of course." Her gaze swept from my head to my feet and back up. I wore a simple camel-colored dress with an Empire waist and chiffon sleeves that split at the top.

"Thank you," I said. She hooked her arm around mine and led us off to the front. We sat at the head of the room, and I watched as the guests, the who's who of Silver Springs, spilled into the hall.

I tried not to bite my nails as all eyes fell on us. I squirmed, sensing a bit of gossipmongering as people looked our way and then whispered in one another's ears. It was obvious what they were saying—Reagan Eckhart died in her shop. That's bad luck. I didn't care. As far as I was concerned, the whole thing was over.

"Holy smoke," Sera whispered.

"What?" I asked.

She nodded toward the entrance. My eyes rested on the double doors, and for a moment I didn't get what she was looking at. My breath flew from my chest as I did, indeed, realize what Sera had seen.

Roman leaned on the lip of the doorway. He gazed into the

sea of gowns and suits. His blond hair hung loose, those darn glasses were, for once, off his face and he wore—dear Lord, the man wore a tuxedo. I melted into a puddle in my chair.

Sera elbowed me. "You all right?"

Okay, so I didn't technically melt, but it sure did feel like it for half a second. "Of course. I'm fine. Why wouldn't I be?"

"Because Tall, Dark, and Incredibly Sexy is on his way over here."

"He is?"

A voice as smooth as velvet and as husky as…well, as husky as husky gets, said, "Hello, ladies."

"Hello," Reid and Sera said. I forced myself to look up. Roman gave me a warm smile. Heat spread over my cheeks as I smiled back. His eyes sparkled, and I looked away, unsure of what to say or do.

"Dylan, do you have a minute?"

Who, me? "Sure."

Roman extended his hand. I slipped my palm over his. He guided me through the throng of people milling about. A cluster of nerves jumbled in my gut. People stared at us as we walked past. Tomorrow the whole town would buzz about the stranger on my arm. The gorgeous, amazing stranger.

"I thought you'd still be mad," I said.

We stepped outside. The scent of honeysuckles clouded the humid night. We walked along a quiet path toward a vacant gazebo. More white lights had been strewn around it, making the intimate space appear magical, as if it belonged in a world of fairies.

Jeez. Now I sounded like my grandmother. Someone stop me.

"Why would I be mad?" he said, holding my hand as I entered the structure.

I shrugged. "I don't know. Maybe because you almost got arrested, you barely got the cuffs off and you don't like witches."

He rolled his eyes. "Enough of that already. I wish I'd never said that."

"It's hard to take back words," I said. "Words hurt. I mean, that whole sticks and stones may break my bones, but names will never hurt me thing just isn't true. Not at all."

He frowned. "I never called you any names."

"Not that I heard," I pointed out. "But you might have in your head."

He raised his hands to stop me from speaking any farther. "Okay. Wait. Let's go back. You look beautiful."

My brows sewed together in thought. "Are you talking about me?"

"Who else would I be talking to?"

"Oh. Well, that's very nice of you to say. You, um…" I swallowed. "You look very nice as well." My gaze drifted to the rise and fall of his chest, and I realized exactly how close we were. I retreated a step and felt his hand squeeze mine. "I didn't expect to see you here tonight."

"You think I'd leave without saying good-bye?"

My heart sank. Good-bye. Of course. He was leaving. I mean, I knew it was coming, but I hadn't wanted to focus on it. "No. I didn't think you'd leave like that."

He edged closer. His skin glowed from the tiny electric lights surrounding us. White reflected in his eyes, and I found myself drowning in his gaze. I couldn't move. It was as if concrete encased my legs, keeping me from inching in any direction.

Roman brushed a stray hair off my cheek. "I also didn't want to leave without doing this."

From the depths of my clutch purse, a cell phone buzzed. I sighed, annoyed that someone had the nerve to interrupt me. "Hold on." I fished it out and saw the name CARRIE flashing. "Let me see what she needs."

He stepped back. "Take your time."

I hit the Answer button. "Hello?"

"Oh, Dylan. I'm so glad I caught you," she said, breathless.

"What's up?" Please hurry, you're killing my chances with this guy who's about to leave town, and who I'll never see again. Sounded depressing when put that way.

"I forgot my dress! It's still at the shop. Can you meet me there in five so I can get it?"

Part of me wanted to say no, but Carrie had worked for me a long time. Plus she put in long hours and always said yes when I asked her to do something. "Sure. I'll see you in a sec." I hung up and dropped the phone back in my bag. "Sorry about that. I've got to meet Carrie at the shop. She forgot her dress."

"Do you want me to come with you?"

I shook my head. "No. I don't need a bodyguard anymore, remember?"

He nodded faintly and stepped toward me. My heart drummed. Roman took my hand. "Dylan, I hope you know that I've changed my mind about not liking witches."

I raised an eyebrow. "Oh?"

One side of his mouth curled into a smile. Dear Lord, if there were awards for sexiest smile, Roman would have won right then and there. I nearly collapsed on the ground. I slowed my breath, trying to force my heart to calm down.

"It turns out I like witches." He drew me to him until my body pressed against the boulder that made up his chest. I stared at his bow tie, not wanting to look up and not wanting to glance away. He hooked his finger under my chin and tilted my face toward his. "In fact," he whispered, "it turns out I like witches very much."

His lips found mine, and Roman, I swear to all things that are true and good in the world, kissed me. Fireworks exploded in my body as his mouth gently caressed mine. I closed my eyes and leaned into the kiss, feeling a world of emotion swirling in me. The past couple of weeks of long talks had all led up to this one glorious moment.

And I had to let Carrie into my shop.

I don't know who stopped kissing whom first. To be honest,

cotton candy and gumdrops filled my mind. I was incapable of focusing on small details. But in the end our lips did part.

"Wow. I guess you do like witches," I said.

Roman smiled. "Told you."

We stared at each other. I was the first to fold. "I'd better go help Carrie. I'll be back in a few minutes."

He kissed my cheek. "Be careful and hurry back."

He didn't have to ask twice.

***

I found Carrie outside Perfect Fit, patiently waiting. "Silly me," she said as I unlocked the door. "I can't believe I totally forgot all about my dress. That was stupid."

I shouldered the door open. "I know. Especially since you've been talking about it all week." I smiled to let her know I was only kidding. "Your hair and nails look great. You're going to look lovely, Carrie."

I crossed the threshold and waited for her to enter. Carrie peered at the top of the frame. She toed forward hesitantly.

I smirked. "Are you okay? Looks like you're waiting for lightning to strike."

She tittered. "No, I just thought I saw a spider in the door. You know how I hate them."

"I know. I hate them too." I crossed to the dress and lifted it from the rack. "Here you go."

Carrie shut the door behind her. She pulled something shiny from her purse. It looked like a long kitchen knife. Like, a really long kitchen knife. Like, one that only a chef would use. Why would she have that in her hand?

"Haven't shaved your legs in a while, Carrie?" I joked. "Had to bring out the big guns, huh?"

Carrie floated across the room as if on wheels. At the same time, everything around me slowed as if I was trapped underwater.

My mind tried to process what was happening. I attempted to move, but the weight of the water, or whatever, held me fast. In the time it took to blink, Carrie had a hand around my collar and the knife pointed at my heart. The world righted itself, and whatever had previously gripped me released its hold.

"Move, Dylan. Do it. Give me a reason to start shredding your skin."

A shrill laugh escaped my lips. "That's a very funny joke, Carrie. But ha-ha. Don't you want the dress?"

Her eyes danced with pleasure. "Really, Dylan? Are you kidding? I mean, your clothes are cool and all, but that's not what I'm here for."

My hopes faded. "I was afraid you'd say that."

She pulled a line of rope from her purse and said, "Sit down and tie yourself up. Don't do a shoddy job. I'll be checking."

My mind raced to put all the pieces together.

"Why are you frowning? Upset that you fingered the wrong person?" She laughed. A shudder moved through my body at the hideous sound. "Oh Dylan, you and your sister are such incompetent witches. Once I kill you, I'll have everything I need. I never meant to kill Reagan; it was always you I wanted."

She pulled up one of my lounging chairs and plopped down on it. She stared at her nails, I assumed to make sure she hadn't chipped one of them. "First off, it's too late for you now, but it was seriously unwise to forget to place the spell of protection on your shop."

I sighed. "So that's why you looked at the door. It wasn't spiders. You wanted to make sure you'd be able to enter since you plan on killing me." I worked slowly, trying to figure out a way to jump her and get the knife from her hands. I wrapped the rope around my ankles at a slug's pace, racking my brain.

"That would be correct. God, I never thought you'd figure out the whole thing about the threads."

Wait a minute. "What do you mean?"

"I mean, the fact that the thread found on Milly looked exactly like one of Queen Esmerelda's."

I worked my hands even slower. "How'd you manage to get one of Em's threads? They disappear after twenty-four hours, and she never did magic when you were nearby."

Carrie smirked. "I've been logging threads for years. Saw Em perform a bit of magic on a table of folks at Java House about three years ago, and snagged it then. Jenny Butts and some women were making a fuss about a baby, and Em performed some magic to quiet them down."

"But that doesn't explain how you had the thread."

She rolled her eyes. "I didn't have it. I wrote down everything about it—the shape, the color, etcetera. It's always good to know what another witch's threads look like. That way you can replicate it and frame the witch for crimes they didn't commit. That's what I did the day I knocked Milly out. Replicated the thread and stuck it in her ear. It's just coincidence no one found my own thread on her."

She crossed one leg over the other and bounced it up and down. "You fell for it, hook, line and sinker. I probably could've convinced you it was that bodyguard of yours, and you would have believed it. I mean, you're a total waste of a witch."

What a meanie. "I gave you a job for three years—you could show a little respect."

"Yes, and in those three years I waited for you to discover what you were, so I could kill you then and take your powers. But that never happened. Finally you announce to the world that you're a witch, and I had no choice but to act fast, before some other witch got the same idea and knocked you off first."

I tied a loose knot around my ankles. "I get all that, but what about my grandma? Why would you freeze her?"

She looked at me as if I was insane. "Freeze your grandmother? I didn't do that. Why would I do that? She's bat crazy." She sighed. "None of that matters now, though. Because once I've skinned you, I'll have everything I need."

Something occurred to me. "You used your nails as an excuse not to touch the dress that killed Reagan."

She nodded. "Yep. Of course my nails had cured. They're gel. The spell I cast wouldn't let me touch the gown again."

Taking a huge risk, I said, "What a crackpot spell. Even once you have my powers, I don't think that's going to cure your problems. You're simply a bad witch. A terrible witch. You couldn't even spell that dress correctly. Good luck with having more abilities. I don't think it's going to help."

Carrie brandished the knife toward my middle. "Shut up. Just shut up. You don't know anything. You didn't even remember to protect this store. I'm actually doing you a favor by killing you now, because as word spreads that you're a total failure of a witch, others will come. Others will try to kill you, and one of them will succeed."

A loud thud came from outside the shop. Carrie turned. "What was that?"

I leaped forward. Well, I didn't exactly leap. I threw myself at her, my legs still entangled in the chair. I reached out, trying to smack the knife from her hand. I managed the next best thing—I struck her arm, and the knife clattered to the floor.

"You little witch," she said as our bodies knotted together.

I hit. I clawed. I scratched. I did everything possible to keep her away from the knife. But with my legs caught in the chair's tines, my abilities were limited.

Carrie kicked me off and clambered for the knife. She snatched it from the floor and rose. My old assistant, my friend and someone I generally liked, towered over me, her face a grimace of twisted shadows.

"Now we'll see who has all the power, Dylan Apel." She raised the knife over her head.

The door of the shop slammed open. Roman stood in the entrance, gun in hand. Carrie screamed. She plunged the knife toward me. I shielded my eyes. I really wasn't interested in witnessing my own death, you know? Just didn't seem like the right thing to do.

Bang! Bang! Bang!

I waited a second, expecting cold steel to enter my body, but nothing happened. One more second passed and I still wasn't injured.

I opened one eye a slit.

On the floor lay Carrie, quite dead.

TWENTY-FOUR

Twenty minutes later I found myself sitting on the steps to the shop, a wool blanket wrapped around my shoulders, a Styrofoam cup of hot coffee in my hand and Roman by my side, his arm hugging my shoulder.

Detective Blount scratched his prickly chin. "We found the knife that Miss Dogwood was going to use to kill you. We'll brush it for prints and hopefully get this wrapped up soon."

Roman released his grip on me. "Dylan, may I see your purse?"

I resisted the urge to ask him why he was interested in my lipstick, but handed it over to him, curious as to what he wanted. He opened the bag and pulled out a small black tape recorder. "I think you'll find this has all the evidence you're looking for." Roman rewound it and pressed Play.

The recorder crackled. It buzzed for a second, and then Carrie's voice came through on the speaker. "Once I kill you, I'll have everything I need. I never meant to kill Reagan; it was always you I wanted."

Blount frowned. "You recorded this without her knowing, I assume. It's inadmissible in court."

Roman crossed his arms. "I don't think this will get to court. That's a confession right there. And you have both our testimonies that Carrie was about to kill Dylan when I stopped her."

Roman handed the recorder over to the detective. Blount palmed it for a moment, and then his lips split into a smile. "Looks pretty open and shut. Well, we've found our killer. You two can come down for questioning tomorrow, and we'll wrap this whole thing up."

We said our good nights. Once the detective was gone, I turned to Roman. "How did that get there?" I asked, meaning the recorder.

He blushed. The assassin actually turned pink with shame. My gut flip-flopped. I wasn't going to like this answer. "I slipped it in when we were at the gazebo."

I raised my eyebrows. "When you kissed me?"

He nodded.

I smacked my lips together. "Let me get this straight. You knew Em wasn't the killer, and you figured whoever it was, they would make their move tonight."

He sighed. "Yes. So I slipped it in your purse, knowing you'd be the target."

"Then you followed me."

"Well, I knew where you were going. I gave you a little head start."

I shrugged off the blanket and stood. "And you waited until I was almost killed to save me?"

A look of panic shone in his eyes. He rose and reached for my hand. I snatched it back. "Dylan, it's not like that. I had to get enough information to prove that the police had found their killer, so that they'd close this case."

"But you—"

"And—" His voice steamrollered mine. "And I needed to make sure the threat against you was clear, so that when I disposed of the killer, there wouldn't be any questions."

Everything had been a lie. He'd kissed me while slipping the recorder in my purse. He'd done it to distract me. Tears blurred my eyes. "But you did it when you kissed me. You didn't even tell me what you were doing."

He stepped forward and rubbed my arms. "Would you have believed me? Kept it in your purse, or would you have ditched it?"

Ditched it for sure. "That's not the point."

He smiled. "It is the point. And trust me on this one, too. Once that cop hears the rest of that tape, I don't think he's going to stay around for much longer."

"Why?" I asked.

"I think he's going to realize Atlanta and its normal crime is a lot easier to deal with than Silver Springs and its cultish criminals. And believe you me, things in town are going to get worse before they get better."

Now he was really annoying me. "Because I'm a witch who doesn't know how to protect myself?"

He gave me a sympathetic smile. "You're learning. But you've got a long stretch to go."

I backed away. "Thank you, but no thank you. If you're style of teaching is leading me on for your own purposes, I'm not interested." I pivoted on my heel and stalked off into the night.

"Dylan, wait—"

But I didn't wait. There was nothing the assassin could say that I wanted to hear. He'd used me to catch a killer. Betrayed my feelings. Someone more levelheaded would probably point out that he'd caught a killer to save my life, but I wasn't feeling particularly sound of mind right now. At the moment fury pulsed through my body. One thing was for certain.

I never wanted to see Roman Bane ever again.

TWENTY-FIVE

After a few weeks everything went back to normal—sort of. Grandma still talked about unicorns, and Milly remained sour as ever, though the gossipmongers had a field day with the fact that Carrie had murdered Reagan. To think, Silver Springs had harbored a murderer right in their very own town! No one, of course, was more surprised than me.

Milly contacted the witch police and explained that the real killer had been discovered. She also told them about Carrie planting the evidence to make Em appear guilty. I feared Em would try to seek revenge, but Sera felt that the Queen Witch possessed more class than that.

She was probably right.

The bell to the shop tinkled. While still staring at the stack of paperwork on my desk, I pasted on my brightest smile and said, "Welcome to Perfect Fit. How can I help you?"

"You can help me by trying not to pin murders on me." Em stood, hands fisted on her hips, a shroud of crimson curls cascading over her shoulders.

Uh-oh. "Hi, Em. Sorry about all that. But Carrie did admit to trying to make it look like you did it."

She lowered her lids and stared down her nose at me. "Was that before the bodyguard I hired to protect y'all killed her?"

I swallowed. My voice came out as a thin, mousy thing. "Yes. That would be correct." So maybe she was mad. Maybe I deserved it. And then again, maybe I didn't. I was conned. Scammed. "I'm sorry, Em. Really." I paused, trying to find something to say that would ease the tension. "Did the police put you somewhere nice? I mean, you're their queen. It's not like they're going to throw you in with all the other riffraff."

She laughed. "They did throw me in with all the riffraff, as they were all out of nice cells for witch queens."

"Oh." Boy, was I in big trouble or what? "Is there anything I can do to make it up to you?"

She smiled. Her eyes twinkled in a way that made me shudder. It appeared I now stood on the bad side of the Queen Witch, and I wished I didn't. She sniffed. "Let me think on it. There may be somethin' you can do to earn my forgiveness."

"Yes, let me know."

She surveyed the room in a silence that lasted long enough to be creepy, and said, "There is somethin' you can do."

I perked up. "What is it?"

She puckered her lips into a kiss. "That's for me to know, and you to find out."

She vanished.

Crap. That didn't sound like something I was going to like at all. As I sat, trying to rack my brain for what awful thing I would have to endure, Sera and Reid spilled into the store.

I rose. "Is everything okay?"

"Dylan, sit down," Sera said.

"Why? What is it?" I asked, now in full-fledged freak-out mode. Had something happened to Grandma? Had she gone to live with the unicorns? Hmm. That wasn't such a bad idea.

"It's nothing serious," Reid said. "Don't get her all panicky."

Sera smoothed her glassy hair. "Sorry." She looked out the window as Tim walked by. He saw her, gave a brief wave and then kept walking.

"It's a good thing Em erased his memory from that night," Sera said. "She did me a favor. Made him forget he ever wanted to try to get back together." She leaned against the wall and crossed one foot over the other. "Now I can officially move on."

"Speaking of Em," I said, "she paid me a visit."

Reid plopped into a chair. "What'd she want?"

I braided the tip of my ponytail in a vain attempt to distract myself. "I suppose to let me know I'd officially teed her off."

"Too bad I can't help you there," Reid said. "I mean, I don't have any powers or anything." She brought the back of her hand to her forehead. "It's the curse of being normal."

"Don't worry," I said. "She'll let us know how to make it up to her. After all, she spent a night in witch jail."

"How bad could it have been?" Sera asked.

I cocked my head at her. "Bad. But I don't want to think about that. What were you going to tell me?"

Reid and Sera exchanged looks.

"What is it?" I demanded.

"You want to tell her, or should I?" Reid said.

"I'll do it," Sera said.

I flexed my fingers like claws. "What is it? The suspense is killing me."

Sera shouldered herself from the wall. "You remember Detective Blount."

"Of course."

"Well," Sera said, "he's leaving."

I stopped braiding my hair. "Oh? Where's he going?"

Reid picked up a magazine and started paging through it. "Says he's going back to Atlanta. He's tired of country life."

"Wow. Roman was right. He kept saying the guy would quit. I never believed him though." Reid and Sera exchanged looks again. "Okay. What is it? What's going on?"

"Thing is," Sera said, "it looks like we have a new detective."

"Already? That was fast."

Reid looked up from a glossy picture of a wedding dress. "It gets better. Just wait."

Confused, I said, "Wait? For what?"

The door banged open. Jenny Butts entered, her hand-pumping ways in full force. Lord, help me now.

"Y'all. Y'all. Y'all. Can you believe it? Of course, I'm sure y'all already know."

I cocked my head. "Know what?"

She stroked her blonde Marilyn curls. "Don't be silly. I'm sure you were the absolute first to know, Dylan. Stop being so coy."

I lifted my hands in surrender. "Would someone please tell me what's going on?"

"Well, silly, if you want to pretend you don't know, that's fine, but I'll go ahead and tell you what you already know—that tall, handsome, male friend of yours is the new chief detective of Silver Springs."

I sank back into the chair. I gave Sera a help-me look. "She's not talking about who I think she's talking about, is she?"

Sera nodded.

"Reid. This isn't true, is it?"

"Afraid so," Reid said. "Roman's the new detective."

Jenny glanced at all of us. "What? What'd I miss?"

I waved my hand. "Nothing. Nothing at all."

Jenny backed toward the door. "Okaaay," she said. "I guess I'll be going then."

After she left, I dropped my forehead to the desk. "Great. Just great."

"It's not a big deal," Reid said. "It's not like you'll be seeing him every day."

Outside, a black SUV stopped at a red light. My heart thudded as the window rolled down. Roman, wearing those stupid black shades, rested his arm on the lip of the door. He looked over in our direction. Our eyes met. At least I thought so. Impossible to tell with him wearing those sunglasses.

He waved. The light turned green, and he drove off.

Yep, he saw me.

Reid was wrong. It looked like I might, in fact, be seeing him every day.

EPILOGUE

"Is everything ready?" I asked Sera.

She finished stacking a trayful of cucumber sandwiches. After wiping mayonnaise on her apron she said, "I think so."

Reid ruffled her burgundy curls. "When will she be here?"

I glanced at my watch. "Any time now. Let's all go into the living room." I ushered my sisters in, and Sera placed the tray on the dining table.

Nan finished tacking a banner to the wall and climbed down from her chair. "I'm all set here."

Grandma put down the gardening magazine she was reading. "Oh? Are we ready? I'm starving."

I tilted my head to one side. "I'm pretty sure we're missing the guest of honor."

"Oh pooh. Who is that?"

Reid said what I was thinking. "The monkey king, Grandma." I snickered.

"Great, can't wait to see him again," Grandma said.

"You shouldn't do that," Sera said.

"What?" Reid shrugged.

Sera pulled off her apron and hung it on a peg. "Tease her. It isn't nice."

The doorbell ding-donged. I gave my sister's hands a squeeze for luck, and we all marched to the door. I opened it. Milly glared at me over her snarling nose. "You wanted to see me?"

I took her by the shoulders and guided her inside. "Milly, we want to officially welcome you into the family."

She looked at the blue WELCOME banner that ran from one side of the living room to the other. Tears misted in her eyes. Nan put a noisemaker to her lips and blew.

Grandma threw up her hands. "Welcome to the family, you old harlot."

That was one way to do it.

Milly caned across the floor. She looked back at us, brought a shaking hand to her lips and did the unthinkable. She smiled.

I walked over and wrapped her in a hug. "Welcome, Milly. We're glad to call you family."

She sniffed a couple of times and said, "Thank you. That means a lot."

I released her, took her hand and said, "Hungry? There's lots of food."

"I'm starving."

Sera crossed to the table and started plating the sandwiches. "Then let's enjoy each other's company as a family."

As we formed a line to take our plates, Grandma pulled me aside. "Here." She stuffed something in my hands.

I looked down at a brown accordion folder. "What is it?"

"Open it."

Sliding off the band that kept it shut, I opened the flap and pulled out a fat manila file that read ROMAN BANE. "Is this what I think it is?"

She nodded. "It's what you wanted to read. Everything is right there."

I started to peel the faded cover back and stopped. This was Roman's life. His life. Every personal detail about it. Everything that had happened to him—from his mother and sisters' deaths to his girlfriend's killing. All of it. Right there in front of me. I could know everything I wanted to know about the mysterious man.

It was none of my business. I placed the file back in the folder and pressed it into Grandma's hands. "No. I don't want it. Thank you, though."

She smiled and vanished it in less than a second.

As we sat down to eat, our plates piled high, smiles splashed across our faces, Sera said, "There's still one thing we never found out."

"What's that?" I asked.

"We never discovered who froze Grandma."

Milly wiped her mouth. "That was me."

Shocked faces turned toward her. "How? Why?" Reid asked.

She shrugged. "Her power was being drained. She needed to be frozen. I knew she wouldn't let me do it, so I disguised myself. Believe it or not, I can do glamours."

"I guess that settles that," I said.

"She's right. I never would've let Milly do it if I'd known it was her. On the lighter side," Grandma said, "I told the monkey king to be here in five minutes for lunch. Will he be too late?"

I glanced at Milly, who forked a beet and said, "No. I think he'll be right on time."

This should be interesting.

AMY BOYLES

Amy Boyles grew up reading Judy Blume and Christopher Pike. Somehow, the combination of coming of age books and teenage murder mysteries made her want to be a writer. After graduating college from DePauw University, she spent some time living in Chicago, Louisville, and New York before settling back in the South. Now, she spends her time chasing two toddlers while trying to stir up trouble in Silver Springs, Alabama, the fictional town where Dylan Apel and her sisters are trying to master witchcraft, tame their crazy relatives, and juggle their love lives. You can find Amy on Facebook at www.facebook.com/amyboylesauthor or email her at amyboylesauthor@gmail.com. She loves to hear from readers.